DAN SHAMBLE, ZOMBIE P.I.
HE'S A STIFF DETECTIVE,
AND HE'S GOT STONES!

Dan Shamble, zombie P.I. He's a stiff detective, and he's got stones!

The cases don't solve themselves in the Unnatural Quarter, filled with ghosts, vampires, mummies, werewolves, and other mythical creatures. It takes an intrepid zombie detective to decipher mysteries, unravel conspiracies, track down cursed objects, and find time for a beer with his best human friend at the Goblin Tavern.

Dan Shamble, zombie P.I., is back from the dead and back on the case in this new collection of eight wacky adventures—featuring a cyclops who lost his eyeball on a drunken bender, an Aztec mummy who wants revenge for too many parking tickets, a crawling hand accused of fingering expensive objects from a curio shop, a distraught mutant fly mother searching for her missing maggots, and the real boogeyman (an insurance salesman) being harassed by his ghoulish aunts. These cases have enough plot twists and stomach turns to keep you guessing, and chuckling, until the very end.

STIFFS AND STONES

STIFFS AND STONES

THE CASES OF DAN SHAMBLE, ZOMBIE P.I.

NEW YORK TIMES BESTSELLING AUTHOR

KEVIN J. ANDERSON

Stiffs and Stones
by Kevin J. Anderson

EBook ISBN: 978-1-68057-738-9
Trade Paperback ISBN: 978-1-68057-739-6
Dust Jacket Hardcover ISBN: 978-1-68057-740-2
Audiobook ISBN: 978-1-68057-741-9
Library of Congress Control Number: 024945244
Cover design by Miblart
Kevin J. Anderson, Art Director
Vellum design by CJ Anaya
Published by
WordFire Press, LLC
PO Box 1840
Monument CO 80132
Kevin J. Anderson & Rebecca Moesta, Publishers
WordFire Press eBook Edition 2025
WordFire Press Trade Paperback Edition 2025
WordFire Press Dust Jacket Hardcover Edition 2025
WordFire Press Audiobook Edition 2025

Printed in the USA
Join our WordFire Press Readers Group for
sneak previews, updates, new projects, and giveaways.
Sign up at wordfirepress.com

CONTENTS

BUMP IN THE NIGHT

I

When the Boogeyman—the actual in-the-flesh Boogeyman—comes into the office and says that he's scared, you'd better pay attention. I could tell this wouldn't be a typical case for Chambeaux & Deyer Investigations.

He came through the door with a cold wind and a ripple of dread. Generally, when I meet a new person, my response is a polite smile and a nod of greeting. This time, as soon as the Boogeyman entered, I felt my skin crawl.

He was gaunt, pale, and hairless. His eyes were sunken into shadowed sockets, his cheeks puckered against his teeth. He looked like a living manifestation of that famous Edvard Munch painting *The Scream*, or maybe a necrotic version of young Macauley Culkin's horrified gasp in *Home Alone*. He wore a trim black business suit with a narrow black tie, as if he worked for a three-letter government agency.

"Help me, Mr. Shamble!" His voice was like a hollow wind blowing through an ice cave. "You've got to help me. I'm terrified!"

For the first time in my career, both as a living detective and an undead detective, I was afraid to take the case—and I didn't even know what it was yet.

Sheyenne, my already-drop-dead-gorgeous ghost girlfriend, rose from the reception desk, and her ectoplasmic form shuddered. Her eyes went wide in instinctive surprise.

Robin, my human lawyer partner, stood at the filing cabinets reviewing notes from one of her upcoming litigations. Seeing the visitor, she reacted like someone who had stepped on a rattlesnake while simultaneously biting into too much mustard on a hamburger.

Alvina, my too-cute vampire half-daughter, jumped down from the worktable where she'd been posting SickTok videos and Monstagram images on her social-media platforms. The kid is an indefatigable optimist, and she never fails to show her pointy baby fangs in a bright smile. She could be bright and saccharin to the point of causing high blood sugar.

She must have had better defenses against the Boogeyman than I did. "I'm not afraid of anything," she said with a sniff. She came forward to face him. "Hello."

"Boo!" said the stranger.

It was like a panic alarm going off in the offices. I had to brace myself not to bolt and flee. When he saw all of us cringe, the Boogeyman raised his cadaverous hands like white surrender flags. "I'm sorry! I didn't mean to scare you. I meant Boo—that's my name. Short for Boogeyman. I was just saying hello. Wait, let me see if I can turn it down, control it."

He closed his sunken eyes and began to breathe slowly, concentrating. He inhaled through his slitted nostrils, calming himself, counting silently. My pulse wasn't racing, since I don't have a pulse, but I could feel the terror begin to subside.

Gathering our courage, Robin and I stepped forward to greet the prospective new client, shoulder to shoulder. "Professionalism beats panic every time," Robin said.

I cleared my throat. "How can we help you, Mr. Boogeyman?"

"Boo," he said, and we flinched again. "Please call me Boo. I'd like to hire your services. I'm … afraid."

Robin gestured the Boogeyman into our conference room, and Sheyenne followed with a new client form. Alvina trotted along, as if her very cheerfulness would help us get through the meeting. Robin carried a yellow legal pad, and I would rely on my intrepid memory (although we relied on Robin's notes as a backup).

Robin got down to business. "What are you afraid of Mr. … Boo?"

"The only thing to fear is fear itself," he answered. "And that's a lot to be afraid of—a lot of fear."

After the gaunt man took a seat, Sheyenne offered him coffee or an energy drink, but he shook his head. "Nothing with caffeine. It makes me anxious." Boo put his bony elbows on the table and nervously straightened his tie. "I want to go straight. I don't want to scare people anymore, at least not unnecessarily. There are enough things to worry about in the world, and everybody needs to dial it down a notch." He wiped a hand along his sunken cheek. "I might give myself an ulcer."

"Tell us more about your job," I said, "so I can get a better feel for the parameters of this case."

"My current job, the one I really love, is as an insurance salesman. Life insurance and afterlife insurance, primarily, but I also handle general casualty and property insurance. I want to give people peace of mind, let them know they'll be taken care of, even if the worst happens—and I'm very good at helping them imagine worst-case scenarios." Boo shook his head. "So many things to be afraid of—all the monsters that have returned to the world, all the people who are afraid of the monsters, and then there are lightning strikes, car accidents, falling meteors. I'm an excellent insurance salesman."

He looked at us, and suddenly the back of my mind was crawling with paranoia about all the bad things that could go wrong in everyday life.

"But I want to *ease* people's fears, not increase them," the Boogeyman insisted. "I want to go straight!" He curled his hand into a sinewy cadaverous fist. "But they won't let me out. They say fear itself is the only thing that holds us together."

Robin paused in her note taking. "Who?"

"My family!" Boo's expression fell into abject dismay, like a kid who had just been told he would never, ever, ever be able to pet a puppy again. "It's a family business."

II

We've taken on a lot of unusual clients, no questions asked—and then we start asking a lot of questions in order to round out the case. Sheyenne presented the Boogeyman with all the necessary forms to fill out, personal profile information, confidentiality releases, payment parameters, and a delineation of the services we would be expected to perform.

Robin planned to prepare preemptive restraining orders for the most pernicious members of Boo's family, while I would offer protective services, as needed. I'm a well-preserved zombie of average height; I wear a trademark fedora and a brown sport jacket with stitched-up bullet holes from one of my previous fatal cases, but I'm not all that intimidating as a bodyguard. Boo could have hired contract golem security, maybe even a rock demon, but he wanted Dan Shamble, zombie P.I. I guess my reputation preceded me.

Ever since the world-shaking event known as the Big Uneasy occurred thirteen years ago, we had all learned to be afraid of many things: monsters under the bed, hobgoblins in the closet, things that go bump in the night.

But that's just everyday life, and here in the Unnatural Quarter, monsters and humans have managed to get along, mostly. Even before the Big Uneasy, back when life was supposedly "normal," people fought constantly, with a plethora of lawsuits and divorces and family feuds. That's what kept my private investigation service and Robin Deyer's legal efforts in business, except instead of representing a couple in a bitter property dispute, we'd now been hired by the Boogeyman, who wanted to extricate himself from his family's expectations.

Boo hunched over the table, reading the fine print on all the forms. He wrote in careful penmanship on every blank line, though he asked to use a felt-tip marker. "It's soft and less hazardous," he explained. "Those pointy ends on pencils or ballpoint pens could poke an eye out."

"I've always been afraid of that," I said.

Boo finished the forms, checked them over, made sure all of the I's were dotted and the T's crossed. Relieved, he looked up at me with a face that only a nightmare could love. "Now we can get down to business."

That was when the absolute fear fest began.

First it came on like a howling, yowling, grumbling, whispering, shrieking thunderstorm that rolled down the halls— and I knew that thunderstorms were definitely not supposed to be inside the halls, particularly not on the second floor.

It sounded like a train wreck of evil cackles bursting through our door. Three separate black whirlwinds, cyclones of smoke and screams, each one capped with a demonic visage of disappointment and wrath. Their horrific faces would have made the Wicked Witch of the West consider an alternate career.

Alvina shrieked in terror, and Sheyenne swelled herself up to place her ectoplasmic form protectively in front of the little vampire girl.

Gooseflesh ran all over my skin. "What are you?" I shouted. I feared I might actually wet my pants for the first time since becoming a zombie.

The three demonic spectres spoke in unison with the voice of a stern teacher assigning detention. "We are your greatest fears. We are your nightmares!"

One drifted forward, her lips stretched over broken teeth. Her eyes blazed red. "We are what our nephew *should* be doing!"

Though scared, Robin was fundamentally unflappable. She seized the half-completed restraining order and flapped it in the face of the horrific spectral women. "I'll file this if you don't leave us alone! I swear I will."

The scary manifestations were not impressed.

Then the Boogeyman came to the rescue. Boo raised himself up, and his gaunt face turned into a shrieking death's head. His neat Men In Black suit rippled out in black tatters like formal attire for the Grim Reaper. Waves and waves of irrational paranoia rippled off of him like an overworked air-conditioner unit on a hot, humid day. *"Go away, Aunties!!!"*

Though the command wasn't directed at us, I wanted nothing more than to pack up my fedora, grab Alvina, and run all the way to one coast or the other.

"You, too, Auntie Em!" Boo added to the foremost spectre. "Can't you see I'm busy here?"

The hammer of fear was like a headwind that drove the ghastly women away. They flitted backward out the door, black smoke swirling and entwining like a nightmarish locomotive in reverse. The foremost female figure swelled up in front of the Boogeyman and cackled, "That's my boy. I knew you still had it, dear." She tangled and twisted and whisked her form as she retreated, following the others down the hall.

Boo sat back down, looking rumpled. He straightened his back-to-normal business suit and shook his head. "Do you see what I mean now? They won't let me alone. I can't have a day's peace just to go to my regular office job."

"Who were they?" I asked.

Alvina added, "You called one Auntie Em?"

Boo looked at the little vampire girl. "Em," he said. "Short for Embodiment of Terror."

"I can see why you'd shorten it," I said.

"My three aunts. They want me to carry on the family traditions, but I can't," the Boogeyman said. "I just can't! Now you see why you have to help me?"

"We do." Robin looked grim and determined.

I gathered my courage and placed a firm hand on Boo's forearm. "We'll get you out of this, one way or another."

Boo stayed long enough to provide the details we needed, even the address where the three unnatural women lived. Robin walked him to the door. "It's a free country. You should be able to choose your own career, even if striking mortal terror is the family business."

"My aunties have high standards, and unrealistic expectations," he said. Looking more relieved than when he had burst into our offices, Boo left humming "The Happy Song" under his breath....

III

The cases don't solve themselves. That's my motto.

I needed to get a clue—or several—and I began by wandering the mean streets of the Unnatural Quarter. OK, some of the streets are actually pleasant, but if Boo's aunties got their way, everyone would quiver in terror—in the Arts and Garment district, in the Old Town restaurants and galleries, in the sprawling suburbs where monsters and humans come home after a long work shift.

I tipped my fedora to a mummy matron setting up a dried flower stand. I passed a writers' discussion club at a Talbot & Knowles Blood Bar, where vampires sipped frothy drinks and debated the ideal number of adverbs per paragraph. Four deadbeat zombie teenagers were tossing dice against the brick wall of a dark alley, but they lost the energy and motivation to pick them up and look at the dots.

It was a pleasant, cloudy day with no undue gloom—just the way the Boogeyman wanted the Quarter to be. I was reluctant to get involved in family matters, but we needed to make the nightmarish aunties back off, not just for our client's peace of mind, but for everybody.

Ahead I saw a beat cop who had waved over a long, old Lincoln sedan. With his ticket book in hand, the policeman leaned into the passenger side window as he lectured the driver, a sweet old spinster. She had hair in a bun, wire-rimmed glasses, a powdered wrinkly face, and a flowered bonnet. When the cop straightened, I recognized my best human friend, Officer Toby McGoohan.

"I can't let you off with a warning this time, ma'am," McGoo said. "Not with all the previous safety citations on your record."

"Please, officer," said the sweet old lady. "It would mean so much to me! Aren't you a good boy?"

"I'm a good *cop*," McGoo said, "and it looks like other cops have been too lenient ten times before. You need to learn how to drive better, if you're going to keep your license, ma'am."

I sauntered up, curious. "Everything all right, McGoo?"

He glanced over at me. "Hey Shamble. I'm just keeping the peace … and keeping traffic moving."

"But I was moving!" the old lady insisted. She gripped the wheel as if it were the only thing anchoring her in place. "Ten miles an hour is still moving, and I was being cautious."

"You were moving far below the speed limit, Miss …" He looked down at the driver's license in his hand. "Miss Flora."

"Floraboding," she said.

The name was suddenly familiar to me. Floraboding, all one word, was the name of one of Boo's aunties, along with Em, for Embodiment of Terror, and Widdershins.

"There's such a thing as exercising a dangerous amount of caution," McGoo said, gesturing to the long Lincoln. "I watched you stop too long at each stop sign. You were going so slowly I caught up to you at a fast walk." McGoo tore off the ticket and handed it to her. "That's what the traffic court calls reckless safety. You make other drivers nervous, and you scare pedestrians because you seem to be following them." His exasperated expression softened somewhat. "Just be a little more considerate, ma'am. Drive faster and more recklessly from now on."

Floraboding frowned like a prune as she tucked the ticket and license back into her purse. Looking closer, I recognized parts of her frightening profile behind the sweet granny façade. "Aren't you one of Boo's aunties?" I asked.

She recoiled in alarm. "Such a good boy. Much too good!" I saw fear wash over her face. "Please don't tell Boo about the ticket. He can't know."

I saw my chance. "Then perhaps, ma'am, if you simply agree to—"

She pushed the button and rolled up the passenger window, cutting me off. She stomped on the accelerator, and the big Lincoln roared off leaving a rubber track on the street.

McGoo nodded. "That's more like it. People won't be so worried about her abnormal driving." He looped his thumbs into his beltloop, leaned back, and said, "Hey, Shamble, what do you call a monster made entirely out of blood?"

Thinking he had actually encountered such a creature on a case, I fell for it. "What?"

"A hemogoblin!"

I was anxious enough that even the stupid joke gave me a moment of relief.

We watched the Lincoln drive recklessly for a block, then Floraboding halted at a stop sign for so long she could have shifted the vehicle into park. Then she eased forward with immaculate caution.

McGoo shook his head. "Some people never learn."

IV

Sometimes you need to confront your fears head on. I had no idea, though, that confronting my greatest fears would entail having a pleasant conversation in the sitting room with tea and cookies.

Since Boo had given us the address of his three terrifying aunts, that afternoon I dropped in for a surprise visit. I considered taking Robin with me so she could serve legal papers, but that would have made the encounter official, and I've found that an off-the-record conversation can accomplish more than getting lawyers involved—even my own firebrand lawyer partner.

I arrived at their old brick townhouse, a place with a lot of character and high rent. Potted geraniums drank up sunshine on the corners of the porch. A cross-stitched sampler hung on the door: "Home Sweet Home." I rang the doorbell, which buzzed like an electric chair.

A sweet, grandmotherly old lady in a flower-print housedress came to greet me. Her gray hair was tied back with a gray ribbon, and she wore lipstick the color of rose petals. She squinted at me. "Hello, dear."

I pulled out my well-worn private investigator license and introduced myself. "Good afternoon, ma'am. I have a few questions on behalf of my client."

A second old lady bustled up to see who was at the door, then a third. I recognized Floraboding in the rear, and one of the other two reminded me of the horrifying face I had seen in our offices, Auntie Em. The third one must be Widdershins.

"We adore company, dear! We'd be happy to answer questions," said Em.

"My client is your nephew, Mr. Boogeyman."

The three old ladies lit up. "Oh, dear Boo! I wish he would come visit us."

"You visited him in our offices … though in a slightly more menacing form."

"Only slightly?" Widdershins clucked her tongue. "I thought we were quite ghastly."

"We've had a lot of practice," said Floraboding.

Em nodded. "Only because the dear boy won't do his job."

"He has another job," I said. "One that he prefers over the family business."

Auntie Em gestured me inside. "Please, Mister ..." She took another look at my license. "Chambo."

"It's pronounced Chambeaux," I said.

Widdershins touched her ear and leaned forward. "What did he say?"

"Shamble," said Floraboding. "His name is Dan Shamble."

I followed them into the sitting room without continuing the argument.

"I'll put on some water for tea," said Widdershins.

"Good thing we have fresh-baked cookies." Em gave me a grandmotherly smile. "We bake a new batch every afternoon, just in case we have company."

The sitting room had a coffee table, sofa (with protective plastic on the cushions), and three rocking chairs, one for each of the deceptively non-terrifying old ladies. The sofa cushions crinkled when I shifted my butt. A grandfather clock ticked in the corner. The air smelled of mothballs. This was not at all the confrontational confrontation I had anticipated.

"If he's here for dear Boo, we have to be hospitable," said Widdershins.

Floraboding sighed. "I wish that dear boy would visit us himself. It's been ages, and his aunties are so lonely." She spread a doily on the coffee table.

Widdershins brought napkins and cups, and Em came in with the cookies and tea. They all sat down in their respective rocking chairs.

That's when the pleasantness ended.

"I came here in hopes of a peaceful resolution, before we file any ugly legal restraining orders," I said. "Will you please leave your poor nephew alone to live his own life?"

The three old ladies swung their sharp gazes at me like ravens that had just discovered a ripe corpse. "The boy has responsibilities," said Auntie Em. "He doesn't understand what he's doing."

"It's just a phase," said Widdershins.

Floraboding set down her teacup and leaned closer to me. "Think about it, Mr. Shamble. What would the world be like without irrational fears?"

I pursed my lips, considering. "Uh, a better world?"

Em glanced up to the window where the lacy curtains were pulled back to show a small back yard enclosed by a wooden fence. She suddenly sat up straight, and her eyebrows arched in alarm. "There's that pesky black cat again! Why does it keep hanging around here?"

I turned to see a large black cat strolling along the fence, peering into the window. It meowed, as if expecting attention.

Widdershins rose promptly from her rocking chair. "I'll take care of it." When the old lady approached the window, the black cat seemed happy to see her, but she looked flustered and embarrassed.

Auntie Widdershins transformed into a snarling, smoky, evil spirit, a black demonic form. Her eyes blazed, and her mouth dropped open to reveal sharp fangs. Noxious green fumes boiled out of her throat as she roared. "Get away!"

The cat's fur stood on end like a cartoon, and it sprang away with a yowl and vanished in a flash.

Widdershins recomposed herself into a sweet old lady, but I knew what terrors lurked inside her. She brushed down her housedress, flustered. "We mustn't let the neighbor animals get too friendly. We have a reputation to uphold, you know. It doesn't look good."

"It certainly doesn't," said Em in a stern voice.

"Absolutely not." Floraboding furrowed her brows.

I felt sorry for the cat.

Em turned back to me. "As you can see, Mr. Shamble, fear is a powerful thing. It unites people."

"We keep everyone on edge for their own good," said

Widdershins, rocking in her chair. "Not just things that go bump in the night, but fears that make your skin crawl."

Em nodded. "Fear keeps everyone alert and wary, so they stay sharp."

"It's definitely not good to let people get too complacent," said Floraboding.

I looked at her, remembering McGoo's traffic ticket for dangerous caution. I wondered if the other two aunties knew how circumspect and safety conscious Floraboding was.

Widdershins got a dark gleam in her eyes, and again the three ladies rounded on me. I could feel the intense emotions boiling in the air.

"Here, let us show you," said Widdershins.

"Before you finish your tea," said Floraboding.

The three transformed into their demonic appearances, black skirling nightmares that filled the quaint sitting room. As I raised my hand trying to fend them off with a cookie, I was suddenly engulfed with pure dread.

I saw pinch-faced, shrewish Rhonda—Alvina's mother, McGoo's ex-wife, and my big-mistake brief lover—barging in to the offices and cooing over Alvina, insisting she had made a mistake and wanting her dear daughter back.

I saw sweet Alvina skipping along the sidewalk, humming to herself—and out of nowhere, a piano dropped from above and smashed on top of her.

Then I saw a nameplate on an expensive wooden desk in a fancy office lined with books, and realized one of my other greatest fears: that Robin Deyer had left us to join a large, corporate law firm.

My blood and embalming fluid turned to ice, and I shook my head to get these images away. But more came.

I saw Sheyenne glowing with romantic energy, then flitting away, leaving me behind. She had found her true soulmate in another ghost, and they wafted off together, heading toward the light. "It never would have worked out, Beaux," Sheyenne said, just before she disappeared.

And, perhaps most frightening of all, I saw McGoo standing on a stage, grinning as he held a microphone. He was pursuing a career as a standup comic.

I lurched up from the old ladies' sofa, fighting off these nightmarish visions. I looked down at a big wet stain on my crotch. In the panic, I had spilled my teacup across my lap—I swear it was just tea.

The three aunties returned to their quaint, endearing forms. They sat back in their rocking chairs in unison, lifting their teacups. "You see, everyone needs a good scare, now and then," said Auntie Em. "But our Boo could do so much better."

The other two old ladies nodded as they rocked and sipped. "It's a family tradition," said Widdershins. "Boo needs to face his responsibilities."

"I wish he'd visit," said Floraboding.

I tried to retain my dignity and ignore the wet stain on my pants as I hurried out of the townhouse. "You will hear from us," I said. These three aunties were going to be tough nuts to crack ... and they were indeed nuts.

V

"Maybe we do need some insurance around here, Beaux," Sheyenne said. "For the office, and the business. You never know when something might go wrong."

"Something always goes wrong," I said. "It's one of the things we can count on."

I was a successful zombie private investigator, but we did not have a lot of spare operating cash. Robin was a passionate lawyer with countless cases, but she accepted too many *pro bono* clients, which kept her heart full and our bank accounts empty.

"How do we afford insurance?" I asked. "We'll just have to live with the risk."

"We should at least get a quote," she said, making up her mind. "I'm coming along with you to see the Boogeyman."

And that was the real reason. After my horrifying tea-and-cookies encounter with the nightmarish aunties, I needed to hear the Boogeyman's perspective. My ghost girlfriend simply wanted to accompany me to Boo's Life and Afterlife Insurance offices, and I didn't mind at all. Whenever my beautiful ghost girlfriend is with me, my confidence increases, and I become a better detective.

Boo's Life and Afterlife Insurance offices were located in an old strip mall next to a pho restaurant, a tanning parlor, and an Egyptian-themed art gallery featuring "Canopic Jars Through the Ages."

We found the very tiny business office, just one little desk where Boo served as the main insurance salesman and policy underwriter, as well as receptionist, accountant, and coffee maker. "Gives a whole new meaning to the term 'small business,'" I said to Sheyenne as we stood in the door. Fortunately, her ectoplasmic form takes up little room, and I just loomed in the doorway.

Boo sat at his desk, across from a pale young human couple who looked nervous and shaky. The Boogeyman saw us and raised a finger. "I'll be with you in a moment, Mr. Chambeaux." Then he turned his full attention to the couple. "Now then, Mr. and Mrs. Vinson, have you given thought to exactly how many terrible things can go wrong every single day? In every corner of your life?

"A meteor could strike while you're out shopping for groceries." He glanced at the sweating, anxious husband. "Why, you could buy a nice bouquet for your lovely wife, and hidden in the flowers might be a … *murder hornet!*" His eyes blazed with the possibilities. "A gas main could explode beneath your house, blowing you all to smithereens. An airplane could crash into the Quarter, wiping out block after block. And you think you're safe at home? You could slip on the wet bathroom floor and fall into a full bathtub—while carrying an electrical appliance!"

"Oh," said the wife. "I hadn't thought of that."

"What if a fire demon moves into the neighboring house and he falls asleep while smoking a cigarette in bed? Or what if a child comes running toward you while holding scissors?"

"So much to worry about," muttered the man.

"And I'm just getting started." Boo calmly pulled out several thick documents. "That's why we have insurance for every imaginable scenario—and I've spent a great deal of time imagining and even creating such scenarios."

"But how much does it cost?" asked the husband.

"You only pay for what you need, Mr. Vinson." Boo's eyes grew brighter as if they had ignited from within. *"And you need everything!"*

Mrs. Vinson snatched at the policies. "Where do we sign?"

Boo flipped to the last page of the thick, legal-sized documents. "If you can pay a deposit this instant, your coverage begins immediately. Otherwise ..." The Boogeyman shrugged his bony shoulders beneath his black suit. "Who knows what could happen when you step out of the offices? There used to be a blacksmith shop upstairs and occasionally an anvil would fall from above."

Mrs. Vinson dug in her pocketbook. "Do you take personal checks?"

"Why, yes I do."

As the couple furiously signed every paper Boo put in front of them, Mr. Vinson seemed in a panic. His expression fell when he glanced at me in the doorway. "Does this insurance cover zombie attacks?"

"Of course. It covers everything," said the Boogeyman. "Nothing to be afraid of."

Sheyenne and I smiled politely as the young couple fled headlong from the insurance offices.

After the clients were gone, Boo collapsed into a shuddering mass of fear. "It's hard to project professionalism when every moment you expect your life to be torn apart! Please tell me what you've learned so far, Mr. Chambeaux. Are the aunties going to leave me alone?"

"I've been to see them in person, but I don't think I scared them."

Boo's eyes went wide as I explained my visit to the three aunts. "You're a brave zombie."

"Either that, or reckless," I said. "Em, Floraboding, and Widdershins tried to terrify me—and they succeeded—but zombies are relentless, especially zombie detectives."

"I wish I'd gone with you, Beaux," Sheyenne said. "I could scare them right back."

"They're just lonely," Boo groaned. "And they take it out on everyone else."

"They did mention that you hadn't visited them in ages. They miss you."

"They must have terrified you greatly when you were younger." Sheyenne drifted closer, concerned. "Did they abuse you? Give you nightmares?"

"Worse," Boo said with a groan. "They cuddled me and hugged me and pinched my gaunt cheeks. They showered me with food and love and gifts—and there's only so much a person can bear! They're too sweet … but only in private."

I recalled the ghoulish spectres that made my skin want to crawl right off my bones. "Too sweet? Not the impression they gave me."

Boo shook his head. "Oh, they wouldn't want anyone to know, because then no one would take them seriously. But when they're around their dear nephew …" He shivered.

Sheyenne remained perplexed. "But if they're really just softies inside, then why do they want you back on the job to strike mortal terror into everyone?"

"They just want to retire," said the Boogeyman. "They're afraid of not being feared."

As I considered their soft spot, an idea occurred to me. "I might know a way to scare them."

<h2 style="text-align:center">VI</h2>

Surveillance is one of the best ways to catch a bad guy in the act, or to dig up dirt on a not-so-bad guy. Or just to see what's going on.

In private investigator school, I took a full unit on Furtiveness. I learned a lot, though my grade was only mediocre because I covertly hid my work from the professor.

I couldn't stop thinking about Auntie Floraboding's odd behavior when McGoo had given her a traffic ticket for reckless carefulness. Shouldn't a manifestation of deepest fears, chaos, and mayhem be a little more *laissez-faire* with safety rules? Having seen the old lady in her most terrifying incarnation, I wondered if she was covering up her real over-cautious personality?

Back at the aunties' cozy brick townhouse, I crouched in the neighboring hedges, keeping an eye out for unexpected social activities. I hid in the shadows during daylight, and I huddled in the gloom as darkness set in. It was a stakeout, just like in countless movies, though without any buddy cop banter. And it was just as boring.

Finally, the front door opened, and one of the old ladies scuttled out, head down. She wore a dark shawl and a lacy hat pulled down to obscure her face. Though she had covered herself up well, I recognized Auntie Em. From what I'd learned in the Furtiveness class, I immediately spotted suspicious behavior.

Em darted forward, crossed the street, then crossed the street again, clearly trying to remain unnoticed, but she didn't elude me. I followed at a safe distance. She could have traveled more swiftly if she manifested her demonic form and swooped like a howling wind through the streets. Instead, the old lady scurried along the sidewalk, moving from one seedy part of the Quarter to an even seedier part. I couldn't imagine what Auntie Em was up to. Off to provoke terror in some unsuspecting homeless camp? Or to startle bar patrons into spilling their beers? Or just to flit past children's windows to give them quick nightmares? Maybe to hide under their bed or in the closet?

No, Em made her way to a soup kitchen—Miss Clara Baxter's Respite for Unfortunate Unnaturals. That was unexpected, and it angered me that the Boogeyman's nefarious auntie would harass these already-suffering monsters. I imagined her swooping in to antagonize them, disrupt the food servers, knock the coffee urns over, and chase the homeless trolls, vampires, and zombies back under their bridges or dilapidated crypts.

I decided to confront Em before she caused too much trouble, but before I could make my move, the old lady entered the soup kitchen, removed her lacy hat, shucked off her shawl, and donned a white apron and gloves.

Amazed and perplexed, I peered through the open door as a werewolf with a sorry case of mange shuffled past me to get a hot meal. Auntie Em stood behind the food line with other volunteers, where she ladled soup and offered plates of bread. She was serving the unfortunate unnaturals—with a smile!

I took furtive photos of her doing her part, sweet and attentive. I was so confused I tapped the bullet hole in the center of my forehead, but I found no thoughts or explanations there either.

How did this behavior fit with the manifestations of terror those three projected in public? Struggling to fit the pieces of the case together, I made my way back to the brick townhouse, wondering what nefarious, or unspeakably kind, activities the other two were up to.

It was full dark now, and I approached from the side of the building, hoping to glimpse the backyard. I heard someone make cooing noises as I crept up to the fence. A single yard light was on to illuminate the small, enclosed yard, which was only big enough for a few potted plants and a small table. Auntie Widdershins was bending down, whispering and whistling. She extended a saucer of milk across the ground.

The pesky black cat stood on the rear fence, his back arched, his ebony fur full and fluffy. "Here kitty, kitty," said Widdershins.

I wondered if she was luring the poor feral animal close so she could terrify it again. But the cat jumped down, circled just out of reach, then approached the saucer, where he began lapping up the cream. "Good kitty, kitty." The old lady reached out with a gnarled hand.

I was afraid she might strangle the cat, or cause him some terrible harm … but instead she scratched behind his ears, stroked him until he arched his back and then brushed against her leg. Even from my hiding place, I could hear him purr.

The cat swirled around, and Widdershins beamed. "Good kitty. Come back for treats whenever mommy calls you." The cat finished the cream, then bounded onto the fence and vanished off on his own nocturnal feline adventures.

Auntie Widdershins took the empty saucer and hurried back inside, thinking that no one had seen her.

I now had all the leverage I needed to get my client what he wanted.

VII

You've seen those old "scary" movies (now viewed as either comedies or documentaries) about rotting, brain-eating zombies terrorizing a town. Sure, under the right circumstances zombies can be terrifying and intimidating—but if I meant to intimidate the Boogeyman's three horrifying aunties, I would confront them with the scariest weapon in our arsenal.

I brought our lawyer.

Now that's intimidating.

Robin Deyer has a knack for making guilty parties cringe and reconsider their bogus pleas when she walks into a courtroom. She's beautiful, professional, and holds all the power because she *knows* she's right and has the passion to prove it to everyone else.

She wore a navy-blue blazer and skirt, white blouse, and carried a briefcase, which seemed as threatening as a mugger's gun. We were going to bring down some fear onto fear itself.

Together, we stepped up to the "Home Sweet Home" cross-stitched sampler hanging on the door and rang the bell.

Auntie Floraboding answered, glanced at the two of us, and her grandmotherly smile expanded into a more vicious grin. "Back for more, Mr. Shamble? One good scare deserves another."

"I believe we'll be doing the scaring today, Ms. Floraboding," Robin said.

The old lady tittered and let us in. "Delightful!"

While the three aunties bustled around as hostesses, Robin and I went into the sitting room. She set her briefcase on the coffee table, snapped it open, and withdrew a manila folder. When the old ladies sat down in their rocking chairs, she flipped open the folder to reveal papers that looked legal and scary. "This is a cease-and-desist restraining order, two for the price of one. You are hereby ordered to stop harassing our client."

"We're not harassing him," said Aunt Em. "We're helping him do his job."

"The boy must learn to take responsibility," said Widdershins.

"He's our dear nephew," said Floraboding.

Robin spread the papers on the coffee table, but I knew our real weapons were still in the briefcase. "You are interfering with Mr. Boogeyman's right to the pursuit of life, afterlife, liberty, and happiness."

"You can't threaten us," snapped Floraboding. "We're the most terrifying presences in the Unnatural Quarter."

"But we wouldn't have to be, if Boo would shape up," Em muttered.

"Oh, you'll want to comply," Robin said. "Once this paperwork is filed, it will become a matter of public record ... and we'll include certain documentation that you would not want anyone else to see."

"Documentation of what?" Widdershins asked.

I took my cue and pulled out the next folder. I shared the photos of Widdershins offering a saucer of cream to the black cat, followed by a shot of the cat rubbing against her legs, and, worst of all, Widdershins grinning with love and happiness as she petted him.

"That cat!" Auntie Em said. "You were supposed to scare it away."

"I ... couldn't," Widdershins mumbled.

"You're supposed to be terrifying," Em continued. "What will people think if they see a manifestation of mortal terror coddling an alley cat?"

"Indeed, what will people think?" Robin asked, dripping with sarcasm.

It was Em's turn. I pulled out the photos of her at the soup kitchen sweetly ladling food, helping out unfortunate unnaturals.

"That's what you do with your evenings, Em?" Floraboding recoiled. "What if someone recognizes you? We'd be ruined! We're supposed to be mayhem and chaos and nightmares."

Before Em could make excuses, I displayed a copy of the traffic citation that McGoo had issued to Floraboding. "And that's a little hard to do when you're one of the safest, most cautious drivers in the entire Unnatural Quarter."

Em snatched the ticket and scanned it, then looked in horror at her sister. "You got a citation for being *too careful*?"

"And a special letter of thanks from the car insurance company," Floraboding said, casting her gaze down. "I don't like to make other drivers worry. I could get in an accident."

"None of this is an accident," I said. "It's all on purpose."

Robin had assured me that blackmail and bluffing was an accepted legal strategy. "The world will know that you're actually just softhearted, sweet little old ladies. Not frightening at all." She snapped shut the briefcase. "And that is just a sample of what we've uncovered. You wouldn't want us to reveal all the other deep, dark secrets we have on you."

"No," Widdershins gasped. "That will ruin our reputations!"

The three aunts sat back in their rocking chairs, looking extremely nervous.

Frowning, I whispered to Robin, "What else do we really have on them?"

She lowered her voice. "There's always something. I'm just letting them play on their own fears."

I nodded. "Seems appropriate."

Em picked up the cease-and-desist restraining order. "Now, now, there's no need for you to file these papers. They haven't been signed or certified yet."

I said, "I came here the other day, hoping you would be reasonable. When that didn't work … Maybe now you three will do the right thing because you're scared."

Robin said, "This all goes away if you leave Mr. Boogeyman alone, let him live his life, and cut down on the nightmares."

The three aunts rocked silently for a few moments, hanging their heads. They glanced at one another, then let out a sigh in unison. "Very well, if that's what we have to do," said Floraboding.

"But we insist one thing in return," said Em. "Our boy Boo has to visit sometimes. He can't be a stranger. He needs to see his dear aunties."

Robin stood up, taking her briefcase and all the papers. "I think we can manage that."

VIII

The following Sunday, Sheyenne and I went out for a walk with Alvina, enjoying a pleasant few hours together. As we passed the townhouse where the three aunties lived, I was glad we didn't encounter any howling or shrieking or nightmarish activity.

The purring neighbor cat emerged from the bushes for some attention. Alvina bent under a ladder leaned against the building and petted the black cat, with one of her feet firmly placed on a crack in the sidewalk. My half-daughter is definitely fearless.

Sheyenne said, "Look, here comes Boo now. His first Sunday visit."

Striding down the sidewalk, the Boogeyman wore a clean black suit jacket and the same old thin black tie. He held a bouquet of wilted lilies in his hands. His skull-like face was pale as always, and he lowered his sunken eyes, as if nervous or guilty.

As the Boogeyman approached, the black cat hissed, arched his back, and sprang away.

Seeing us, Boo paused, drew a deep breath. "Now I have to face the music." He shuddered, looking at the "Home Sweet Home" sign on the townhouse door.

"It'll be a nice time," I said.

"It'll be a nightmare. Auntie Em will pinch my cheeks, and Auntie Floraboding will exclaim about how much I've grown, and Auntie Widdershins will insist that I need to eat more." His shoulders slumped, but then he raised his chin, summoning his courage. "But I can face this."

"It won't be so bad," Sheyenne said.

"Oh, it'll be bad, but I can give as good as I get." He spotted the black cat crouched by the corner of the townhouse and said, "Boo!" The cat yowled and bounded away. "I'm the Boogeyman."

He rang the bell as Sheyenne, Alvina, and I kept walking. We glanced behind us to watch the three aunties greeting Boo, hugging him, cooing over him, pinching his cheeks. They dragged him inside where he would have to endure the smothering kindnesses.

"Nothing to be afraid of," Alvina said.

I looked down at the kid. "Oh, there's plenty to be afraid of, but no need to worry about it."

The vampire girl skipped ahead, and I glanced up to make sure no pianos were falling out of the sky. I cocked my fedora and strolled along with my ghost girlfriend at my side. "Nothing to worry about," I said.

FIRE IN THE HOLE

I

The slime on the amphibian's face glistened in the office lights, but I could still see the tear spill out of his yellow eye. It ran slowly down the spots on his cheek.

I hate to see a salamander cry.

"It'll be all right, young man," I said, ushering him into Chambeaux & Deyer Investigations. "Tell us about your case."

Feeling supportive, even paternal, I put an arm around his small shoulders. That was unfortunate, because it left a sticky smear on my sport jacket sleeve, but the client always comes first.

"Come in," said Sheyenne, my ghost girlfriend, as she flitted forward from the reception desk. "You're safe here. What's your name?"

The young salamander walked upright, balanced by the thick tail that protruded through the rear of his patched trousers. Frayed old tennis shoes barely covered his webbed feet.

"I'm Syl." He sniffled, and the slime made a thick liquid sound in his sinuses. "I can't stand it anymore at home." His black forked tongue flicked in and out of his wide mouth, and another viscous tear rolled down the opposite spotted cheek. "I need to be emancipated!"

Sheyenne used her poltergeist powers to close the door, so he felt an added measure of safety. His slitted eyes flicked back and forth like a hunted animal. His head was slung low, as if he'd been browbeaten too many times.

Robin Deyer, my firebrand human lawyer partner, emerged from her office. She straightened her trim business suit. "It's our mission to help unnaturals everywhere," she said, her dark brown eyes already flashing. "Don't you worry, Mr., uh, Syl. Come into the conference room. We want to hear all about it."

"I just don't think I can face him alone," Syl said. "He's such a domineering presence." He hung his head even lower.

"Who?" Robin and Sheyenne both asked in unison, as if they meant to tag-team strangle whoever was picking on this endearing new client (although when dealing with monsters, strangling isn't always an effective option).

"My Pa!" Syl said. "If he knew I was here, he would whup the spots right off my hide."

A girl's cheery voice came from the back of the office. "Oh, he's so cute!" Alvina, my adorable vampire half-daughter, skipped out of the kitchenette, where she had been playing a slow game of tic-tac-toe with the sentient kitchen mold growing on our wall.

Startled, Syl spun about, thrashing his thick tail. He saw only what looked like a ten-year-old girl, although now that she had turned into a vampire, Alvina would never grow up. She came right up to Syl and reached out to shake his webbed hand. "Oh, it's sticky and slimy."

Syl nodded. "I put on a fresh coat so I'd look presentable. I wanted to make a good impression, so you'd take my case."

Robin gestured to the open door of the conference room. "Let's get all the details." She carried a yellow legal pad as well as the magic pencil that would transcribe her notes.

Even if this sounded like a strictly legal matter, I liked to sit in on intake meetings. Cases often spiraled out of control, and we might still need my skills as a zombie detective.

Over the years, Chambeaux & Deyer Investigations had seen many unusual cases. There was no shortage of work since the Big Uneasy—when an unusual alignment of planets, the correct phase of the moon, and the accidental spilling of a virgin's blood (a fifty-year-old clumsy librarian, but a virgin nevertheless) on the original *Necronomicon* brought back all the mythical monsters, ghouls, ghosts, vampires, werewolves, mummies, demons, etc. At first there had been a great uproar, but eventually all the unnaturals settled down in the Quarter and just tried to live their lives and get along.

I'd been a down-and-out P.I., and I set out my shingle here because I had no better place to go. When one of my cases went sour, someone came up behind me in a dark alley and shot me in the back of the head. But after the magic of the Big Uneasy, you can't keep a determined detective down. I clawed my way back up out of the grave as a zombie. Back from the dead, and back on the case.

Now, Sheyenne drifted into the conference room with a pitcher of water, green tea for Robin, bad coffee for me, and a juice box (special blood-orange blend) for Alvina. Syl took the pitcher of water and slurped some with his forked tongue and smeared more over his drying slime.

After bracing himself, he began to explain. "It's my Pa." He put his slimy elbows on the table surface. "He constantly criticizes me, crushes my spirit, makes me work sixteen-hour days. He locks me in my muddy tunnel room … and he yells a lot."

Robin's expression darkened with anger. "Does he beat you?"

"Sometimes with a belt, though he usually wears bib overalls, which don't have a belt. There are patches on my back where he really did knock the spots right off."

Then something changed in the salamander's demeanor, and

he sat up straighter. He squared his shoulders. "But I'm learning how to find my inner spirit, how to be strong, and how to stand up for myself! I've been taking self-esteem lessons."

"Good for you," Sheyenne said.

Alvina's grin showed her baby-teeth fangs as she slurped her juice box. Robin's enchanted pencil furiously took notes all by itself on the legal pad.

"I never would have been able to get this far without my guru," Syl said. "I know I can be brave. I can find the backbone because—" He pounded the conference room table with a small fist. "I may be an amphibian, but I am also a vertebrate!"

I wanted to cheer him on. "Indeed you are."

Then Syl lowered his spotted head again. "But I don't know the legal details. I want to be emancipated from Pa so I can live my own life, but I'm not considered an adult." He sniffled again, and two more gelid tears rolled down his face. "I'm too young."

"How old are you?" Robin asked.

"Ten."

"He's my age!" Alvina chimed in. "Or as old as I look."

Robin clucked her tongue. "I'm afraid that's too young for the law. Ten years old is still considered a child."

Syl flicked his forked black tongue out of his mouth. "But I'm not a child! The expected lifespan of a common salamander can be twenty to thirty years, so I've lived at least a third of my life. Surely that means I'm an adult? Relatively speaking?"

Alvina, who spent far too much time on Wikipedia, said, "Well, it depends on what kind of salamander. The giant Chinese salamander can live up to two hundred years."

"Then I'm screwed," Syl moaned. "I'll just have to go back to the ashram and keep learning how to be strong."

Robin considered. "Hmmm, I can make the case for you. An unnatural salamander is a different creature altogether, and the law is vague. I can argue that you qualify as an adult, subjectively speaking."

Syl beamed with renewed hope. I folded my gray hands on the table. "I can arrange for protection, if you do need a zombie private investigator."

"Oh, thank you!" Syl pressed his hands to his heart. "That helps me gain the confidence to find my inner me."

He had a definite spring in his step as he glided out of our offices.

II

That night I went out for a quiet midnight walk in the Unnatural Quarter. It was long after dark with the moon just rising—the busiest time for people and monsters to be out and about. The Talbot & Knowles Blood Bars did a brisk business, and the nightclubs were open and noisy. Little shops of horrors, as well as grocery stores, served plenty of customers.

I wore my sport jacket with the clumsily stitched bullet holes across the front, tilting my fedora just enough to cover the bullet hole in my forehead. I had recently been freshened up at the embalming parlor, and I felt good. I take great pains to maintain my appearance, mostly for the benefit of my ghost girlfriend. I'm not one of those rotting shamblers who eat at fast-food restaurants and refuse to take care of themselves.

The energy of the Quarter always helps me concentrate. As a detective, I can learn many details about cases and contacts just by wandering around, picking up the vibe. Besides, it keeps the rigor mortis out of my joints and makes me limber.

I bumped into Officer Toby McGoohan in his blue patrolman uniform standing on a street corner. All week he'd had the midnight shift. I raised my hand in a wave. "Hey, McGoo."

"Hey, Shamble." A grin spread across his freckled face.

Nearby, under an ornate wrought-iron lamppost, slouched a skeleton saxophone player with the instrument pressed against his teeth. He attempted to blast out a mournful, if clichéd, rendition of "Feelings," although the sax remained mercifully silent, because the skeleton had no lungs.

"Do you know how many lawn gnomes it takes to screw—" McGoo began, but before he could finish laying out his joke, we were interrupted by an enormous fire dragon that suddenly appeared overhead. Its breathy roar was accompanied by the crackling sound of serpentine flames. The thing looked like a reptilian inferno in the air.

All activity stopped in the streets. Several people screamed. Vampires and werewolves ducked for cover, and a considerate hunchback threw a flameproof tarp over a terrified mummy so his bandages would not catch fire.

The huge flame dragon was diaphanous, constructed entirely of fire, smoke, and burning gases. It roiled along above the rooftops in the Quarter, its long tail thrashing, its fiery jaws opening to exhale a gout of orange flames. The dragon was full of fire and menace, shooting sparks and cinders as it drifted overhead like a low-flying aircraft. Fires began to spread from rooftop to rooftop.

It was a disaster.

On the other hand, the monster's arrival had interrupted McGoo's dumb joke, so I would count that as a small victory.

McGoo placed one hand on each of his service revolvers, but neither the regular bullets nor the silver bullets would have any effect on this elemental creature. "What is that thing?"

"It's a *fire dragon*, obviously," I said. "But let's not worry about genus or species right now. We've got to protect the city!"

"Thanks for the help, Shamble," McGoo said, and we both started running.

Panicked people ran for shelter, though there was little to be had. A quick-thinking frog demon was resourceful enough to pop open a manhole. "Down here, down here!" he shouted, ribbeting like a frog. He leaped into the sewers with a loud splash, and a crowd of terrified pedestrians followed him.

The fire dragon moved across the sky like an alligator cruising through a swamp. It flapped its enormous flame wings, shot sparks in all directions, and ignited more fires.

McGoo was on the radio. "Call out the fire department. All divisions!" He listened to a squawk of static and yelled back, "It's a fire dragon! Better send the special unit!"

Taking our cue from the clever frog demon, the two of us popped open more manhole covers, directing the evacuation down below. We sent as many people as possible into the flowing tunnels of sewage, where they would be safe and comfortable.

Even as shockwaves of panic spread, the elemental flame dragon seemed unaware of the destruction and terror it was causing. Instead, it just drifted over the rooftops as if it, too, was out on a quiet midnight stroll.

I had no idea how to fight it or scare it off. The fires were spreading from roof to roof, and if something weren't done soon, the whole Quarter would become an inferno.

Then the creature flapped its wings and rose higher into the sky. As we watched, it simply dissipated into wisps of flame and thinning smoke.

But even though the threat was gone, the fires still raged. We heard a wailing, ear-splitting siren as the fire truck rolled up, a bright red tanker vehicle. A pale-skinned banshee with dark stringy hair clung to the side of the truck and let out a warbling wail that cleared all traffic and shattered nearby windows.

As soon as the driver screeched to a halt and the banshee stopped wailing, the tank hatch popped open. From inside, silvery frolicking water sprites burst upward as if they were riding a geyser. The water sprites giggled, playing together and dancing in the air as they pulled the water from the tanker and spread it out into streams.

"We've got this, hee-hee!" said the lead sprite, a chubby, silvery-skinned woman who flicked her fingers and sprayed water everywhere.

Other sprites reached to the sky and called in clouds, which galloped in from the horizon. The water sprites circled around each other as if playing Ring Around the Rosie, spraying water onto the burning rooftops.

Steam filled the air as the fires were extinguished. The playful sprites swooped down, chattering and spreading more water. Soon, a downpour burst out of the first black thunderhead, and the sprites elbowed one another, as if it were just horseplay in a swimming pool.

"It's great to see people who love their jobs," I said to McGoo.

The water sprites swept over the burning rooftops and extinguished the fires. In fact, the giggling creatures seemed disappointed that they were so swift and effective, which ended their play too soon.

Drenched, McGoo and I stood in puddles on the street. The water sprites spun around together and then sullenly returned to the tank in the back of the fire truck.

Next to us by the lamppost, the skeleton jazz musician continued swaying with his saxophone, playing his imaginary tune. We looked at the blackened rooftops, saw wisps of smoke still roiling up, but at least the fires were out.

"That could have been a great inferno, Shamble," McGoo said.

"Instead, it's just a scorch—at least this time." I shook water from the brim of my fedora. "Let's hope that fire dragon never returns."

III

Sometimes clients need more than our usual services—instead of just investigating nefarious activities, we can also provide moral support. When Syl the salamander asked if we would stand beside him for his graduation/ascension ceremony at the Wham-Bam Ashram, how could we refuse? The slimy little kid already had self-esteem issues.

"My Pa won't support me," Syl said on the phone to a very warm and understanding Sheyenne. "And I wouldn't want him there. He'd just complain and ruin everybody's state of bliss."

Sheyenne and I agreed to go to the ashram, while Robin burned the midnight oil (and the morning oil), studying case precedents for the emancipation of unnatural youths and larvae.

Alvina bounced up and down and really wanted to go, but it was McGoo's night to watch her. (He's her other half-daddy, and since neither of us actually knows who her real father is, we take turns.) Sheyenne and I decided it might not be a good idea to have the bubbly little vampire girl there. If there was going to be a lot of meditation and nirvana and bliss, it would be too much for a rambunctious kid.

We arrived at the Wham-Bam Ashram just after dark, with the full moon rising. Surrounded by beautifully landscaped gardens, it was an aesthetically pleasing structure set on a hill— and hills are hard to come by in the Unnatural Quarter, which is surrounded by swampland. The ashram was an impressive Asian pagoda with curved, pointy roofs, and the first floor was an open-air pavilion. The zigzag walkway up the hill was marked by a string of paper lanterns, lit by swarms of rent-a-fairies.

Although the architecture was non-culturally specific, it seemed just the right place to study enlightenment. Apparently, before the Big Uneasy, the ashram building had been a high-end tea house that had gone out of business.

Sheyenne glowed with satisfaction as she drifted beside me. I walked under the archway into the grand open pavilion floor of the Wham-Bam Ashram. Incense rose from fragrant torches burning in wall sconces.

I picked up a program sheet on the welcome table.

Enlightenment Ceremony
Graduation and ascension of our karma-positive students
Hosted by Guru Grbth

We entered, not sure where to go or what to do. Ahead, dozens of people were gathered in concentric circles around a central dais. Around the edges was an audience of parents, spouses, and demonic symbiotes who had come to show support for the graduates. I saw two proud-looking vampires, a scaly water creature who spritzed himself from a mister, and even a nervous-looking older human woman who seemed to be the aunt of one of the students.

On a raised central platform sat an enormous, burly ogre whose shaggy head was the size of a suitcase, covered with dreadlocks and fur—Guru Grbth, I assumed. His thick lower lip was like an inflated firehose. His eyes were as big as dinner plates. He wore a loose robe comprised of at least two bedsheets' worth of tie-dyed material, pastel pinks and blues and yellows. Somehow, perhaps with the aid of a forklift, he had lowered himself into a lotus position on a bamboo mat. He rested a huge, spiked club the size of a telephone pole on one knee.

Seated in circles on the floor were the ashram students, wearing white robes that covered their hairy, scaly, slimy, or pallid bodies. The students bent close to one another, whispering in barely contained excitement.

Syl sat in the outer ring, his slime glistening in the torchlight. He turned his head with unexpected flexibility and spotted us. He sprang to his feet and scampered over to us, his big tail waving from beneath the white robe. "You came! You really came to support me!"

"Of course we did, Syl," said Sheyenne.

"This means so much to me!" He reached out and shook my hand in a grip that felt like a glove filed with mucous.

"We'll help you stand up for yourself, kid," I said.

His tongue flicked out. "Guru Grbth is already teaching me

how to find my inner strength and delve to the depths of my soul. By meditating and using magic, I can find my true inner salamander."

Wind chimes tinkled and jangled, adding to the mood. The spectators around the room muttered in rising suspense, or maybe it was boredom, because everyone had waited so long for the ceremony to begin. On the dais, the guru shook his shaggy head and let out a belch.

"That's Guru Grbth?" I asked. "A little hard to pronounce isn't it?"

Syl nodded. "When you reach a certain stage of enlightenment, you no longer need vowels in your name."

"Really? What's the next stage?"

"Then you don't even use consonants." Syl tightened the sash of his white robe, keeping his voice low. "I've been sneaking away from home and taking these classes, and I've learned so much. I'm proud of my classmates, too. We've had werewolves with hair-loss problems, vampires with hemoglobin intolerances, ghosts who are afraid of their own shadows." He nodded to the other graduation candidates sitting in the circle, patiently waiting for the ceremony to begin.

"Even some mummies, I see." Sheyenne indicated a pair of old cloth-wrapped bodies that looked like dried collections of twigs.

"Oh, those two—some of Grbth's most famous students. They've attended for five years running."

"It takes that long to graduate?"

"Not really. They just got down into the lotus position and have never been able to get up again."

In the back of the room, an Igor assistant swung a mallet and bashed a large copper gong, which nearly deafened us. It did accomplish its aim of hushing the audience. Syl shook my hand again, then scurried back to his place among the students.

Grbth's deep and resonant voice rumbled out. "We begin with a brief meditation." He lifted one massive hand and curled his thumb and forefinger together in an *O*. With his other hand, he raised the spiked club and bashed it on the floor while humming a drawn-out, thunderous "BOOOOOOOMMM!"

All of the students repeated the same sound, and the ogre bashed his club again, calling out the meditation syllable. "BOOOOOOOMMM!"

I turned to Sheyenne. "I thought they were supposed to chant *Om*."

"This sound is more definitive," she said.

After several minutes of this, the Wham-Bam Ashram was shaken to its foundations, and I worried the tall pagoda would come tumbling down. Finally, the ogre guru stopped. With astonishing nimbleness, he unfolded himself and rose to his feet, letting the tie-dyed robe hang around him like the tent of a Woodstock ghost.

"We are gathered to celebrate the graduation of a new group of students. I taught them the ways of enlightenment, inner peace, and strength. They have unlocked the true potential of their souls, and tonight they will each be presented with … the Amulet of Importance."

In his sausage-like fingers, Grbth lifted a tiny gold chain with a little locket in the middle.

The enlightened students tittered and gasped. The other spectators, including myself and Sheyenne, were both impressed and confused.

The ogre swung his large eyes over the gathered students, peaceful yet extremely proud. "You have all learned how to be your true selves. I know you will do great things for monsters everywhere."

"BOOOOOOOMMMM!" yelled a werewolf student, whose fur bristled in many different directions.

"BOOOOOOO!" yelled a ghost, drawing the sound out to a pleading moan good enough to haunt a castle.

"Booooooommm!" squeaked a lawn gnome, wobbling back and forth.

The petrified mummies rasped out the cheer themselves, and soon everyone joined in. Syl seemed delighted.

Grbth called the students by name, and each filed up to the central dais. Uniformed Igors stood at the base of the dais and handed each graduate a printed certificate and a little gold chain.

Syl was one of the last. Swelled with pride and confidence, he swiveled his spotted head to reassure himself that we'd stayed through the ceremony. I gave him a congratulatory nod.

The little salamander stepped up to the dais, leaving faint slime tracks from the holes in his tennis shoes. The guru ogre bowed his wagon-sized head. "You, Syl, are one of my greatest students. You have truly learned from me. You already have the power within yourself." Grbth took the gold chain from the nearby Igor and draped it over the narrow amphibious head. "With this Amulet of Importance, I say that you are ready for the world. Go face whatever challenges arise."

The gold chain slid down the slime-coated neck. Syl's forked tongue flicked in and out, then he danced off the stage, letting the next enlightened graduate come up behind him. He scuttled back to join us, glowing with excitement.

"We're very happy for you," said Sheyenne.

"Congratulations. You did real good, kid," I said. "I'm sure your father would be proud of you, too."

Syl's head drooped. "I have to change into street clothes. My Pa would say it's all a waste of time. He doesn't know this is how I spend my allowance."

I felt sad and disappointed to hear this. "It'll get better. We'll help."

IV

Even after Syl the salamander had graduated into self-confidence and the next stage of enlightenment, complete with his Amulet of Importance bling, his life was still downtrodden drudgery.

I came upon the poor slimy kid just after I had finished serving an eviction notice to a rowdy frat-boy poltergeist. The ghost had died of alcohol poisoning during a college party and was still so spiritually inebriated he didn't even know he was dead—nor was he happy to get the eviction notice. Nevertheless, the unpleasant deed was done, and Sheyenne could send a bill to the client. I felt as if a burden had been lifted from my shoulders.

Then I saw Syl slogging along the streets in his patched pants and tattered sneakers. His body was splattered with mud, which did not actually look out of place among the spots. He pushed a wheelbarrow piled high with thick mud, head down, forked tongue lolling out with exhaustion. As he drove his load down the street, some of the mud dribbled off the sides and splattered onto the pavement.

"Hi Syl," I said. "Looks like you're hard at work."

The young salamander looked up at me. "Sorry I can't stop and talk, Mr. Shamble. I have to haul two more loads of mud today or my Pa will get mad."

He was not at all the bright and confident salamander I'd seen the night before in the Wham-Bam Ashram. I tried to sound encouraging. "My partner is still researching the age re–quirements for a sentient salamander to apply for emancipation from an abusive parent. But seeing this ..." I shook my head. "We might have an argument both ways. If the court insists that you're underage, then we can charge your father for violating child labor laws."

"Just doing my chores," Syl said as he plodded along, and I shambled beside him. "It's not a job, because he doesn't pay me. Except my allowance. That's how I paid for my teachings from Master Grbth. Worth every penny."

The overburdened wheelbarrow creaked. "Where are you taking this load?" I asked.

"I'm hauling mud from the swamp on the west side of town to the swamp on the east side of town."

"And why would you take mud from the west side?" I asked, wondering if it was a better quality of muck.

Syl kept trudging along. "To make room for the mud that I carry back from the eastern swamp. My father says the swamps are due for a full-fledged mud exchange, and I'm the one who has to do it. I've been at this for two years now."

My heart went out to him, and I knew Robin would be furious when she heard this. "Not today, kid. We'll deliver this load and then go home. I want to meet your father." As a zombie I can be looming and intimidating, though I prefer not to be confrontational. I decided to make an exception for stern salamander parents, though.

We walked along, chatting, and I tried to lift his mood. Syl was very proud of the tiny gold amulet dangling from a chain at his neck.

When we got outside of the Quarter to the eastern swamp, I helped the salamander push the heavy wheelbarrow over to where a long shovel had been stuck between mangrove roots. Together, we dumped the mud into the murky swamp with a big brown plop.

Syl looked forlornly at the shovel. "I've got to load up again and head back to the west side. Five loads each day. That's my quota."

"Today we're changing the quota," I said in a hard voice. "Leave the wheelbarrow here. I want to have words with your father. I'll take the heat if he gets upset."

Syl's tongue flicked in and out. "Mythical salamanders had a lot of heat, but my Pa and I are just mud salamanders."

"You're not 'just' anything, kid. We're getting you out of this mess."

Agitated and uneasy, Syl led me along a well-worn path into the dreary mudflats, the neighborhood where he had grown up and where his father—whose name was Neb—had built a hovel. It was all they could afford, since Neb was lazy and refused to work.

STIFFS AND STONES 41

The hovel was a rounded hummock of mud covered with moss and dead patchy grass. Empty cans of beans and Vienna sausages were scattered around the lawn; the most prominent feature was an old rusty wheelbarrow propped up on cinderblocks, its axle broken.

The muddy mound was not at all like an English barrow. I had seen some of the nice, remodeled barrows that a group of entrepreneurial wights were offering for short-term rentals on AirBNBarrow. This one, though, did not look like that.

"That's my home," Syl said. "A nasty, dirty, wet hole, filled with the ends of worms and an oozy smell." He blinked his yellow eyes. "Not like the comfortable holes I read about in *The Hobbit*."

The hovel was made even nastier by the surly-looking salamander who sat in a metal lawn chair on the front porch next to the round door. Neb wore a pair of faded bib overalls with no undershirt so I could see the spotty flesh in his armpits. His spots were gray and leprous looking, and his eyes blazed with a tinge of red.

The pudgy salamander let out a grumbling hiss, then wrenched himself out of the chair, thumping his thick tail back and forth. "What are you doing home, boy?" His forked tongue lashed out of his mouth. "You ain't put in a sixteen-hour day yet!"

"I want you to meet somebody, Pa." Syl clutched the arm of my sport jacket and tugged me forward.

"Don't want to meet nobody, and I warned you never to make friends."

I loomed in front of the elder salamander as best I could. "I'm Dan Chambeaux, private investigator."

"You're a zombie," Neb snapped.

"And you're very observant," I said. "We're looking into your son's welfare and possible abuse. Slavery isn't a sign of being a good parent."

"I'm his guardian. The boy has to earn his keep." Neb

lurched closer, trying to be menacing, but I can be menacing too. I held my (muddy) ground.

Neb glowered. "I took care of that boy since he hatched. His mother abandoned the whole clutch of eggs after she spawned. No-good whore! Left me with barely enough of our eggs to eat, but I missed this one." He nudged an elbow toward the sulking and intimidated Syl. "So, he hatched, and I had to take care of him. I raised him to do a good day's work and to take care of his Pa." He snapped at the spotted young salamander. "Go crawl into the hole and lock yourself in your room. You're grounded!"

Syl's eyes lit up. "Really?" The delight was plain in his voice. "Then I can finish reading *The Hobbit*!" He ducked through the round door and slithered into the tunnel beneath the hovel.

Neb glared at me. "And you mind your own damn business!" He slouched back down into his metal lawn chair.

I certainly knew my own damn business. I turned away, thinking of the additional details I could report to Robin so she could file amended paperwork for Judge Hawkins.

V

That night as Sheyenne and I were reading Alvina a bedtime story after she crawled into her large cardboard coffin box—the vampire girl had asked for *Children's Selections from the Necronomicon*—the enormous fire dragon appeared again over the Quarter. It looked even larger than the first time.

When I looked through the dingy windows of my upstairs apartment, I could see the blazing reptilian entity rising over the rooftops.

Alvina peered next to me. "Oh, it's like a nightlight!"

Fire alarms rang throughout the city, and banshee sirens wailed. At least the water-sprite firefighters were going to have fun tonight.

"Keep Alvina safe," I said to Sheyenne as I hurried for the

door. "I better go see if I can help. I'm sure McGoo is already running to the scene."

"What can you do about it?" Sheyenne asked, concerned.

"Well …" I paused and pondered. "McGoo and I stood there and watched last time, and that was pretty effective."

I was out the door before she could make a counter-argument.

I lurched off at full speed, slipping into "fast zombie" mode. The elemental dragon beat its blazing wings like huge sails. It craned its serpentine neck, opened its jaws, and coughed out even brighter fire. Sparks flew from its lashing tail.

The ethereal creature circled overhead, bellowing into the night, but it didn't attack. A monster of such great size could have blasted the whole Quarter into cinders if it wanted to. But when the fire dragon trumpeted out a call and blasted flames into the sky, the sound didn't seem angry or vengeful. Rather, it felt more triumphant, like a celebration of freedom or confidence (not that I'm an expert on elemental dragon sounds).

I could see where the creature was heading—straight toward the tall pagoda tower of the Wham-Bam Ashram.

While the rest of the UQ emergency-response teams raced to quench fires and rescue innocent victims, I decided to head the thing off at the source.

I wondered if Grbth could help. After all, the ogre guru was so enlightened he no longer needed vowels in his name.

As I raced up the steep, zigzag path to the tiered pagoda, I wished the ashram had simply chosen a straight line instead of a sidewalk that symbolized the winding journey of life. The paper lamps along the walkway were dark; apparently the rent-a-fairies weren't working tonight.

The fire dragon circled high above, bellowing out more fire, thrashing sparks from its tail. I could hear the furnace crackling of its passage.

I ducked into the open pavilion, which was nearly empty. On

his bamboo mat on the raised dais, the huge ogre was again sitting in a lotus position, still holding the spiked club.

"Hello!" I called out. "Mr. Grbth, there's a fire dragon overhead! Better get out before it destroys the whole ashram."

The ogre raised his head. Despite the crisis going on throughout the Quarter, he seemed utterly at peace, content with his role in the universe. His heavy-lidded eyes opened and closed with the deliberate slowness of an electric garage door. His voice rumbled out. "I am aware of all things. That is one of the benefits of achieving nirvana. I no longer need security cameras."

I felt suddenly suspicious. "Do you have something to do with that fire dragon?"

Grbth hung his huge head. "Yes, I am partly responsible. I must take care of this unsettling ripple in the stream of peaceful consciousness." He looked toward the roof of the pagoda and the many levels of the pavilion above. "Sometimes my followers don't even know their own strength, once it's unlocked."

"Your followers?" I asked. "One of your students is doing this?"

"No—one of my graduates. Now I must meditate." Grbth closed his eyes again and raised the spiked club. He pounded the floor with a resounding thud. From the depths of his solar plexus emerged a rumbling meditative sound. "Boooooooommm! Boooooooommm!"

The vibrations did something strange to the air, and I felt dizzy. I backed away, worried that the fire dragon would incinerate the ashram at any moment. The unfazed ogre had fallen into a deep meditative state, and I could see there would be no convincing him. Since he was the size of a small automobile, I certainly couldn't move him against his will.

When I dashed outside, I gazed up at the pinnacle of the pagoda, where the fire dragon loomed in the air. Elsewhere in the Quarter, emergency crews had responded, and the water sprites worked alongside conventional fire-suppression crews to extinguish the flames. But unless the restless elemental creature was stopped, it would keep spreading fire wherever it went.

But as I stared up at the dragon, another figure rippled in the air. A huge, intimidating form rose up through the pavilion's open windows and balconies, until it coalesced in the sky to become a misty but terrifying manifestation of Guru Grbth.

The huge ogre had created an astral projection of himself and now hovered in the open air to face off against the dragon. Planning ahead, Grbth carried an astrally projected spiked club. It was like a scene from one of those Godzilla versus Monster of the Week movies, and I prepared myself for a smackdown.

The fire dragon flapped its enormous wings, scattering sparks and little flames. The spectral ogre loomed closer, reached out a muscular arm.

I cringed, looking for cover.

The shimmering guru gently patted the fire dragon on its flaming head.

Astral Grbth mumbled a soothing meditative sound, and the elemental dragon circled closer, thrashing like a dog wagging its tail. The ogre stroked his hand down the dragon's spine.

"There, there …" boomed Grbth's voice. "Focus. Find your center. You have unlocked your inner strength. Now you must control it."

The fire dragon flapped its wings and rolled in the air, so the astral ogre could scratch its scaly belly. More sparks flew. The flickering dragon rumbled and purred, then pulled away, drifting higher. It flapped giant incandescent wings and rose into the air where it spread out, faded, then dissipated into mere curls of smoke.

The astrally projected ogre nodded in satisfaction, and then he, too, faded into nothingness.

I bolted back into the ashram to find Grbth stirring on his bamboo mat. He stood up with a groan and a grumble, placing a hand against the small of his back as if he had pulled a muscle.

"All taken care of, for now," said the ogre guru. "Sometimes they get excited once they reach enlightenment, but with great power comes great responsibility." Grbth scratched his shaggy beard and belched. "I need to have my students start meditating over comic books."

"What are you talking about? Who was it?" But I already knew. "It's Syl, isn't it?"

The big ogre nodded. "Yes, poor boy. Terrible home life. He needed self-esteem and self-protection. Here at the Wham-Bam Ashram, I teach my students to find the strength within. Syl discovered and released his inner salamander."

VI

I couldn't do this alone. After rushing back to the office, I rounded up Robin, who was now armed with all the paperwork she had filed—as well as an emergency protective order she had just received from Judge Hawkins. That would help poor Syl even more than his Amulet of Importance.

As we set off for the salamander hovel in the mudflats, Sheyenne demanded to go along. And since Alvina was not technically able to stay by herself (and it was far too late to get an emergency babysitter), my half-daughter tagged along as well, even though sinister swamps and fire dragons and abusive amphibious fathers weren't exactly the best things for a little kid to be exposed to.

When we got to the barrow-shaped hovel, it was clear we had found the right place. On the ground, the slurry of stagnant water and brown ooze bubbled like volcanic mud pots. The air sparkled and flashed overhead, manifesting just a hint of the fire dragon. Alvina watched the light show and grinned with fascination.

With her ghostly speed, Sheyenne drifted ahead of us. "Hurry Beaux!" she called back. "I hear shouting! I don't want Syl to get hurt."

Robin stalked forward, clutching the legal briefcase against her side. "That Neb Salamander is going to be in more trouble than he can imagine. We'll sue every last spot off of him."

A geyser erupted in the mudflat, and sulfurous steam hissed out. The fiery dragon flickered in the air again. We reached the round door set into the grass-covered mound just as another mud pot burbled open and swallowed the broken old wheelbarrow propped on cinderblocks.

Behind the sealed round door, Robin and I could hear shouting. "Get to your room, you worthless slimy son of a—"

I pounded on the door. "Neb, open up! Zombie detective!" It wasn't as intimidating as yelling "Police!" but at least he would know we weren't door-to-door salespeople.

The shouting stopped, and I heard squishy sounds approaching. Robin opened her briefcase and pulled out the legal document, holding it like a battle axe.

The round door swung inward to reveal the dank, muddy tunnels inside. "What do you want?" Neb demanded. He still wore the same old bib overalls.

"This is a legal decree." Robin thrust the protective order forward. "Your son Syl has requested emancipation from you. He is to be cut loose immediately. You no longer have any parental rights."

"Emancipation!" Neb growled. "That's too damn many syllables. Let me see that." He grabbed the document out of Robin's hands, leaving slimy prints on the paper.

"We also have it digitally recorded," Sheyenne added.

From the back of the tunnel, Syl slunk forward. Seeing us, he seemed to find inner self-confidence. "I hired them, Pa, because I don't want to live with you anymore. You don't treat me right. I'm my own person."

Neb crumpled the emancipation decree and threw it into the mud outside. "I am his guardian. He's mine to do with as I please. He's too young to face the world alone."

"He was old enough to face you," I said. "Syl is stronger than you can imagine."

"I found my inner salamander!" Syl clutched the little gold Amulet of Importance around his neck.

Overhead, the sparks and wispy flames coalesced, creating the fire dragon. "That's me." He jabbed a webbed hand toward the astral manifestation. "That's who I am inside—a fire dragon! And I'm not afraid of you anymore."

Neb was certainly afraid, however. "Why you ungrateful little—"

The fire dragon roared, and a whoosh of diaphanous flames swept across the mudflats. Neb ducked back into the tunnel.

Robin extended a hand and took Syl's slimy fingers, pulling the young salamander out into the night, while Sheyenne and Alvina came closer to support him. Robin said, "You can start over, Syl. You're legally and completely free. The judge agreed with our case."

"What am I supposed to do?" Neb squirmed. "Haul all that mud myself? Wheelbarrow after wheelbarrow, from one swamp to another? It's ridiculous."

"It's ridiculous," I agreed.

"But Syl won't be part of it," Robin said.

Sheyenne drifted down and picked up the wadded emancipation decree. "I did mention that we also have a digital copy."

I said to surly Neb, "Maybe if you went to the Wham-Bam Ashram, you could work hard, meditate ... and find your own inner *worm*."

"Wait, there's something I still need from my room." Syl withdrew his hand from Robin's and ducked back into the dank tunnel.

While we waited, we faced off against Neb, but the abusive amphibian didn't have the vocabulary to express what he really felt.

Syl emerged a moment later holding a beloved battered paperback copy of *The Hobbit*. "Now we can go—for good."

We walked proudly away from the mudflats, and Alvina

skipped along next to the young salamander. I could tell they would stay friends. Syl was so happy, he even managed to whistle a cheerful tune with his forked tongue.

"We'll set you up in temporary lodgings, and I'm sure you can get a job. You'll have countless opportunities," Robin said.

"I'm a salamander," Syl said, taking it as a badge of honor. "The future is bright as mud."

As we strolled along, the fire dragon appeared again overhead, glowing bright and happy. Golden sparks flew in all directions. With a companion like that, I knew Syl wouldn't have any trouble at all.

HAND JOB

n the Unnatural Quarter, it seems like every monster and mythical creature wants to tell their life (or un-life) story—from werewolves spinning a hairball of a tale, to ghosts waxing spiritual, to vampires with a pointed biography.

But when a disembodied crawling hand—C.H. for short—decided to write his tell-all memoir, communication proved difficult. Still, at Chambeaux & Deyer Investigations, we were happy to help.

The precocious appendage entered our offices riding the back of a fat white sow, so I immediately knew the situation was well in hand. The pig prodded the door open with her nose, while the crawling hand gripped one of her ears between thumb and forefinger, in case the ride got bumpy. Behind them came a plump, smiling witch with an outburst of steel-wool hair under a pointy black hat adorned with stars and moons. The witch's long hooked nose sported a stylish wart, and her voluminous black dress smoothed and also widened her hips.

I had just stepped out of my office, ready to don my fedora and wander the streets of the Quarter in search of mysteries, or maybe just lunch at the Ghoul's Diner. But I was always happy to chat with the Wannovich sisters.

"Mavis," I said with a grin on my cold gray lips, "and Alma! A pleasure to see you ladies. And C.H., it's been a long time!"

The disembodied hand twitched on the pig's neck, and Alma, the sow, reacted as if it were a back rub.

Mavis and Alma Wannovich were busybody witch sisters active in social circles around the Unnatural Quarter. They were both lonely spinsters and, like every human and unnatural, they wanted a little romance in their lives. Alma had once attempted to cast a love spell from a popular manual, but the spell backfired due to an unfortunate typo, and the result irreparably transformed her into a large sow. Although Alma had adapted to her porcine circumstances, she and Mavis had sued Howard Phillips Publishing for failure to run a proper spell-check. As a result, the Wannovich sisters now held senior editorial positions at the company, achieving some success with a ghost-written series of my fictionalized and occasionally ridiculized cases as "Dan Shamble, Zombie P.I."

Mavis cackled a greeting. "Mr. Chambeaux, while we appreciate your harrowing adventures, you'll just be a side story in our new epic autobiography of Mr. Crawling Hand, titled *Hand Out*."

Riding the pig's back, C.H. tilted onto his wrist stump to extend a forefinger, twirling it in triumph.

My beautiful ghost girlfriend Sheyenne rose up from the receptionist's desk, sparkling and ectoplasmic. Most new clients react more positively to a sparkly, curvaceous, blonde poltergeist than to a zombie with a bullet hole in his forehead. "We'll help in any way." She beamed. "C.H. is an upstanding, five-fingered citizen."

I reached out to shake the hand's hand, which lifted him off Alma's back. I said, "C.H. certainly helped me out down in the sewers when we fought against Ah'Chulhu and his evil real-estate plot." I set C.H. on Sheyenne's desk to give him more room to scuttle about. "So tell us about the project."

Alma bent her flat nose to the rug and snuffled around, grunting an explanation, which Mavis translated. "Mr. Crawling Hand came to us with a book proposal for his memoir. As a small, detached limb, he surreptitiously observed many important events, and he'll point the finger at some of the criminal activities he witnessed."

On Sheyenne's desk, C.H. fluttered his fingers, trying to communicate. It looked like he was playing a fast arpeggio on a piano.

Mavis's brow furrowed as she tried to make sense of the motions. "Ummm, he says it will be a sensitive story, compassionate, and very … touching."

"Will there be a digital edition?" I asked.

The witch gave a vigorous nod. "And a braille edition. C.H. has also agreed to do special signature sheets for us."

The hand scuttled across the desktop and picked up one of the pens next to Sheyenne's computer, proudly tucking it between thumb and forefinger as he pretended to sign his autograph.

"But he won't be narrating the audiobook," Mavis added.

"Understandable," I said. "Not everybody has the voice for it."

"I can't wait to read it," Sheyenne said. "Do you need us to give background interviews and pertinent information?"

"So long as we don't breach any legal or ethical agreements." Robin Deyer emerged from her office. She was a beautiful African American woman with large brown eyes and neat hair clipped back with barrettes. She wore a smart navy business suit and carried a legal briefcase under her arm, although I knew she wasn't due in court until tomorrow morning.

"Of course, Ms. Deyer," said Mavis. "Due to the privacy issues, we will only expose the juiciest parts to scandal."

Robin gave a satisfied nod. She has a warm heart and a legal mind like a steel trap. Ever since the Big Uneasy, she had set her sights on finding justice for the downtrodden, which in this case meant the various unnaturals for whom old human law did not apply.

While Alma snorted and snuffled, a shrill squeal came from the conference room, and our little vampire girl darted out, wearing her pink unicorn sweater. Her blond hair was in bouncy pigtails, and her baby fangs were bright white against her lips. "Piggy, piggy!" My half-daughter Alvina had a special bond with the Wannovich sisters, particularly Alma, and she threw her arms around the sow's neck. "I'm doing homework about pig demons and frog demons. Do you want to see?"

Alma pricked up her ears and snorted. The kid was excited as she led the sow into the conference room, where her homework notes were strewn across the table.

C.H., meanwhile, gestured wildly, raised fingers in a peace sign, then curled into a fist and rolled around before balancing himself on a pinky. Mavis looked confused. "Sorry, I can't tell what he's trying to say."

Robin leaned closer. "Ah, he's using standard GSL. I'm well-trained in unnatural sign language."

"What does the G stand for?" Mavis asked.

"Goblin, in most instances, although it's applicable to gargoyles, gremlins, ghosts, and garglebeasts, but it has recently been expanded for use by any unnaturals who have at least one hand." She nodded toward C.H. "There's a simplified version for people with tentacles."

Delighted that he could now be understood, the crawling hand made gesticulations, finger movements, the hang loose symbol, and death-metal devil horns.

"What he says is compelling and alarming," Robin translated as C.H. continued his silent soliloquy. "He comes from a broken home, a divided family. There's crime and treachery—and lots of sex."

"Sex?" Sheyenne's pale glow intensified as she flashed me a glance.

Alvina popped her head out of the conference room. "Sex?"

"You go back in there, kid," I said.

Alma nudged the little vampire girl back to the report on pig and frog demons.

The severed appendage pranced about, and Robin explained, "He says he has a lot to tell."

C.H. hopped down onto Sheyenne's keyboard, and his fingers danced across the keys. Along the bottom of her screen, which currently held an overdue invoice from a harpy who was suing her equally unpleasant ex-husband for unpaid child support, the hand typed, "It was a dark and stormy night, and all good hands were sound asleep on their velvet pillows—"

Then our door burst open, and UQPD cops swarmed in, led by Officer Toby McGoohan. "Halt! Police!" I realized this was not a friendly visit, though he smiled when he saw me. "Oh, hey, Shamble!" He seemed surprised to find me standing in my own offices.

C.H. froze on the keyboard, his first two fingers lifted in surrender. Mavis raised her hands after straightening her pointed hat. Robin instinctively placed herself between the police and our clients, though none of us knew what this was about.

Snorting, Alma waddled out of the conference room with Alvina right next to her. The kid flashed a pointy smile at McGoo. "Half-daddy!"

"Hi, darlin'. Sorry to interrupt your homework." He pulled a folded paper from the pocket of his blue uniform shirt. The other cops with him—a vampire, a werewolf, and a pimply-faced human—had their guns drawn, ready to face some imaginary threat.

McGoo cleared his throat. "I have an arrest warrant for the appendage that goes by the name of Crawling Hand, aka C.H.

He's been implicated in a smash-and-grab robbery at an Egyptian antiquities boutique."

C.H. rocked back on his wrist stump and splayed his fingers, either in denial or surrender.

"I'm sure he has an alibi," I said.

"He was caught red-handed." McGoo withdrew handcuffs from his belt and clipped the silver bracelet around the end of the severed wrist.

Robin was indignant. "We'll get to the bottom of this, C.H. I will act as your attorney."

"Oh, that's nice of you," said Mavis.

McGoo picked up the crawling hand, but the handcuff fell right off the empty wrist. "No resisting arrest now! I've got you in my grasp."

C.H. was trembling. Still holding the cuffs, McGoo snatched up the hand separately as the other policemen retreated to guard the hallway.

II

While C.H. was booked and fingerprinted, then placed in a holding cell, I faced McGoo at his cluttered desk in the squad room, demanding to know details of the crawling hand's supposed crime.

In her ectoplasmic form, Sheyenne hovered next to me, just as worried. "You're sure you have evidence against this particular separate hand, Officer McGoohan?"

"Oh, it's this hand, all right. The night guards identified him from mug shots."

I pressed, "I want to know what he was accused of stealing."

McGoo contemplated a stack of forms and files on his desk and scooped it all into the trash can. "I have more paperwork to do at the scene of the crime, Shamble. Come on, I'll take you there myself. The evidence techs are still bagging and tagging. One of the messiest crime scenes I've ever experienced."

I couldn't imagine that the clever, nimble hand would be involved in bloody work. "Was it a violent robbery?"

"No, but the mummy proprietor is a very disorganized hoarder—you'll see what I mean."

Ready to go, McGoo tucked his blue cap over his short red hair. He grinned a lot, usually at his own inappropriate jokes, which had gotten him in deep trouble in the past. We had been close friends when I first set up my detective agency in the Quarter, and he walked his daily beat. We remained friends even after I was shot in the back of the head when a case of mine went sideways. I'd clawed my way out of the grave and started work as a zombie P.I. My own cases frequently required the resources of the police department, and McGoo just as often leaned on me for off-book investigations.

Now he led me and Sheyenne at a brisk pace across the Quarter, then down a back alley crowded with boutiques and curiosity shops. Yellow crime-scene tape was draped around the front of Notions of the Nile, whose sign was decorated with hieroglyphics that looked suspiciously like Egyptian emojis.

Sheyenne flitted inside, passing through the crime-scene tape and even the solid wall so she could move among the crowded artifacts. McGoo and I followed her, but we had to go through the regular door. Looking around, my ghost girlfriend said, "How would anyone find a specific thing in all this clutter?"

Gremlin evidence techs moved about using magnifying glasses and museum brushes to study mounds of artifacts, rolled rugs, vases, urns, tapestries, carvings, ashtrays, cat toys, pharaoh love seats, and macramé hangings. With my analytical detective mind, I classified all the items as *Junk*.

The gremlins darted from shelf to shelf, dusting for fingerprints. They took photographs with large cameras, then used their iPhones to click selfies in front of a display of "I ❤ Egypt" sphinx curios.

"Hey, careful with that!" cried a rattling, raspy voice, and the gremlin techs chittered at one another. A thin, desiccated figure wrapped in dingy linen strips creaked forward, making insistent gestures with petrified hands. "Every item is categorized according to rarity and discount code." He turned to McGoo with a whistling huff through his sinus cavities, as if blaming him. "I've been robbed, Officer! I'm already a victim— do not make me a victim again with your oafish incompetence."

McGoo lifted his chin. "I prefer to think of it as *exceptional* incompetence."

The mummy hobbled forward on rattling, bandage-wrapped legs. Seeing my fedora, he assumed I was a private detective of some importance. "My name is Akhenatenominimum. Or Tony, for short."

I was glad to know the short version. "Pleased to meet you, Tony." I grasped his hand, careful not to break any of the desiccated bones.

He turned his coal-black eyes to me, as if hoping for better service. "I was robbed last night! Come, look at my curio case that holds the most valuable items in my shop."

Tony creaked over to a nook near the front of the store. "Notions of the Nile caters to only the most discriminating aficionados of ancient Egypt."

Next to an antiquated cash register, a glass cabinet held items of exceptional value, including some rarities that were priceless (or at least, they had no visible price tags). The top pane had been shattered, leaving a wide, jagged hole.

"That severed hand smashed the glass with his knuckles and snatched my most valuable artifact! A precious rolled scroll from ancient and magical times, sealed in a bright green scarab case."

"And what was this artifact, Mr. Akhenateno—uh … Tony?" I asked.

"It was very valuable!" the mummy exclaimed.

"Other than that …" I prodded.

"It was sealed by incredibly powerful wizards of the Nile, written down from a revelation by the well-known pharaoh fitness expert, Na-Pu-Ko-Tak." He paused, as if waiting for us to be impressed.

"I've never heard of him," Sheyenne said.

McGoo shrugged. "My mummy knowledge ends with Boris Karloff and Brendan Fraser."

"Na-Pu-Ko-Tak wasn't all that well-known," Tony admitted. "But he was very smart and gifted in the dark arts. On that scroll, sealed for millennia inside the valuable scarab case, was written the *secret of immortality!*"

"Hmmm, it does sound like a powerful spell," I said.

Sheyenne looked around. "Are you sure it's not just lost here in the clutter somewhere?"

McGoo crossed his arms over his chest. "We'll find it, sir. Our evidence techs are the best in the business."

From the other side of the shelves came a loud crash as a cat-shaped urn fell, knocking down piled scrolls and a set of matching Egyptian cigarette cases.

"We found fingerprints all over the place!" called out one of the gremlins. "Smudges everywhere. We'll identify 'em."

The other gremlin tipped over a rack of pharaoh-designed leisure suits. "That detached hand should've worn a glove."

If the fingerprints matched, C.H. would be in even more trouble. I knew I'd have to talk with the alleged witnesses and get the full story.

McGoo tried to reassure the brittle mummy proprietor. "We already have the perpetrating limb in custody. Once we interrogate him, we'll learn where he hid that scroll with the secret of immortality."

III

Since Robin was the severed limb's attorney of record, and I was his zombie detective, we went to see the prisoner. We needed face-to-face time with the hand. My determined lawyer partner was already building up a five-point defense for her client. She had filed paperwork to get C.H. free on bail, but the UQ Police Department, not to mention the HR Department, had a strict policy against loose hands.

The cold austere cell in the back of the precinct building had cinderblock walls and a concrete floor. A scuttling hand could easily have slipped between the wide iron bars, but C.H. had been placed in a gilded canary cage that hung from the ceiling. The rest of the holding cells looked empty, although one apparently held an invisible man who had been arrested for indecent exposure.

C.H. looked forlorn in his hanging cage, but when he saw us, he waggled his fingers in a hopeful greeting. His knuckles were scraped, as if he had tried to batter his way out of confinement.

Robin stepped into the cell. "We're here to discuss your case, Mr. Hand. I promise we'll use every possible defense strategy to get you out of here."

"Robin even knows some underhanded tactics," I offered, taking a seat on the lone bench against the cinderblock wall.

C.H. rattled around inside the cage, gesturing and pointing in convoluted gestures, which Robin interpreted for me. "He insists it wasn't him. He claims he's been fingered for someone else's crime."

Sadly, I had heard such stories before, and so had Robin.

I spread my hands. "But two witnesses identified you."

C.H. tapped his fingers in an insistent denial on the newspaper that lined the floor of the cage.

Robin interrupted, "Don't worry, Dan will verify their story. Here in the Unnatural Quarter, night security guards tend to blow things out of proportion."

"At least the ones who survive," I said.

C.H. made more urgent gestures, and Robin said, "He insists it's a case of mistaken identity. Many hands look alike."

"How many disembodied ambulatory hands are running around the Quarter?" I asked.

Robin pointed out, "They can't run, Dan—they're hands."

"Good point, but not the point."

The crawling hand gave a detailed, emotional explanation. Robin listened and watched, though she looked dubious. "He claims it must be his twin brother named Lefty."

"Lefty?" I peered into the cage. "So an identical twin?"

"Fraternal twins. They were separated at birth, but Lefty has led a far more sinister life, crawling around in the seamy underbelly, sticking his thumb in the shadows. He has his fingers in every kind of black-market pie."

"That sounds suspicious—and also convenient," I said, looking at the abbreviated hand. "But you're a left hand. Are you saying your brother Lefty is the same?"

Through insistent gestures, C.H. explained that, no, his twin was the *right* hand, but had chosen his nickname strictly to confuse matters, proving how sinister he really was.

I was ready to begin my investigation. "Any idea where to find your brother?"

In a weird wobbling movement, C.H. made a thumbs-down gesture.

Robin wasn't discouraged at all. "You know that Dan is the best zombie private investigator in the Quarter."

"It says so right on my business card," I said. "Zombies are relentless and persistent, and I never give up on a case."

I rose from the cold bench, feeling the stiffness in my knees. I needed to go back to the All-Day/All-Nite fitness center in order to keep the rigor mortis at bay.

A ghoul jail attendant opened the door and shuffled forward, carrying a tray of food. Though he wore a UQPD uniform, the gray-skinned, drooling unnatural had been assigned to administrative duty, since ghouls weren't good at high-speed foot chases or shootouts.

"Lunchtime," the ghoul said, dragging out the word like a dead body. He banged the tray against the bars of the cell. He used an iron key to ponderously work the lock, then swung the creaking door open. He shuffled in and dropped the tray on the metal bench far from the canary cage. I saw it was a special meal of hand rolls and finger food.

C.H. made listless, forlorn gestures, and Robin translated, "He says he's not hungry. He'll eat later."

We followed the ghoul attendant out of the cell. The barred door slammed shut with a loud, foreboding clang.

IV

Since there had been so much chaos at the scene of the crime, I needed to have another look around at the Notions of the Nile.

"I want to go along," Alvina said with the boundless enthusiasm of an undead ten-year-old. (She was now almost thirteen, but she had stopped aging after a botched transfusion infected her with vampire blood.)

"You'll get in the way," I said. From past experience I knew she would eventually talk me into what she wanted.

"But I'm your investigation research assistant. Pleeeease?"

"You'll poke around and go where you're not supposed to go."

She placed her hands on her hips. "That's what an investigation research assistant is supposed to do!"

She had me there.

Glowing, Sheyenne came up beside us. "Beaux, she could use some fresh musty air among all the relics, and she'll get extra credit at the Nosferatu Academy."

I could never resist these two most important women in my life, and I knew when a battle was lost. "All right, kid, though I don't think Akhenatenomininimum is the type of dried-up old soul to be impressed by cuteness and sweetness.

"But I'm so good at it," Alvina said.

That was another thing I couldn't argue with.

We set off for the ancient Egyptian boutique. Down in the shadowy back alley, with its drab awnings of various novelty shops, we came upon Tony peeling away the yellow crime-scene tape draped around his door. On a signboard, he had scrawled fresh words in chalk: "Today only. Post break-in sale."

Alvina said in a stage whisper, "He looks like his linen wrappings could use a wash."

The ancient bag of bones turned about with an indignant sniff that sounded like a hollow whistle through his sinus cavities. "They are *vintage,* young lady."

I stepped closer. "Hello. We spoke yesterday, Mr. Akhenatenominimum. I'm Dan Chambeaux, zombie private investigator."

"Call me Tony. It's much easier."

"Akhenatenominimum!" Alvina said, showing off.

The mummy proprietor exhaled a long, dry sigh. "I'm just happy to get back to business. I've got a life to live, you know—and I've had one for thousands of years."

I tipped my fedora in a respectful gesture. "We'd like to ask a few more questions, sir, and have another look around."

Tony shuffled back into the shop, oddly unenthusiastic. "The UQPD has the case well in hand. I just want this whole thing behind me."

"But we're sure they arrested the wrong hand!" Alvina said, bouncing after him.

Inside the cluttered Notions of the Nile, the stacked shelves looked as if they'd been ransacked. Clothes racks were toppled over, urns in disarray, sarcophagi half-open and filled with old magazines. I wondered if the gremlin evidence techs had caused this whirlwind of damage, or if this was just Tony's organizational system.

A piece of plywood covered the smashed glass top of the display case, but I bent down to look at the remaining valuable items through the side. "Are these other artifacts worth anything?"

Alvina wandered off to poke among the exotic objects. She found a cartoon mummy Pez dispenser, but despite her persistent clicking, it was out of candy.

"You can see all the prices there," Tony said as he opened a ledger book and started to add columns. He seemed intent on ignoring me.

"Why do you think the alleged hand stole only the scarab case and not any of these other valuables?"

"It wasn't an alleged hand," Tony said. "It was a real hand. How else could it break the glass?"

"But why would it leave all these other rarities? Doesn't make sense."

The old mummy made another whistling huff through his sinus cavities. "He took the most valuable ancient scroll. How much do you think a single hand can carry when it's on the run?"

I repeated Robin's wisdom. "It can't run. It's a hand."

Still, Tony had a point.

I looked at the plywood top covering. "If that little scroll held the secret of immortality, why didn't anybody open it up and read it before now? That's a pretty interesting secret. You'd think someone would peek."

"The coded hieroglyphics of Na-Pu-Ko-Tak are only visible under the light of an Egyptian full moon, which occurs rarely and unpredictably."

I nodded, as if I understood what he was talking about. "And what's an Egyptian full moon?"

"A full moon high in the sky covered by a veil of thin clouds, so that everyone sees it the way a mummy would look at it through gauze wrappings."

"Now it makes sense," I lied.

At one of the back shelves, Alvina stood on tiptoes to pull down a carved wooden box. She slid open the lid. "Look, half-daddy, I found a creepy dried monkey's paw!" She held the desiccated, curled thing. "I wonder what it's used for. I wish—"

I cut her off immediately. "Put that back, kid."

"But why?" she whined. "The discount says 'partially used.' What does that mean? I wish—"

"*Now*, kid! That's not part of the case."

With a sigh, the vampire girl tucked the shriveled monkey's paw back in its box and returned it to the shelf.

Even though Notions of the Nile had no customers, Tony was impatient to get back to business. "There's really no need for further investigation, Mr. Shamble."

"It's Chambeaux," I corrected, as usual.

"Everything is taken care of. I've already filed the insurance claim, and I have a very good policy that covers break-ins."

That made me suspicious. "But how do you place value on the secret of immortality?"

As he waved, Tony's gnarled hand looked remarkably like the shriveled monkey's paw. "They have adjusters for that."

As she rummaged among the canopic jars, Alvina found a small sarcophagus. "Look, it's a mummified kitty! Can I have a pet, pleeease? I've always wanted a kitty."

"Not today, kid." She had asked for a pet before, but Sheyenne, Robin, and I were worried that she wouldn't take care of it. Still, a mummified cat was lower maintenance than most other animals.

I motioned for the vampire girl to leave. "I'll follow up if I have any further questions, Mr. … uh, Tony."

"Akhenatenominimum!" Alvina said.

"I am having a special post-burglary sale, Mr. Shamble," the mummy pointed out. "Surely you have loved ones who are fond of old things?"

"My ghost girlfriend certainly is," I quipped. "But I'll have to be enough for her."

V

I arranged to meet the rent-a-cop witnesses at a popular gypsy coffee cart. The gaudy red wagon was strewn with Christmas tree lights and ornate colorful hexes. Hanging wind chimes tinkled in the breeze, accompanied by the hiss and snort of an espresso machine inside.

Two night security guards waited for me—a sleepy, pot-bellied human and his stoic golem partner, Bill and Urg. We had crossed paths before. Now, they loitered at the coffee cart, obviously waiting for me to buy. It was worth the investment so I could get an honest report from them.

"You two always find yourselves in the middle of dire circumstances," I said.

Bill shrugged. "We're night security guards who work around a bunch of monsters. It comes with the job."

Urg added in his deep, resonant voice, "That's why we get hazard pay."

While Bill studied the lengthy hot drink menu on the side of the gypsy cart, I said, "I want to talk with you two about the Notions of the Nile burglary. You were at the scene of the crime when the display case was broken?"

"Yup, we saw it with our own four eyes," said Urg.

In front of us at the coffee-cart window, an Igor in a lab coat ordered a triple shot, half-caffeinated, extra foam, extra hot, dark-roast/light-roast blend latte with a caramel macchiato mark, double-cupped, and with a straw. That meant I would have plenty of time to talk to the two guards before it was our turn to order.

Bill patted his potbelly. "Urg and I were in the back of the store, taking a careful inventory of the candy, snacks, and soda section when we heard a crash. We ran out and saw the hand right in the middle of the curio case."

The golem gave a ponderous nod. "It happened right there, before our four eyes."

Inside the coffee cart, the gypsy barista bustled around with a flurry of cups and measuring devices, pumping from bottles, stirring with a long spoon, and adding a hiss of steam. A bright red scarf was tied around her head, and her earrings jingled as she worked to prepare the high-maintenance order.

Bill continued, "I yelled for him to halt, but he didn't hear me … probably because a hand doesn't have ears. The appendage kept doing his nefarious deed, and when I ran closer, he attacked me. That thing had a vicious thumb!"

"It tried to strangle Bill!" Urg said. "Wrapped around his throat and squeezed!"

Swallowing hard, Bill rubbed his neck. "He had a real strangler's grip."

"But not much leverage, fortunately," Urg said. "I was able to knock the hand back onto the counter."

Finally, the gypsy barista set the finished hot beverage onto the window shelf, and the Igor departed without leaving a tip or even saying thanks. The gypsy barista leaned out and shook her fist at him, yelling a curse.

The Igor tripped on an uneven section of sidewalk and fell flat, spilling his drink.

When I stepped up to the window, the barista crooked a finger at me. She wore so many metal bracelets in a row it looked like a Slinky on her wrist. "You better not have a complicated order."

"Just a coffee, ma'am," I said and glanced at Bill. The golem wouldn't be drinking anything.

"Large coffee," he said, "with cream and two sugars."

Knowing the barista was in a touchy mood, I dropped a five-dollar bill in the tip jar first, just to get things on the right foot. Mollified, the old woman ducked back into the cart.

"Even after I knocked the hand away," the golem continued, "it grabbed that scarab case and scuttled off as fast as five fingers could go."

"Well," Bill said, "three fingers, because he was holding the stolen property in two of them."

"How do you know it was my client who committed this crime?"

"We saw him with our own eyes," Bill said, still sweating

with his recollections of the ordeal. "Identified him from a mugshot. Crawling Hand. Unmistakable."

Urg said, "It was a hand job, all right."

While we waited for the coffee, Bill rubbed his throat again. "You can even see the bruises from when he tried to strangle me."

Indeed, the long purplish marks clearly outlined four fingers and the indentation of a thumb. As a detective, I held up my left hand, trying to match it with the bruise pattern. When I pressed it closer to Bill's throat, he flinched back, clearly not wanting to be strangled again.

But I spotted an important clue. "This isn't right … I mean left. Look at the position of the thumb and the fingers. It's the wrong direction. My friend C.H. is left-handed, but these marks were made by a right-handed strangler."

Almost certainly one named Lefty.

Bill rubbed his neck with one hand, then rubbed it with the other. "You're right, Mr. Shamble. Was he maybe a backhanded strangler?"

"Sure looked like C.H. from the mug shots," Urg said. "I was never good at right and left." He glanced down at his shoes.

I knew I would have to investigate this further.

The gypsy handed us our cups of coffee, and we walked off, but the dark, bitter brew was no match for my thoughts.

Bill took a sip from his cup and let out a long sigh. "Good coffee. Almost worth getting strangled for."

"You've been very helpful," I said. "But the police will want to question you again."

"We'll get around to it later," Bill said. "We have to be off now."

The golem nodded his big clay head. "Afternoon gig, guarding the toxic waste dump."

Back at the Chambeaux & Deyer offices, I couldn't wait to share my strong new evidence with Robin—but before I could say a word, Sheyenne rushed forward to tell me about a discovery of her own. "Beaux, I ran a full search to find C.H.'s missing evil twin!"

The little vampire girl bounced up beside my ghost girlfriend. "I helped, too! I know all sorts of interwebs tricks."

They were a great team. Sheyenne explained, "We searched for any evidence of loose hands or other single appendages in the criminal records, but C.H.'s brother is clean."

Alvina piped up, "Then we ran a search on the registered owners of illegal and black-market businesses, but we still didn't find any hand records."

They didn't seem disappointed at all. "That's a lot of things you didn't find," I said. "Why are you so excited?"

"Because Alvina suggested something that never occurred to me," Sheyenne said, and the kid grinned, making her little white fangs protrude. "We looked for *legitimate* businesses owned by detached hands—and we found one!" With her poltergeist powers, she handed me a scrap of paper on which she had written a name and address. "And this is where you can find him."

In her office, Robin hung up the phone and came out to join us, wearing a glum expression. And I hadn't even told anyone my good news yet.

"That was a disappointing call from the crime-scene lab," she said. "The fingerprints found on the smashed display case are definitely identical to C.H.'s. We'll never be able to prove he's not guilty now."

VI

More determined than ever, I braced myself as I approached the shop door. A manicure salon, of course—Fancy Fingers. The chemical smells wafting out rivaled anything produced by a mad scientist's lab.

Inside, intense black lights shone down onto tables with finger bowls, rubber mats, and jars that held implements reminiscent of Nazi torture devices. An extensive rack of nail polish showed an array of colors like an apothecary's selection of deadly poisons.

Most of the stations were empty, but a hatchet-faced, severely beautiful Bride sat erect in a chair as a clumsy troll manicurist used thick fingers to rub lotion into the stitches that circled her wrists. Her Nefertiti hairdo had been done up to emphasize the white zigzag, and intense eyeshadow and lipstick indicated that the Bride was getting ready for a night on the town.

A second troll woman, obviously the receptionist, lumbered up to me with a menu of services. "New customer?" She frowned at my grayish hands. "You need a lot of work."

"Self-improvement is on my To Do list." I looked past her to see the actual person, or partial person, I had come to see. "I'm here to speak with your boss."

On a purple velvet cushion rested a splayed, detached hand —a right hand. On either side, two pale vampire princesses caressed, massaged, and pampered Lefty. The hand relaxed on the pillow as the vampires kneaded his knuckles and fingers. Lefty's nails were perfectly manicured, as expected.

As I pushed my way around the troll receptionist, the vampire princesses looked languidly at me, their dark eyes pools of night. They smiled like predators.

I stood before the purple cushion. "Mr. Lefty, I'm Dan Chambeaux, private investigator. I've been engaged to look into a burglary at Notions of the Nile."

Lefty tapped his forefinger on the velvet cushion, indicating disinterest. I continued, "Eyewitnesses saw a disembodied hand matching your description at the scene of the crime. Do you know anything about that?"

Lefty aggressively extended his middle finger at me.

In a sultry voice, the left vampire princess said, "We can translate for you."

"No need," I said. "The point was clear. Fingerprints at the scene have been linked to a client of mine, Crawling Hand." I leaned closer to the cushion. "But if you're his twin brother, wouldn't the fingerprints be the same?"

Lefty extended his middle finger at me again, then added more gestures with his pinky and thumb.

"That's not how fingerprints work, Mr. Chambeaux," said the vampire princess on the right. "The prints on a left hand are not the same as the prints on a right hand."

"Ah, but does that still hold true if they're twins?" I said, demonstrating my complete ignorance of forensic science.

"Crawling Hand is Lefty's fraternal twin, not identical twin," said the other vampire.

I seized on the little victory. "So you admit they're brothers!"

"Again, that's not how fingerprints work," one vampire princess said without even glancing at Lefty's frenetic gestures. The second princess added lotion to the back of the hand.

"It could be a genetic anomaly," I said, "or a plot contrivance."

"Lefty has an alibi for the night of the crime," said the first princess. "He was with us, giving a massage."

The second vampire purred. "He's very good with his fingers."

"Do you know anything about a stolen scarab scroll?" I pressed my bad luck. "The secret of immortality, written down by a famous pharaoh ... whose name I can't remember right now."

Again, the extended middle finger. Lefty seemed to have a limited vocabulary.

"What else can you tell me about your brother, C.H.?" I prodded.

Lefty just flicked his forefinger, as if snapping away an insect.

The receptionist troll loomed behind me, as did the

manicurist troll. The two vampire princesses flashed their long fangs and held up their lacquered claws in a threatening gesture. Even the intimidating Bride had risen from the manicure station, upset that I had interrupted her beauty services.

"Well, I think that answers all my questions," I said. Inhaling a deep breath of the toxic nail polish and cuticle-softening fumes, I backed out of the Fancy Fingers manicure shop.

Hands down, that was a very uncomfortable and unproductive interview.

VII

Night had fallen by the time I headed back to our offices. I was still trying to get my hands around what I had learned and what I suspected. C.H.'s estranged twin brother was definitely sinister, and I had a gut feeling he was involved in the stolen Egyptian immortality scroll. Even though my undead digestive system is rather sluggish, I've learned to go with my gut instinct. Was the mummy Tony also in cahoots? Perhaps a scheme to get an insurance payout?

On my way back, though, the bright marimba tones of an incoming call interrupted my walk. When I saw the caller ID, I hoped it was official business rather than a stupid joke. "Hey, McGoo, what's up?"

"Shamble, get to the jail! Quick! It's about your amputated friend!" I heard police shouting in the background, alarms ringing.

"What's the matter? Is C.H. all right?" I was stumped. "I have new evidence—"

"Just get here!" He hung up before I could ask more incisive detective questions.

When I arrived, the jail was in an uproar. Uniformed cops ran about like a stirred-up hornet's nest. They pointed their guns in all directions, as if to defend against a full-frontal terrorist attack. In the back, I heard a loud gunshot, and everybody froze, holding their breath. Then a meek voice said, "Sorry!"

When he came to meet me, McGoo's cheeks were flushed such a bright pink that his freckles almost disappeared. I looked at the chaos around us. "Did you tell another one of your jokes, and it bombed big-time?"

"This is serious, Shamble. No time for stupid things!"

I wanted to argue that there was always time for stupid things, but I followed him toward the back. McGoo was panting hard. "There's been a jailbreak, Shamble. Dangerous fugitive."

I slipped a hand into my sport jacket pocket and felt the comforting grip of my .38. "C.H.? But he's a cute little guy."

"He already tried to strangle a night security guard. We have no idea what other reckless damage he could cause!"

"About the strangling, I've got an update—"

He hurried me to the jail in the back of the station. In the crawling hand's cell, I saw the gilded canary cage suspended from the ceiling, but the wire-frame door had been bent and twisted, then pried open. The cage was empty.

"Imagine the brute strength that would have taken, Shamble," McGoo said.

I admitted it was impressive, and one-handed at that. After C.H. had broken loose, he must have swung on the cage, dropped to the cell floor, and scuttled out between the bars.

"He's on the loose, and he could be anywhere—lurking behind a file cabinet, hiding in the shadows under a desk, just waiting to grab an innocent officer's ankle!"

I still felt sympathy for the detached appendage, though. "He was desperate, McGoo, and I can prove he's innocent. Well, Robin can."

"Innocent? Now he's a fugitive—that changes everything. We're putting out an all-hands bulletin. We'll comb the Quarter until we have him back in cuffs."

Several other well-armed UQ policemen hurried up, guns drawn.

I could see I would have to solve this myself and clear the crawling hand's name.

VIII

While armed UQPD patrols combed the Quarter for the digital fugitive, I suspected the precocious appendage would go back to the scene of the crime, even if he wasn't guilty. C.H. was not afraid to get his hand dirty.

I moved at a brisk, cadaverous pace through the dark streets. Deciding to be surreptitious, I circled around to the back alley behind the front alley that held the Egyptian novelty shop. There, the shadows were even deeper, the rats scuttled louder, and the garbage smelled even more rancid. Many denizens of the Unnatural Quarter found it pleasant.

I glanced at the night sky, where a veil of high, thin clouds partially obscured the full moon. An Egyptian full moon—exactly the phenomenon that Akhenatenominimum said was necessary for the revelation of the immortality scroll. *Interesting and convenient*, I thought. It wasn't a particularly rare meteorological phenomenon, after all.

I lurked in the deepest gloom, keeping my eyes open. Next to me, I found a polite, displaced hunchback without a current physical address. He scooched to one side to give me more lurking room.

Before long, the back door of Notions of the Nile creaked open, and two figures emerged. I pressed my back against the slimy brick wall to stay unobtrusive.

"You got enough room there, bud?" the hunchback asked.

"Yeah, I'm fine, thanks."

The two figures wore Temporary Security Agency uniforms, and under the hazy light of the full moon, I could discern Bill and Urg.

"I didn't expect we'd get a night off," said the golem security guard.

"Don't complain," Bill said. "That mummy is still paying us overtime. Let's go to the Goblin Tavern. It's safer there."

The two walked the other direction with a spring in their step. I would rather have been at the Goblin Tavern as well, finishing my second beer by now, but the escaped crawling hand took priority.

After the security guards departed, I waited in the shadows for a long, anticlimactic moment.

"I've got an extra blanket, if you want to relax," the hunchback said. "It gets chilly some nights."

"I don't expect to be here long," I said.

"Suit yourself," he said.

My legs and back were stiff, as usual, and I began to reconsider hunkering down, when the back door creaked open again, and a wobbly stick-like figure emerged. I poked my head forward, staring intently.

"Is he the one you're waiting for?" the hunchback whispered.

"I don't know for sure," I whispered back. "I'm just looking for something suspicious."

"Looks suspicious to me."

"I agree."

Tony poked his bandaged head out into the faint light of the alley. He turned his gauzy eye sockets to the sky, then used a claw-like finger to pry the bandages open so he could see the moon better. "It's the prophecy! Woo-hoo!"

The desiccated, decrepit curio-shop owner wobbled away in the opposite direction, heading out the other end of the alley. Just as I suspected, Tony was involved somehow—and he must know where the stolen pharaoh scroll had been taken.

Before I could follow him, I heard a rustling sound among the yellowed newspapers, candy wrappers, and other scattered debris in the opposite gutter. A pale left hand pushed aside the detritus, emerging from his hiding place. I would have recognized C.H. anywhere.

As the hand surreptitiously tip-fingered forward in pursuit of the suspicious mummy proprietor, I strode over to him. "C.H., do you realize how much trouble you're in?"

The disembodied hand froze, knowing he had been caught. In desperation, he raised two fingers in a peace sign, and I saw they were flecked with blood. Among the strewn garbage of the alley, I saw the furry bodies of three strangled rats. C.H. must have been bored while he was waiting.

"Look, I know you're innocent, even with the fingerprint evidence," I said. "I'm sure your right-handed brother Lefty is behind this, but we have to get proof before the UQPD captures you again. They're hunting you now."

C.H. gave me the "OK" sign with his thumb and forefinger.

I snatched him up. "We'll make better time this way. I can take bigger strides."

The hunchback called from the deep shadows. "Nice meeting you."

"Same to you. Have a fine night."

With the hand in hand, I hurried after the surreptitious Akhenatenominimum.

IX

For a shriveled-up denizen of ancient Egypt, Tony kept up a fast pace as he moved through the side streets. I hung back far enough so he wouldn't spot me tailing him.

C.H. fidgeted and squirmed in my grip, and I explained that his brother had a secret lair, which was where I assumed the mummy was going now. The crawling hand twitched in surprise, and I patted his knuckles to reassure him.

We stealthily approached the rear of the Fancy Fingers manicure salon just as Tony was surreptitiously unlocking the back door's heavy deadbolt with his own key. The old-fashioned door had an open transom window at the top, which allowed noxious manicure fumes to roil out into the night. After a quick glance around, the mummy opened the creaking door and ducked inside Fancy Fingers. I moved to get into position as he pulled the door shut behind him, but I was dismayed to hear the heavy deadbolt click back into place.

Why did evil masterminds and their mummy henchmen pay attention to security measures at the most inconvenient times?

I pressed my ear against the door and listened, worried that one of the burly troll manicurists might be standing guard. When all seemed quiet inside, I fished out my set of trusty lockpicks and got to work. Though my fingers were numb, I was highly proficient, under normal circumstances.

This wasn't one of those circumstances. The deadbolt foiled my every attempt, and I even bent one of the picks. (Fortunately, I ordered them in economy-sized packs.)

The disembodied hand squirmed and pointed upward, indicating the open transom window. I raised my eyebrows. "You think you can get in there, C.H.?"

He nodded up to his first knuckle. It seemed like a Hail Mary gesture to me, but I tossed the disembodied limb. Even though it was a clumsy throw, C.H. snagged the lip of the transom window, curled his fingers around the edge, and used his thumb and upper-finger strength to lift himself over. He swung down and dropped inside.

"Don't forget to unlock the deadbolt!" I said in a loud whisper.

I heard scuttling, scuffling sounds on the other side, and then the deadbolt snapped open with a grating click. I turned the knob and cautiously pushed the door open, wincing at the overpowering smell of formaldehyde and nail polish. I found myself in a dark storeroom for Fancy Fingers. "C.H.!" I whispered.

I saw the little hand darting toward the main salon, from which I heard voices and saw flickering candlelight under the pulsing black lights. The sounds of off-key, vaguely Egyptian chanting thrummed in the air. I crept forward and peeked through the back storeroom door, trying not to make a sound.

The manicure stations had been pushed against the walls, and the rack of nail polish bottles was now filled with black candles. The two troll manicurists must have gotten the night off because I didn't see them anywhere, but the sleek, deadly vampire princesses filled all of the security needs and also served as arm candy, or in Lefty's case, hand candy.

They were preparing for an important ceremony, or a masquerade party. Akhenatenomininimum awkwardly draped a hieroglyphic-embroidered shawl over his shoulders and donned a funny ceremonial hat. In one gnarled fist, he gripped a golden ankh that looked like a handheld can opener.

I didn't spot C.H., but the manicure shop was so cluttered with shoved-aside paraphernalia that the crawling hand had plenty of places to hide.

The hand at the center of attention, though, was C.H.'s sinister brother Lefty. He rested on the purple velvet cushion on top of a raised speaker's podium in the middle of the manicure room. Cementing his appearance as an evil mastermind, Lefty stroked a scrawny hairless cat with thumb and forefinger, while one of the vampire princesses intoned on his behalf, "Pretty kitty, pretty kitty."

In front of the purple cushion sat a green enameled case shaped like a big scarab beetle. This made me want to do an unnatural fist pump, because if nothing else, I had just found convincing proof that C.H. was not the culprit from the curio shop.

"Pretty kitty, pretty kitty," intoned the other vampire princess.

Lefty tapped his forefinger on the cushion, growing impatient. Tony adjusted the funny colorful cap on his bandaged head and stepped forward. "I'm ready, boss."

The mummy was obviously not ready, though, because he dithered with his ankh and then went over to the nail polish rack of black candles, pausing to relight one that had guttered out.

Using the brief delay, I ducked back into the storage room

and urgently called McGoo, whose number was on speed dial for magical emergencies such as this. When he answered, I said in a harsh whisper, "McGoo, come to the Fancy Fingers manicure salon! It's an emergency—and bring lots of men."

"Shamble, you know we have a mixed-gender police force."

"Then be inclusive and bring all of them!" I told him to Google the address before I hung up, then crept back out to observe the ominous ceremony.

By now the two vampire princesses had donned striped pharaoh headdresses, which made them look culturally confusing and downright silly.

After straightening his bandages, Tony approached the velvet cushion and raised both hands as if worshipping the god of cuticles. The hairless cat blinked its large eyes at him, as if the ankh were a cat toy.

"In the name of the pharaoh Na-Pu-Ko-Tak," Tony intoned, "I, his descendant Akhenatenominimum, will recite the coveted secret of immortality!"

Lefty rocked back on his stump and splayed his fingers and thumb in a high-five gesture before reaching forward to clutch the scarab case. Tony installed the golden ankh in an empty slot in the nail-polish rack.

Lefty's fingers twisted, strained, and fumbled with the latch. Seeing the detached hand's frustration, the nearest vampire princess flicked open the hasp so he could pry the case open to reveal a tightly rolled scroll not much bigger than a stubby cigar.

I had hoped there would be some kind of pre-show before the ritual, so McGoo and his reinforcements would have time to get here, but Lefty was determined to get on with it. He hooked his forefinger around the scroll and picked at the blob of brown sealing wax with his fingernail, but the ancient seal was petrified. A vampire princess tried to help him, but Lefty kept trying until the glob cracked. He flicked away the broken wax and tried to unroll the stiff papyrus paper with two fingers.

Finally, he peeled the scroll open enough to display a confusing incantation in hieroglyphics.

"Let me have a look at that, boss," Tony said.

Before the mummy could pick up the ancient scroll, though, I spotted a flurry of movement across the floor. C.H. darted along, getting up a fist of steam, and sprang into the air to the top of the speaker's podium. The hand landed on the cushion next to Lefty.

The sudden movement startled the hairless cat, who sprang onto the chest of the nearest vampire princess. Letting out a loud yowl, the cat clawed at her cobwebby gown, but she batted it away, knocking the cat into the nail-polish rack of lighted black candles, which toppled over onto the linoleum floor.

Now palm to palm with his mortal enemy, C.H. locked his fingers around Lefty's. The two hands squeezed and crushed in a vengeful grip, first swatting fingers and then engaging in a furious round of thumb wrestling.

Deciding it was time for me to intervene, I lurched into the ceremonial/manicure chamber. "Zombie detective!" I shouted. "Stay where you are!"

But Tony moved faster than I had ever seen a mummy move. While the two amputated hands were busy with their mutual five-fingered death grip, the corrupt curio-shop owner snatched the scroll and held it up under the pulsing black lights.

I tried to intercept him, but the two vampire princesses blocked me, baring their long fangs. They did indeed look silly in their striped pharaoh headdresses. "Better not try it," I warned. "I have formaldehyde in my veins, and I wouldn't taste good."

Akhenatenominimum spread the scroll as he tried to read it aloud. "Behold, I have the secret of immortality!"

Finally, I heard the wail of police sirens coming closer. McGoo never failed to be not a moment too late.

The pair of wrestling hands rolled off the cushion and crashed onto the floor, where they broke apart. Lefty tried to flee, but C.H. pursued him, landing with his palm on the back of the other hand, using the full force of his knuckles to push him down.

Tony cleared his throat. "The secret of immortality is ..." He drew out the moment in ridiculously clichéd suspense, just trying to translate the old-fashioned hieroglyphics under the bad lighting. "Sorry, this is an old folk dialect."

Outside, the police sirens reached a crescendo as tires screeched to a halt in the street. Doors slammed, and cops shouted as they rushed the front door of Fancy Fingers.

"The secret of immortality is ..." Tony was in a rush now, translating on the fly. He paused as the words sank in. "Uh ... Eat lots of fruits and vegetables, and exercise more." The mummy hung his head, reading the scroll again with his sunken eye sockets. "That's it?"

One of the vampire princesses said with bitter disappointment, "Vegetables?"

"That secret's been known for centuries," I said. "But few people are willing to pay the terrible price for immortality."

The front door crashed open, and McGoo charged in, followed by his gang of uniformed cops. They all had their weapons drawn, with good reason for once. "Halt! Hands in the air!"

Akhenatenominimum complied with such urgent swiftness that he tore the ancient papyrus scroll in half. Seeing all the guns pointed toward them, and knowing that every UQ police officer had several rounds of silver bullets, the two undead princesses also surrendered.

C.H. lifted himself off of his brother's hand, rocking back on his wrist stump and holding up two fingers in surrender. Lefty, though, seemed completely defeated after the revelation of the much-anticipated, but ultimately unimpressive, secret. Exhausted, he splayed limp on the floor.

McGoo pointed his police special revolver at C.H. "There's the fugitive!"

But I stepped in front of the hand. "Not so fast, McGoo. You've got it all wrong, and I can prove it." I pointed to Lefty instead.

McGoo dangled a set of handcuffs. "As long as I can arrest somebody and close the case. You've got a lot of explaining to do, Shamble."

"How about I do it over a beer at the Goblin Tavern?" I said. "After you get Lefty here booked and fingerprinted."

My best human friend couldn't agree fast enough.

X

Seated on our usual bar stools in the noisome atmosphere of our favorite watering hole, McGoo and I accepted the foamy beers that Francine the bartender had poured us without even asking. The Goblin Tavern was a place where everybody knew your name, but didn't hold it against you, where drinks flowed freely for all types of humans and unnaturals.

After a long slurp, McGoo let out a satisfied sigh, then wiped his upper lip. "So, Shamble, we had the wrong hand after all."

"As I tried to tell you multiple times." I didn't let him off the hook. "It was an honest mistake—and a clueless one."

"This was a case where the left hand really did know what the right hand was doing," McGoo said, "but we didn't believe him."

"Good thing Bill and Urg revised their story as soon as they saw the new suspect," I said. "And Lefty's fingers exactly match the bruises on Bill's throat."

Alvina trotted up, standing on her tiptoes so she could reach the bar. "Francine, can I have another Shirley Jugular, please?" She waved her empty glass after she plucked out the maraschino cherry and popped it in her mouth.

"Of course you can, sweetheart," said Francine in her husky, cigarette-damaged voice. She made another bubbly, frothy children's drink and handed it to the vampire girl.

I leaned closer to my best human friend. "You know, your part isn't going to look good when C.H. writes his memoirs, McGoo."

He frowned down into the beer while I took a long drink of mine. "Maybe C.H. will agree to an edited version for the general public."

Robin slid onto the bar stool next to him. "That might be arranged. This hand job had a happy ending. I'll discuss the matter with the Wannovich sisters. As publishers, they'll want to do the right thing."

"And a heroic cop character will increase sales," Alvina said. With her Shirley Jugular, she ran back to the dartboard, where she threw sharpened wooden stakes at a target.

Robin ordered a club soda with lime, then set her briefcase on the bar and removed her yellow legal pad, studying notes for an upcoming court appearance. Sheyenne flitted in to join us, though she rarely hung out at the tavern. On date nights, I took her to fancier places.

But I was happy for an evening with my friends and family, the ghosts and goblins and all the other unnaturals. One more case closed.

Zombies are often restless, but this zombie detective felt content at the moment, filled with job security.

BULL RUNS

I

Our company car at Chambeaux & Deyer Investigations had more miles under its hood than I've had bizarre cases.

The "Pro Bono Mobile" was a 1972 Ford Maverick with a lime-green paint job held together by patches of rust. The suspension sounded like a moaning ghost on a depressed day, and the tires were as bald as an orc. The car might have been an eyesore elsewhere, but the sagging, decrepit vehicle did not look out of place among the sagging, decrepit inhabitants of the Quarter.

But it got us where we needed to go, when the engine ran. (That was one of the reasons I usually chose to walk around the Unnatural Quarter, even with my stiff, undead legs.)

We parked the Maverick a block away from our main offices, not out of shame but because I could rarely find a closer spot. Right now, I enjoyed the stroll to the car with my ghost girlfriend Sheyenne. We were going together to serve a restraining order to an unruly werewolf who kept causing problems at a local dog kennel during his full-moon transformations. Sheyenne carried the paperwork using her poltergeist powers, and I adjusted my fedora as I walked next to her. We thought it would be a nice day, just another case.

But as we approached the car, I saw the parking ticket tucked under the windshield wiper—and the burly minotaur meter maid looming there, filling out his logbook.

Sheyenne groaned. "A parking ticket looks bad on our Chamber of Commerce record."

"I'll take care of it, Spooky," I said as I stepped forward. I'd faced many tougher cases.

The minotaur huffed through his big nostrils, making the metal nose ring flap up and down like a doorknocker. "This your car?"

His curved horns looked as if they belonged on the front of a Texas Cadillac. His blocky face was framed by large, twitchy ears. He had no pants, so as to accommodate his whiplike tail and stocky, furred legs, but he did wear a white Parking Enforcement shirt.

"It's our company car," I admitted. "Chambeaux and Deyer Investigations. I'm Dan Chambeaux, zombie P.I."

The minotaur snorted again. "I've heard of you. Zombie detective."

I was about to give him my business card, thinking we might resolve this, but Sheyenne drifted forward. "Excuse me, but why are we getting a ticket? I don't see any sign that says No Parking."

"Abandoned vehicle," said the meter maid. "Some gremlin filed a claim for scrap."

"It's not scrap!" Sheyenne said.

The stocky minotaur stepped onto the curb. "Your back passenger tire is blocking the sewer drain. A family of mutant lab rats complained that they can't access their home."

I reached into my pocket for the keys. "I'll move it right away. There's no need for a ticket."

Sheyenne waved the pending werewolf restraining order in

front of him. "We're on our way to deliver important legal documents."

I pulled out my wallet and fished out a twenty. "Let me get you a nice dinner for your trouble. On a meter maid's salary, it might be nice to—"

The big bull snorted wisps of smoke through his nose. "Don't call me a meter maid. I've got more testosterone than you could imagine! I'm Parking Enforcement, name's Dustin." He snatched the ticket off the windshield and shoved it into my gray hand.

"Sorry, I meant no offense." Minotaurs can be touchy. In the many years since the Big Uneasy, I had learned to deal with the temperaments and eccentricities of all forms of unnaturals.

As I held the parking ticket, the minotaur stomped off to harass other motionless vehicles, but he paused, twitched his tail, and lowered his horns in contemplation. "I've been meaning to look you up, Dan Shamble. I want to hire you for a case."

That changed things.

Sheyenne's glow brightened. "We're always happy to accept new clients. Come to the offices after we deliver this restraining order. We can discuss the matter then."

"I want to discuss the matter now," Dustin said.

I knew not to wave any red flags in front of a minotaur. "That works for me, too. What seems to be the problem?"

"It's not so much a problem. It's distress."

"Distress?" I looked at the burly brute, trying to imagine what could intimidate a half-man/half-bull.

"Intestinal distress," said Dustin. The answer made me queasy. "Some of my minotaur friends have been getting sick. Parking Enforcers talk, you know."

"How are they getting sick?" Sheyenne asked.

When Dustin hunched his shoulders, his white parking enforcement shirt stretched to the point of ripping. "Bad stomach flu. Hit seven of us so far. Completely incapacitating." He snorted again. "It must be poison in the food supply."

"That would be serious," I said. "I have no idea what minotaurs eat."

"Specialized diet," Dustin said. "Blood bales from a local supplier." A pink tongue the size of a hand towel licked around his lips. "I want you to look into what's making my friends sick."

"Zombie P.I. on the case, as soon as I digest the information." I held up the citation. "In the meantime, do you think you could …?"

The minotaur turned about. "I have to keep my integrity, Mr. Shamble." He stomped off, and I was left with a parking ticket and a new case.

II

Since we had an impatient minotaur, I started the case right away. After Sheyenne and I delivered the restraining order to the embarrassed werewolf, we headed back to the offices.

Sheyenne filled out the paperwork for Dustin as a new client, while I researched the dietary habits of minotaurs. For that, I used my research assistant Alvina, my cute little vampire half-daughter (don't ask).

Wise in the ways of the internet and social media, the kid cheerfully accepted the assignment. In ten minutes, she gave me a printed report on the food preferences of man-bulls and, most importantly, the primary supplier of blood bales—Melody's Weeds.

"I even got the address!" Alvina waved the paper in front of me. She would have just shown me her phone screen, but she knew that I was old school and still preferred printouts.

"Melody's Weeds? Sounds like a marijuana shop."

"We can ask if they provide that service, too," the vampire girl said. "I'm going with you to investigate."

"No you're not," I said. But as usual I lost the argument.

Since I had found a good, and legal, parking place for the Pro Bono Mobile after serving the restraining order, I didn't want to move the car. Alvina was filled with enthusiasm and energy, so I decided it would be a good day to walk.

With the cute kid skipping by my side, we left the inner Quarter and headed past cluttered, vacant lots with signs that said, "Graveyard space for lease."

Eventually, we arrived at an old barn on an acre of land surrounded by a split-rail fence. The area was overgrown with unruly brown weeds, dead crabgrass, vines, thistles, and dandelions. Loose tumbleweeds clustered against the faded barn like a football pileup. Above the open barn doors, MELODY'S WEEDS was painted in big letters.

"She should hire me to do yardwork," Alvina said. "I could use some extra money."

"With the condition of that yard," I said, "you'd earn enough money to buy us a new company car."

"But I like the Pro Bono Mobile!"

"So do I, kid. Let's go inside."

The air was redolent with weed dust and pollens. The wind rattled the dead vegetation, and Alvina chased after a bouncing tumbleweed.

Reaching the entrance, I called out by way of greeting, "Hey, your barn door's open!" Alvina joined me as we entered the dim, dusty interior. I sneezed so hard that a little squeak whistled out through the bullet hole in my forehead. Inside, stacked bales of reddish hay looked like compact boxes of vegetation.

In the middle of the barn stood a large processing and baling machine that looked like it had been designed by Rube-Goldberg Farm Products. In the back was a small office and another room with a securely locked door.

"Here to buy some weed, shoppers?" said a singsong female voice.

An ethereal wood nymph glided forward—Melody, I assumed. She had delicate features, faintly green skin, and intense emerald eyes. Her expression had a distinctly stoned look. Her unruly hair was studded with little flowers and entangled vines. Her dress was made of bark and moss.

"We're here to investigate minotaur food," Alvina said.

The wood nymph swirled closer, inspecting us. "Strange. Neither of you appears to be a minotaur."

"It's for a school project," I said quickly. My half-daughter was often useful in my investigations.

Alvina caught on. "We have a special unit on creatures with horns, big ones."

"You've come to the right place! Melody's Weeds is the primary supplier of basic foods for half-human, half-bull hybrids. They have specialized tastes, carnivores that chew a cud."

I looked at the stacked, reddish bales of hay. "And what exactly do you feed them?"

"A special recipe." The wood nymph had a hum in her voice. "Let me show you the process. It's time for the daily harvest."

"Need an extra hand for yardwork?" Alvina bobbed her cute blond pigtails and flashed a smile that showed small, pointed baby fangs. "I have reasonable rates."

Melody chuckled. "Oh, I have everything quite in hand."

I remembered the condition of the yard. "It sure looked out of hand outside."

"Follow me." The wood nymph brightly led us back out into the sunlight. "My blood bales are packaged and shipped fresh every day."

As I looked around the tumbleweeds, crabgrass, and dead vegetation, I said, "I could suggest a landscaping service."

"Oh, that won't be necessary!" The wood nymph waved us

back. "Please stand against the wall of the barn. Those thistles can be nasty when they go flying."

Though I didn't know what Melody meant, I tend to follow instructions when I hear a veiled threat.

After Alvina and I pressed our backs against the plank siding, the wood nymph sang a singsong tune, and a whirlwind swept up. Gusts of wind circled the area inside the split-rail fence, uprooting the dried weeds. Crabgrass and thistles flurried into a tornado of dead vegetation, and the tumbleweeds bounced up like thorny bubbles. The storm of vegetation poured through the open barn doors and into the cavernous interior.

As soon as the last of the tumbleweeds vanished inside, Melody gestured for us to follow. She skipped into the barn, and Alvina skipped after her, while I just shambled along. After all the weeds were gone, the yard around Melody's Weeds looked remarkably clean and tidy.

Inside, the large baling contraption sucked in the blown, uprooted weeds and churned and crunched, chopped and processed. Above, a big tank marked GRADE A/TYPE A BLOOD squirted into the mix. The other end of the machine rattled and hummed, then coughed out a dense, twine-wrapped block that looked like a reddish shredded-wheat loaf. A conveyor stacked the finished bale on top of the pile, just as another one emerged.

"Impressive operation," I said.

Smiling, Melody turned to Alvina. "Did you get what you need for your school report, little girl?"

"Still researching," she said.

I raised the important question. "Do you have regular inspections? Have you ever had any complaints about food poisoning?"

Her flower-entangled hair fluttered about in indignation. "Food poisoning? I run an absolutely pure, all-natural operation here. Completely organic weeds and blood. No artificial colors, flavors, or preservatives."

Considering what Dustin had told me, I didn't believe her for a minute. I needed a sample from one of these bales. I glanced at Alvina, and my detective's assistant understood what I was thinking. A rambunctious vampire kid is good at creating diversions.

Giggling, she ran to the wall of bales and started climbing up, scrambling from one step to the next. "I'm queen of the mountain!"

With a hoot of surprise, Melody ran after her. "Come down from there. It's dangerous."

I took the opportunity to step closer to the baling machine. As the next bloody package popped out, I pulled off a handful of processed weeds and stuffed it in my jacket pocket. Mission accomplished.

"Come on, Alvina," I said. "You can climb bloody bales some other time."

The kid obediently sprang to the floor, brushing weeds and red smears off her pink dress. She trotted up to join me.

"Thanks for your help, Melody," I said, "and sorry for the disturbance."

"Your little girl needs to be more mellow," the wood nymph said in a slow, relaxed voice. "I could offer some ..."

I whisked my half-daughter away before her curiosity sank in.

III

Back in the offices, Robin was ready for battle. She's a lovely woman with dark hair, brown eyes, and coffee-colored skin. The crusader set in her jaw made legal opponents tremble with fear, but an unnatural in trouble couldn't have a better defender than Robin Deyer.

"I'm going to fight this with everything I've got." She clutched the parking ticket. "Chambeaux and Deyer will not stand for injustice."

"It might be easier just to pay it," I said. "Use your energy to protect monsters and save the world."

Sheyenne joined us. "It's a hundred and fifty dollars, Beaux."

My nostrils flared. "In that case, I support your endeavors, Robin."

She headed back into her office with its shelves of law volumes. "I'm going to take photographs of exactly where the car was parked. The zone was not clearly marked—you can't be expected to know all the nuances that only meter maids understand."

"Dustin prefers the term Parking Enforcer," I said.

"He's just swinging his … bull around. We're going to court, Dan. I already filed notice. We appear in two days, and you need to be there as my witness."

That made sense, since I was the one who had parked the car.

I reached into my pocket and pulled out the handful of compressed sticky weeds. "Here's a sample of the blood bales that minotaurs eat. But how do we prove food poisoning? Am I supposed to do a taste test?"

Sheyenne beamed, ectoplasmically. "Lucky for you, I have friends in the weed-analysis lab."

"Weed-analysis lab? There is such a thing?"

"It's a specialty service." Using poltergeist powers, she whisked the blood-bale sample into a manila envelope. "I'll get it over there and ask for expedited processing." Her gorgeous blue eyes shone. "We will add the extra fee to Dustin's bill."

"Can you pad it enough to pay for the parking ticket?" I grumbled.

Carrying her laptop, which was adorned with rainbow and unicorn stickers, Alvina turned the screen to us, bubbling with energy. "Look what's on the Unnatural Quarter events page—a charity race this weekend!"

She set the laptop on Sheyenne's desk, and I looked down at the picture. "The Running of the Bulls."

"It's a 5K minotaur run to raise money for disadvantaged monsters. Can we go? *Pleeease?* I need it for my school report."

"Kid, we just made up that school report to fool the wood nymph."

Alvina put her small hands on her hips. "It's not nice to lie."

Sheyenne came to her rescue. "We don't have plans this weekend. We can watch the minotaur race if you want, honey."

To me, it sounded like a lot of bull, but maybe it would connect with Dustin's case. Meanwhile, I was more concerned about our upcoming parking court appearance.

IV

Unnatural Quarter Parking Court was an afternoon matinee offshoot of the much more exciting traffic court. The Honorable Angela Stone presided, a hard judge but fair—but I was more interested in *winning* than in having a fair judge. The courtroom's wooden benches were crowded with plaintiffs, mostly unnaturals who made a grumbling cacophony of growls and haunting squeaks.

Several nervous-looking humans clustered in the back, like sheep about to be slaughtered. Clearly regretting their decision to fight the violation, two of them had a quiet conversation with the goblin bailiff, who directed them to the clerk's window outside, where they could just pay their fine and flee.

Robin took a seat in the second row, concentrating on her notes. She had been in many courtrooms and litigated numerous criminal cases, so this was old hat for her. Since I was just a zombie detective, this experience was a brand-new hat for me.

I heard indignant werewolves and ghosts, none of whom admitted being in the wrong. In the bench behind us, a tusk-faced demon commiserated with a sullen vampire. "I had ten minutes left on the parking meter, and I can prove it. Time dilation is one of my demon spells."

"I paid for my permit through sunup," the vampire said. "Look at me. See this pale skin? Do you honestly think I would be late?"

In the front row, where he could directly face the judge, sat an angry Aztec mummy. His bandages were frayed and haphazardly looped, and his leathery face exposed crooked brown teeth in a rictus that would never be confused with a friendly smile. His ember-red eyes burned as he muttered, "I better not have to pay this ticket. It's unjust!"

I tried to spot Dustin in the crowd. A minotaur shouldn't have been hard to find, even in a crowded courtroom, but I didn't see him anywhere.

Since he was the Parking Enforcer who had issued our ticket, he would have to formally affirm the codes we had violated. Our guilt or innocence (or at least our parking ticket) would depend on the minotaur's testimony. I wouldn't be sharing any updates on the food-poisoning case, though, since today we were adversaries.

The goblin bailiff yelled out in a warbly, hollow voice, bringing the court to order. "Park your butts in your seats or you'll receive another violation!" The unnaturals promptly obeyed.

The doors from the judge's chamber squeaked open behind the bench, and the judge rolled forward. Angela Stone was a heavy, gray stone angel, like an extravagant ornament from a cemetery. She had become animated during the Big Uneasy, but even though magic had brought her to life, her joints had little flexibility. Her marble wings remained half extended. Somehow —no doubt with an assistant—she had donned her black judicial robe, which had long slits cut in the back. Rather than sitting, because it wasn't entirely clear she had legs carved inside the flowing stone dress, she stood behind the bench.

Judge Stone grasped the gavel in a marble hand and slammed it down. "Come to order! Everything must be in order, neat and tidy. Everyone must follow parking rules, or else." She rapped the gavel again for good measure. "The first case is …" She scrutinized the stack of papers in front of her.

The Aztec mummy sprang up from the front bench. "It's me! I'm first! My name is Monty—right there on the docket!"

The stone angel's face did not change, carved in a calm, angelic expression. Nevertheless, she was clearly angry. "I will have order, sir."

"Yes, in order! And I'm first in order." The mummy, Monty, was agitated and full of energy.

Judge Stone looked at the docket. "Very well, you are first. We see you so often here … Monty, that I can understand why you think we're on a first-name basis. This is your eighth parking ticket in the last three months."

"It's excessive, Judge. You know it is."

"It is only excessive sir, because you continue to park illegally."

"That remains to be proved," Monty said. "I challenge it. Bring my accuser."

With great effort Judge Stone straightened her angel wings as she referred to her paperwork. "I call the minotaur Dustin from Parking Enforcement." She looked out at the benches and waited.

And waited.

Others in the courtroom began to mutter, looking around. I still didn't see any minotaur. "Dustin?" the judge called out, frustrated. "Are you here to testify?"

It became apparent that the bull-headed meter maid hadn't bothered to show up.

"He's out sick," called the bailiff after glancing at a text on his phone.

"Sick?" Judge Stone sounded exasperated. "Then I have no choice but to find for the defendant." She turned her emotionless stone face toward Monty, who was squirming with excitement. "It appears you've gotten off again, sir."

"Justice has prevailed!" Monty crossed his scrawny bandaged arms over his hollow chest, as if expecting cheers and applause. He received none. He tore the ticket in half, then stormed out of the court.

I tried to get my head around what had just happened as the judge scanned the courtroom. "Does anyone else intend to call Dustin in the matter of parking enforcement?"

I raised my gray hand, and five other unnatural defendants stood up, wearing uncertain smiles.

Judge Stone's marble face somehow managed to convey a frown. "Very well. Your cases are all dismissed."

I was pleased with the result, but Robin looked disappointed. She held her stack of papers. "But I built a complete defense. I have contradictory public ordinances and photographs of where the car was parked. I even have a testimonial from the rat family affirming that they could indeed get into their sewer home. We would have won our case."

"The results are what matter, not the method, Robin. Sometimes the cases do win themselves."

Conceding, she packed up her paperwork. With our parking violation rescinded, we could work on our more important clients.

Considering my investigation into the mysterious minotaur intestinal distress, I was worried that Dustin had fallen ill, too. Now that we were no longer courtroom adversaries, I would do a welfare check on him, first thing.

V

With her usual diligence, Sheyenne had filled out all of the personal contact details in the minotaur's new client form—including Dustin's mobile number. The phone rang five times, until a miserable voice responded, sounding like a belch inside an empty oil barrel. The long, nauseated groan might have been a greeting.

"Is this Dustin? Are you all right? It's Dan Chambeaux."

The response was another mournful, gurgling moan, and finally he articulated, "I'm sick as a dog, Shamble … or as sick as any other animal that gets real sick, real bad."

I was deeply concerned. "I'll be right over." Considering the urgency, I decided to take the Pro Bono Mobile, even if it meant losing our good parking spot.

His house was in a green, well-landscaped part of town. (Parking Enforcement must pay better than I had imagined.) Dustin's front yard was a massive hedge maze with an entrance gate marked with "No Solicitors." But I was a detective, not a solicitor, so I made my way into the green labyrinth.

Trying to find the door, I blundered into blind ends, retraced my steps, tried other pathways, always keeping my eyes on the destination. After fifteen minutes, I finally reached the minotaur's ornate front door, which was framed with tiles done up in a Greek key pattern.

I rang the doorbell beneath an intercom speaker. I was anxious and frustrated, especially after all the time I had lost wandering in the hedge maze. I rang again and again. Eventually, the intercom crackled, and the sick groaning voice answered, "Shamble?"

"It's me. I came to check on you," I said.

With a click, the door automatically unlocked. "Listen carefully." With plodding words, the minotaur said, "Left—left —right—left—right—right, then left again."

"What does that mean?"

Dustin didn't answer.

I stepped into the foyer and an even larger household maze, this one with wood-paneled walls. Now I understood his instructions.

Wishing I had a better short-term memory, I turned left and hurried down the hallway, then left again. Tapping the hole in my forehead to jog loose my recollection, I turned right, then left, and blundered my way through.

I arrived at the center of the minotaur Parking Enforcer's labyrinth, his man-bull cave. With all the wood paneling, it reminded me of a basement den. In Dustin's case, though, it had become a sick room.

The minotaur slumped in a half-reclined easy chair with a crocheted afghan wrapped around his shoulders. His white UQ Parking Enforcement shirt had been tossed on a chair next to a dresser. A box of tissues sat on a TV tray beside the chair, and a laundry-basket-turned-wastebasket held mounds of used tissues.

Dustin let out a pathetic lowing moan like a lost cow looking for its herd. "I hope zombies can't catch this bug, Shamble. Sickest I've been in a long time. I've got the runs." With a clawed hand he snatched a tissue from the box and blew gouts of green snot out of his bull nose. "The runs … from both ends."

Trying to reassure him, I said, "I'm looking into your case." At the side of the room, I saw two compact blood bales, one of them partially eaten. "I went to Melody's Weeds and sneaked a sample, which is being processed now. We'll find out if there's food poisoning."

With a groan, Dustin grabbed a bucket at the foot of the chair and stuck his bull snout into it, ready to vomit, but he controlled himself. "You'll find something … but you have to prove it!"

"Sorry you were too sick to come to parking court," I said, not sounding sorry at all. We had benefited to the tune of a hundred and fifty dollars because of it.

Dustin let out his lowing moan again. "Got to get better by Saturday. Need my full strength back."

Since it was already Wednesday, such a rapid recovery seemed unlikely. "What's on Saturday?" I asked.

He set the bucket down, panting hard. "Bull Run—the biggest charity event of the year, at least for minotaurs. The Running of the Bulls, five kilometers through the streets to raise money for disadvantaged minotaurs." Dustin slumped back in the chair. "Gotta get better by then."

"Just rest. That's the best thing. Be sure to drink your electrolytes—"

Suddenly, Dustin wrapped his beefy arms around his gut and rolled out of the seat. I heard a wet, gurgling sound like an unbalanced washing machine coming from his intestines. "Excuse me, gotta … go!" Barely able to stay on his feet, he staggered away in a wobbly stampede, swaying and groaning.

Dustin vanished into the labyrinthine halls. I heard him bump into the paneling, then turn right. He kept going, then returned the same way and tried a different hallway. He moaned. "I know it's here somewhere! Have to find it." He crashed into the paneling and tried a different route.

I let him continue his desperate search for the bathroom, while I meticulously retraced my steps to the exit.

VI

"I want to sue the city!" The angry Aztec mummy was dry as a husk—otherwise spittle would have sprayed from his shriveled lips. "I need you to do it for me, Ms. Deyer."

Monty shuffled into our offices with the rattle of dried bones and rustle of tattered linens. Even though his parking ticket had been thrown out, the old mummy was still unreasonably outraged.

We met in the conference room with the door closed. (I didn't want Alvina to hear the vitriol he was spewing.) Sheyenne had offered coffee, tea, or water, but Monty wasn't interested in rehydrating himself.

Cool and calm, Robin sat with her yellow legal pad ready. "We're happy to help you, sir. Why exactly do you want to sue the Unnatural Quarter?"

"For harassment! I'll sue the minotaur Parking Enforcers in a one-man class action. The meter maids are all out to get me."

Robin pretended to take notes. She liked to wait until a conspiracy theory took clearer shape before she wrote a detailed summary.

"But your last parking ticket was dismissed," I pointed out, "and so was ours. Dustin is genuinely sick."

Robin leaned forward, still waiting for Monty to make his case. "Is there still an outstanding problem, sir?"

Monty reached into his brown bandages and pulled out an envelope, which he slapped on the conference table. "I got another violation just this morning! Nine parking tickets in the last year—it's profiling because I come from Central America!" He fumed.

"And were you parked illegally?" Robin asked.

"What's that got to do with anything?" The mummy squirmed in the chair. "Every time I park my car, I get a ticket. I want to force the city to leave me alone." He pulled out another sheet of paper that listed all nine of his parking tickets, along with the names of the minotaur meter maids who had issued them.

Robin tapped her magic pencil on the legal pad, then released the implement so it could start writing its own notes and impressions. She skimmed the parking citation. "This seems quite clear. Your car was parked in a plainly marked No Parking zone."

"But *I* parked my car there, so obviously you can't say there was *no parking*."

"What was your previous ticket about? The one that was just dismissed?" I asked.

"I parked in an unloading zone," the mummy said. "It was right next to my apartment door, so I was unloading a burden from my feet."

"Not a legally defensible strategy," Robin pointed out.

"The city needs to learn its lesson. I want to get my revenge. Those minotaurs, the unreasonable parking zones, all these citations. How do I make them stop?"

"By parking legally from now on?" I suggested.

"That won't make them pay!" Monty stood up with a huff and a puff of dust. "So, you aren't going to take my case?"

Robin said, "We're eager to deal with any injustices to unnaturals, but I'm afraid we can't sue the Quarter for responding appropriately to your own illegal actions."

Furious and dissatisfied, Monty stormed out of the conference room. For once, I was glad *not* to have another client.

VII

When the blood-bale analysis came back in only two days from the weed unit, I knew Sheyenne must have some special pull with them. No doubt she flirted with a shy lab geek, since she is particularly gorgeous, even for a ghost.

"Did they find food poisoning?" I asked as she studied the chemical analyses.

Sheyenne had been in med school before being murdered, and her expertise came in handy. She studied the results. "No botulism, salmonella, *E. coli,* or the usual suspects that make people sick from their food."

I took the sheet from her spectral hands and skimmed down the incomprehensible numbers. "Yeah, I don't see anything either."

But I could not forget how utterly miserable Dustin had been. I hoped he'd managed to find the bathroom in the maze of his home before it was too late.

"This is an especially unusual result." Her glowing finger touched a highlighted column on the left. "A high concentration of rare fungal spores."

"Is that suspicious?" We had watched Melody gather all kinds of weeds and debris from the barnyard—thistles, nettles, thorns, crabgrass, groundcover, everything mulched in her processing machine.

"*Fungal spores*, Beaux. If those were agricultural weeds used for bovine customers, why would there be mushrooms?"

"Another mystery to solve," I said. I was accustomed to taking on cases that I didn't really understand.

"That wood nymph is definitely adding something to the blood bales, and the minotaurs are eating it."

I took the lab printout as evidence. "I'll investigate. But why would spores make the minotaurs sick one at a time, instead of all at once?"

"I don't know. Be careful, Beaux. It might be dangerous."

"I'll take a police escort," I promised.

Officer Toby McGoohan, or McGoo, is my best human friend. He was transferred to the UQ Police Department, not as a promotion but to sweep him under the rug when his off-color jokes had offended the wrong people.

I approached him on the street corner as he walked his daily beat. He has a round freckled face, which flushes easily in embarrassment. Fortunately, he's too thickheaded to get embarrassed often.

"Hey Shamble," he said.

"McGoo, I need your help. Would you go with me to investigate suspicious activities at a local weed farm?" I explained the basics of the case.

McGoo shrugged. "Sure, I could use an herbal pick-me-up."

Together, we went to Melody's Weeds, passing vacant lots and rundown open areas until we saw the fenced yard around the weathered old barn. In just two days, the noxious brown underbrush had grown up like a forest. Dandelions shot fluff into the air, tumbleweeds crowded up against the barn wall, and thistles grew tall among the crabgrass.

"You didn't tell me I needed to take allergy medicine as part of the case," McGoo said, then sneezed.

"Being a policeman in the Unnatural Quarter is a high-risk job." I wasn't sure how Melody would react when accused of causing severe intestinal distress to numerous minotaurs, but I was determined to get answers.

The barn door was open like a toothless mouth, and we entered the cavernous farm warehouse. The big baling machine sat waiting for another mouthful of weeds. Previously, the walls had been stacked with reddish bales, like part of an Egyptian pyramid, but most had been delivered to minotaur customers. Considering the overgrown barnyard, she would be harvesting a fresh stockpile soon. I had to stop her from making other minotaurs sick.

"Hello, Melody? It's Dan Chambeaux," I called out. "I need to ask you some more questions."

McGoo shouted, "And he brought police backup this time." He meant to sound intimidating, but then he sneezed twice.

The wood nymph glided out of the back room behind the baling machine, quickly closing the door. An eerie pale blue glow came from the secret chamber.

"That must be quite an extensive school project," she said in her singsong voice. "I didn't know my process was so interesting."

I stepped closer to her with McGoo at my side. "It's not your process I'm concerned about, but *diarrhea*."

Melody blinked her swirling greenish eyes, confused.

"It's a fluid situation," McGoo said.

I fluttered the sheet of lab results in front of her face, hoping that she understood the analysis as little as I did. "Your blood bales are contaminated, and minotaurs are getting sick. I snuck a fresh sample last time I was here, and look at these lab results. How do you explain them?"

The wood nymph seemed frightened, and I was dismayed that the numbers seemed to make sense to her. "But there's nothing in my blood bales that could cause harm. Minotaurs have very robust digestive systems. They can handle the thorniest thistle or the sourest burdocks."

"What about the spores? Explain these suspicious spores." I pointed to the appropriate column, glad that Sheyenne had highlighted it for me.

Melody backed away from the baling machine. "But those spores are harmless!"

"Since when are spores ever harmless?" I asked. I'd had several unpleasant encounters since the Big Uneasy.

"But … they're just rare mushrooms from my private fungus garden. They require special cultivation. My customers never know the difference."

"What kind of mushrooms? We know your minotaur customers have gotten individually sick—there's a pattern here."

Melody insisted, "I'm a wood nymph. I would know if my mushrooms were harmful." She glanced anxiously toward the closed door of her special room.

"Better come clean, ma'am," McGoo said.

"I grow the mushrooms for elite clients and for my own enjoyment. That's all. I put the spores in the blood bales, and the minotaurs help out. They're a necessary part of the growth cycle." Reluctantly, she opened the door of her private room, letting the bluish glow spill out.

McGoo and I pressed closer. Within the dim, eerie room, spindly mushrooms grew from numerous flat beds: they had rounded colorful caps, frilled undersides, twisted lumpy stalks. Some waved gently like seaweed in a current.

"I'm not a fan of mushrooms," McGoo said. "Not even on pizza."

I couldn't disguise my wonder at the unusual fungus garden. "What do you mean the minotaurs help out?"

"These mushroom spores require a particular and unique fertilizer, and a digestive triggering process—and as you can see, they're thriving. If I didn't put the spores in the blood bales for the minotaurs to eat, I would never have this garden."

"I don't understand," McGoo said. I was glad he brought up the matter first.

"It's the fertilizer!" she said again.

"What kind of fertilizer?" I asked.

"Bullshit—very rare and specialized."

"Bullshit isn't rare around here," McGoo said.

"You mean, the minotaurs …?" My brow furrowed around the bullet hole in my forehead.

"The minotaurs consume them when they eat the blood bales. The spores pass through their digestive system, which activates them, and then they come out in the dung. I carefully gather it when I can—quite an unpleasant task, believe me—and I bring it here. All these mushrooms require a lot of bullshit to grow."

"It does sound like a lot of bullshit," I said.

"But I've been doing this for years!" Melody said. "The minotaurs never got sick before."

"You didn't just give a particularly contaminated batch to Dustin?"

She scratched her weed-entangled hair. "Dustin's had the same weekly order for years." She indicated the large baling machine on the floor of the barn, the remaining stacks of blood bales. "If my process is contaminated, why would only one minotaur get sick?"

"There have been seven others," I said, but my voice faltered. "But … only one at a time." Food contamination did not make much sense as the answer. I glanced at the lab printout, hoping some new solution might occur to me. In defeat I turned away. "I'll let you know if we have any other questions."

Melody's good cheer seemed unflappable, even after our bizarre accusations. She called after us in her singsong voice, "Good luck with your daughter's school report."

VIII

Back at the office, I sank into the problem like a swamp monster in quicksand. There had to be some connection, some explanation for the sick minotaurs.

Alvina insisted that I play two games of Angry Vultures with her, which helped clear my mind. Afterward, I sat at my desk and combed through the lists.

In his initial case paperwork, Dustin had given us the names of the other seven minotaurs who had suffered violent and inexplicable intestinal distress. They'd all recovered quickly, though, and I hoped Dustin would be back on his feet, or on his hooves, in time for the Running of the Bulls.

I scanned the list of minotaur victims, deciding to interview them all, find out what else they had eaten for any ideas of what could have gotten them sick. Maybe they drank from an unsanitary trough and swallowed an amoeba parasite? Perhaps we needed to do a laboratory fecal analysis. We could get a fresh sample, if Dustin had not, in fact, made it to the bathroom in time. But I would leave the handling of bullshit to the wood nymph.

It had been a lucky break for us that Dustin got sick on exactly the day he was due to testify in parking court against us … which made me remember that Monty had gotten a similar advantage.

As a detective, I am good at making unexpected connections. It seemed an odd coincidence that Dustin and seven minotaurs had fallen ill at separate times, and the angry Aztec mummy had gone to court for eight parking tickets.

I called out, "Sheyenne, do you still have Monty's list from when he wanted to sue the city over his parking tickets?"

She clucked her ectoplasmic tongue. "We keep everything, Beaux."

"How do we compare those parking court dates against the dates the other minotaurs got sick? And which meter maids issued his citations?"

"I can do that," Alvina piped up.

"Yes you can, kid," I said, and Sheyenne handed her the list.

The little vampire girl quickly accessed public records, found the parking violations, the court dates. "Look, each one of those tickets was dismissed!"

Alvina's laptop screen showed that whenever the Aztec mummy had a case in parking court, the minotaur witness failed to show up, and Monty won by default.

Each time, the Parking Enforcer had called in sick.

A smile crept across my stiff, embalmed face as I hugged Alvina. This time it wasn't bullshit at all.

IX

I always feel a thrill when I solve a case. I was confident I'd found the desiccated old culprit, though I wasn't sure how Monty managed to get the minotaur Parking Enforcers violently ill. I couldn't quote chapter and verse in the criminal code about imposed diarrhea infractions, but McGoo would come up with something when he handled the arrest.

Our responsibility at Chambeaux & Deyer was to the client, and my first priority was to inform Dustin. I knew exactly where he and his minotaur friends would be. It was time for the Bull Run.

Alvina was jumping up and down with excitement. "We've got to get there early! I want a good view, and the sidewalk is already crowded." Robin had gathered folding lawn chairs and a little tripod camping stool, though we didn't need to bring a seat for the kid, because she would never sit still anyway.

We trooped out into the main street, making our way to the starting line of the charity race. It was a festive event, and many unnaturals clustered together, jostling to get a better view. I even saw a few human tourists.

Minotaurs in sleeveless exercise shirts with number placards gathered shoulder to shoulder, snorting and stomping. They lined up, ready to charge off, with their nose rings jingling and their eyes blazing.

I hadn't had a chance to give my final case report to Dustin, but I was glad to see him among the runners, fully recovered. His long ugly face was full of excitement for the run.

"Look at how horny they are!" Alvina said.

"You're right about that, kid."

On a stepstool beside the starting line, a lawn gnome held up a starter pistol that was almost as big as he was. "On your marks!" the gnome cried in a hollow voice. "Get ready for the fifth annual Running of the Bulls!"

Dustin noticed us standing on the sidewalk. He snorted, then bowed his big-horned head, hunched his shoulders, and got ready to run.

The starter pistol cracked with a recoil sufficient to knock the lawn gnome off of his stool. Fortunately, an alert bystander caught him before he could shatter on the concrete.

The minotaurs were off, snorting and puffing, their feet thundering on the street. Panicked spectators scattered out of the way, afraid the monsters would stampede into them. The race swept past us as the minotaurs picked up speed.

Ahead, a bandage-wrapped figure suddenly staggered out from a wide cul-de-sac, waving his gnarled hands. He clacked his bony jaw as he yelled out, "You are all to blame! All you minotaurs who harassed me and wronged me."

Monty strutted into the street and glowered at the oncoming minotaurs. They snorted and bellowed, paying little attention to their desiccated nemesis.

I yelled, "Monty, get out of there!" But the roar of the crowd was too loud, and the bulls were too focused on their run.

Monty was single-minded, too. He unrolled a clattering, design-inscribed codex that had sections flagged with yellow highlighter notes. He began to read and chant in front of the cul-de-sac. "I am Montyzuma, and I will have my terrible revenge."

He finished chanting his long Aztec curse from the codex.

The line of minotaurs, still clustered together on their run, swayed in their tracks as the magic struck them. They grumbled and looked at each other. Their ears flopped and pricked up.

Then, Dustin grabbed his stomach, wrapping massive arms around his gut. The other minotaurs began lowing and groaning. A succession of loud, gurgling flatulence erupted from them like a fusillade of cannon shots.

The mummy hopped up and down with glee, jangling his marked-up codex. "That is just the beginning of Montyzuma's revenge!" He cackled. "You have harassed me for the last time." He attempted to loom at the mouth of the cul-de-sac, though he was rather short.

The minotaurs swayed and moaned, stomping their big feet, and then a flare of urgency rippled through them. They let out a simultaneous bellow that signaled a call of nature and changed direction. They charged directly toward Monty, bound by a common intestinal emergency.

I realized where the mummy was standing. The cul-de-sac behind him had been set aside with a bank of portable latrines for the Bull Run crowds.

Seeing their only chance for relief, the minotaurs galloped forward, their bull heads down, horns extended.

The Aztec mummy waved, trying to get out of the way. "No, no!" he cried, but the minotaurs charged right over him.

Most of them made it to the Tow-a-Toilets in time.

X

When the wood nymph brought a crockpot filled with savory-smelling mushroom soup, she meant it as a peace offering. "My special recipe. Once you taste this, you'll see that I only intend to bring joy to others with my special fungus."

"I'll pass," I said. Like McGoo, I wasn't a big fan of mushrooms, especially if the spores thrived on bullshit.

Alvina lifted the lid and poked among the bobbing fungus

STIFFS AND STONES   109

caps. Sheyenne frowned down at the soup. "None for me either. I was killed with toadstool poison."

"Leave it in the kitchenette," Robin said from her office door. "I might need a snack later." Her voice became stern. "But from now on, you must make full disclosure of any additional ingredients in your blood bales."

"I understand that," said Melody in her melodious voice. "In fact, I plan to make it a selling point!"

She flitted out of the office just as a tattered, brown wreck of tangled rags stumbled in.

"Monty!" I said. "You're looking much better than expected." Though he did smell much the worse for wear; he was a walking skid mark.

The last time I'd seen him, trampled by minotaurs in distress, he had been little more than a stained smudge on the pavement. But he had already endured as a mummy for thousands of years, and he was resilient.

That meant Montyzuma could face the punishment for his intestinal crimes.

"I know, Mr. Shamble. I came to make amends. I understand now that what I did was wrong. I have to pay all of my back parking tickets, even the ones that were dismissed." He sulked, still not convinced, but he had given up his revenge.

I had explained everything to McGoo, who wrote up an arrest warrant. As soon as the trampled Aztec mummy reanimated himself, McGoo put his narrow wrists into handcuffs.

"And community service," Monty said. "I'll be sweeping streets and working on urban beautification projects for the next year." His narrow shoulders slumped. "I just wanted to apologize to you all." He lowered his wrapped head. "And ask for one small favor."

I let Sheyenne handle the matter, since she is a more forgiving person. "What is it Monty?"

He reached into his rags and pulled out a small paper card. "Could you validate my parking?"

MYSTERY MEAT

I

The giant fly was frantic as she buzzed into the offices of Chambeaux & Deyer Investigations. Her long translucent wings vibrated like stained-glass windows made of Saran wrap. She clutched her top two sets of articulated arms in dismay. "My maggots are missing!"

She accepted a tissue from Sheyenne, our receptionist (and my ghost girlfriend), so she could dab tears from her multifaceted eyes.

I shambled into the front office when I heard the loud buzzing sound, and I could immediately see that this human-sized insect needed our help. As a zombie detective, I'm ready to solve even the oddest cases.

The mother fly buzzed back and forth in the reception area, bouncing off the window in desperation, then coming back to where Sheyenne and I could soothe her.

I said, "Take a breath, ma'am, so we can figure out how to assist you." I extended my pallid hand, then pulled it back, not really wanting to be grasped by those clenching claws.

"My babies!" With great effort, the large fly forced her wings to settle down. Her proboscis uncurled, then curled like a New

Year's Eve party favor as she took a deep breath. "The whole brood! They're all I've got. I need to engage your services, Mr. Chambeaux. You're the best zombie detective in the Unnatural Quarter."

I guess my reputation preceded me. "So, it's a missing persons case, then?" I asked.

"Missing maggots," the agitated insect corrected. I almost made a wisecrack about needing to call out the SWAT team, but that was in poor taste.

The mutant bug's name was Mama Fly, because apparently flies are so common and have such small brains that any one name will do the trick. At least Mama Fly was easier to spell than some of our Lovecraftian clients, like Maug-Shugguleth.

Robin Deyer, my passionate human lawyer partner, emerged from her office ready to offer advice. As usual, this case would be a team effort.

After we calmed her down, Mama Fly managed to offer explanations. "I need a private investigator, and I need a fly spotter." She still looked as if she might hurl herself against the already-flyspecked window, so I eased myself back toward it and opened the glass, just in case.

"Tell us what happened to your maggots," Robin said. "How many of them? And what did they look like?"

Here in the Quarter, we were used to monsters, demons, ghosts and mythical beasties of all kinds. There were new cases every week to keep me, Robin, and Sheyenne busy.

Even so, I'd never had to search for missing maggots before.

"My babies wriggled off to the playground, just like always," said Mama Fly. Her proboscis uncurled and curled again. "And they never came home! I've talked to other flies in the neighborhood, and they're buzzing with gossip. At least two other maggots disappeared at the same time."

"And when did they disappear?" I asked.

"This morning—hours ago! But a mother knows when

something is wrong. We need to search the entire Quarter. Find them! You have to hurry—it's urgent."

Robin and Sheyenne determinedly took notes.

"I understand your worry, Mama Fly," I said, "but there's no immediate reason to suspect they're in danger. We have time."

"No we don't!" The fly's wings fluttered again. "Our lifecycle is only a few weeks, and they need to pupate! There's not a moment to lose. Oh, my babies!"

Now we understood her extraordinary urgency.

After we took down the pertinent information, Mama Fly buzzed off.

II

In the Unnatural Quarter, a disappearing creature—even an insect one—was not an uncommon occurrence. I put out word on the street to my meager network of informants. At the UQ Police Department, I met with Officer Toby McGoohan and gave him a heads-up. I even filled out a missing larvae report.

As a zombie detective, I am good at aimlessly shambling, and I would start pounding the pavement soon, but Robin and I needed to strategize our approach. Because it was lunchtime, we met at the Ghoul's Diner, our usual unpalatable eating place. My little vampire half-daughter also joined us; Alvina is the only one who actually likes the miserable food served by Albert Gould, the proprietor—but the kid usually orders a prepackaged box of Unlucky Charms, because she likes the way the cereal made the milk turn blood red.

The diner was filled with the usual (actually, unusual) lunch crowd: vampires slurping blood soup or taking IVs to go, two slender female werewolves eating salads, a lanky necromancer who came in every day to order the "dead things" special. My taste buds haven't worked since my death, so I'm pretty much immune to whatever flavors show up in the mess served by

Albert. It's the company I like, and eating at the diner with friends, partners, or clients was just part of the ritual.

We found an empty booth. I took one side, bending my stiff knees and tucking myself into the corner. Alvina scooted in next to me, bubbly and squirmy as always, while Robin capped the other end.

"Those poor little maggots," Alvina said. "So cute and cuddly! I hope we find them."

"We'll do our best, kid." I nudged her with my elbow. She nudged back. It was a sophisticated game we played. She's a few years older than her ten-year-old appearance, but now that she'd been turned into a vampire, she would never grow older. Even so, Alvina wore "cute" as a badge of honor, and she was good at it.

Robin set her briefcase on the sticky Formica tabletop, but before we could discuss Mama Fly and her offspring, Esther, the obnoxious harpy waitress, sashayed over and glared at us. "I suppose you want coffee instead of just the water!"

"You haven't brought us water yet," I said.

"Quit complaining," Esther snapped. "You get your coffee, but refills aren't free today." I usually couldn't stomach more than one cup anyway. Esther shrieked toward the kitchen where Albert was slaving away, dripping slime and rotting tissue into everything he cooked. "Three lunch specials!"

"Lunch special," Albert replied in a slow, slurred voice. The gaunt ghoul seemed to thrive on the drudgery, though his sullen face was capable of no expression other than sullen disappointment.

"No, I want a box of Unlucky Charms," Alvina said.

Robin straightened, not fazed by our shrill waitress. "I'd like my usual peanut-butter-and-jelly sandwich. With a pickle."

"Make your own damn peanut-butter-and-jelly sandwich," Esther said. "We don't serve that here. This is a fine restaurant."

"I order it every time I eat here," Robin said, still

maddeningly calm. "A peanut-butter-and-jelly, please, and a pickle."

Esther fluffed her feathers, which were razor-edged and gleamed like metal dipped in an oil slick. "If I give in to one of your stupid customer demands, then you'll always want something special, and you probably won't tip!"

"I won't tip unless I get my peanut-butter-and-jelly sandwich." Robin had faced the most combative litigants in court, so she had no trouble facing off against a waitress.

"Unlucky Charms, please," Alvina repeated.

I did my best to mollify Esther. "I'm okay with the special, Esther. Bring it on."

Esther stalked off. "It better be a damn good tip!"

Robin took out her papers, and we reviewed notes of where maggots were frequently seen, places where flies frequented. We studied a small map of the Quarter to determine where to start our efforts.

Eventually, Esther came back with Alvina's box of cereal and a carafe of milk, as well as Robin's PB&J. She placed a blue plate in front of me with a large round slice of meat marbled with paler swirls, garnished with just a dab of gravy. It looked juicy, almost tasty.

"What is this, Esther?" I could even smell it ... and it actually smelled good.

"Lunch special—just what you ordered." She turned around.

I poked at the meat with a fork. "What *is* the lunch special?"

"Mystery Meat."

From behind the counter, Albert looked up and groaned. "Lunch special. Mystery Meat."

I might have been intrigued, but the ghoul's lunch specials were often questionable, and some questions are better left unasked. This meal seemed less offensive than usual, however— the flesh not so gray and without the usual colors of decay or the smell of rot.

Curious, I used my knife to cut off a piece, which was tender and meaty all the way through, and the smells were even savory. I popped a bite into my mouth and chewed. I blinked in surprise. "This is actually palatable."

"New source," Albert said. "Mystery Meat."

I took another bite, tasting it more, even savoring the meat. "In fact, this is delicious."

"I thought you couldn't taste anything," Robin said.

"Usually not, but this …"

Alvina stole a bite and agreed that it was yummy—high praise indeed for someone who prefers breakfast cereal with artificial colors and flavors.

"Mystery Meat. Good protein." Albert grinned, which was unfortunate, because his snaggly, rotted teeth were enough to make anyone lose their appetite. "Bug based."

I hesitated. "*Bug* based? You mean I'm eating … insect steak?"

Distracted in the kitchen, Albert used his forearm to whisk a handful of skittering cockroaches from the kitchen counter directly into the stewpot. "You always eat insects here."

I knew that, even though I hadn't wanted to see.

Robin had an opinion. "Insects are a viable protein source, Dan. Considering food shortages, climate change, and agricultural disasters, traditional sources of meat like massive cattle herds are costly, not to mention destructive to the environment. In recent years, we've seen many advances in delicious meat substitutes: plant-based, soy-based, even textured algae products."

Demonstrating her vast knowledge from Wikipedia, Alvina said, "Lots of cultures eat bugs. Crickets, grasshoppers, earthworms, beetle grubs, termites."

"You're making my mouth water, kid." I looked down at the half-eaten Mystery Meat steak on my plate.

Robin said, "Be open minded, Dan. Unnaturals eat rotting flesh and brains all the time. Don't be queasy about a different, environmentally safe kind of protein."

I grudgingly took another taste, which was not bad at all. I offered a bite to Robin since she was so insistent, but she politely declined. Instead, she bit into her PB&J, followed by half of the dill-pickle spear.

The moment we were finished, Esther sauntered by to snatch our dishes like a shoplifter. When she looked down at my lunch plate, her already pinched face tightened even more. "You cleaned your plate! Now what am *I* supposed to eat?"

She huffed off, and we quickly laid money on the table so as to avoid facing her again with the actual bill.

As we left the Ghoul's Diner, I heard the rumble of a large engine and saw a delivery truck in the back. It was pulling away after having dropped off large crates. The side of the truck said *Gold Boris's Abattoir. Home of Mystery Meat!*

Curious, I watched the truck roar off to make its other deliveries.

III

Though we had already started work to find the missing maggots, Mama Fly was impatient and desperate. She buzzed back into the offices carrying a stack of printed flyers. She wore a red polka-dotted scarf tied around the top of her head, just above her multifaceted eyes.

Sitting at her homework table, Alvina started to giggle. "Flyers! I get it." She'd been posting notices about the missing larvae on her Monstagram and SickTok accounts.

Sheyenne chided, "This is serious business, sweetie."

It wasn't any worse than my SWAT team joke, but at least I'd kept that one to myself.

Mama Fly's wings fluttered. "I don't understand."

"F-L-Y … ers?" Alvina said, waiting.

Mama Fly shook her head. "I'm a fly. I don't know how to spell." She set the stack of papers on Sheyenne's reception desk. "But I had help with these."

Each flyer had a bold headline: "Missing. Have you seen this maggot?" Beneath were photos of featureless pale worms, long thick grubs with slightly pointed heads, no eyes, small rounded mouths.

"Oh, you have pictures—that'll help," I said. Every one of the grubs looked identical.

Mama Fly said, "I'll leave these here with you." Her wings twitched and fluttered. "I have to get to work processing the town manure pile." The proboscis uncurled and curled in frustration. "The boss wouldn't give me time off."

I took the flyers. "We'll put these all around the Quarter, ma'am, and continue our vigorous search. But I need some more information. You said your grubs were at the playground when they vanished. Could you give more details about exactly where they were last seen?"

"At the maggot playground." Mama Fly's insectile forelimbs twitched with worry. "Everyone knows Dumpster Row. Where else would maggots play?"

As the insect flitted off, I picked up the stack of paper and looked at Alvina. "Kid, you want to come along? Let's go post these flyers."

IV

I'm always glad to have quality father/half-daughter time, so Alvina and I spent the afternoon walking through the Quarter and taping Missing Maggot notices to wrought-iron lampposts, on the sides of abandoned buildings, onto crypts in the Greenlawn Cemetery—all the places where they would get the most traffic. Even, with Albert's permission, on the door of the Ghoul's Diner, right next to a new poster that advertised "We now serve Mystery Meat on select menu items."

I remembered how good the food had tasted, though I still found something unsettling about it....

We decided to investigate where the grubs had disappeared.

Maybe other children had seen the poor maggots on the playground. Alvina would be my secret weapon, since she was cute as a button and had good rapport with the offspring of any species.

Following directions, we made our way to an industrial part of the Quarter, where fly-by-night businesses were housed in corrugated metal buildings. Dumpster Row was not at all the playground I had expected (though it was true to its name). The open paved area was like an airport long-term parking lot for garbage receptacles, filled with row upon row of dumpsters, as if the receptacles had reproduced like … well, like flies. Green ones, brown ones, orange ones, and others so rusty I couldn't tell what the original color had been.

Alvina shaded her eyes to look down the endless rows. "Is this where dumpsters go to die?"

"Let's not be morbid, kid," I said. "Maybe they're all just asleep."

The sun had set, and twilight layered extra shadows and gloom onto the complex. I saw small forms scurrying between the containers, squirming underneath them, ducking between and rushing over them. Likely, packrat demons, scavenger squids, or gremlin treasure hunters who would ransack the dumpsters for collectible trash.

Alvina skipped ahead, banged on one of the dumpsters, then went to the next one. She lifted the groaning lid and peered inside before she dropped back down and let the lid slam. She shook her head. "Nothing interesting. I wonder who would want to play here?"

"Giant maggots, I suppose." I cupped my hands around my mouth and shouted, "Hello? Any maggots out here?"

I heard a faint rustle and stirring, a few muffled bumps on metal walls, but there were hundreds of dumpsters here, and I had no way of identifying where the sound had come from. More shadowy figures scuttled around the containers.

Adjacent to Dumpster Row, a neon sign on the corrugated

roof of the nearest industrial structure flickered on, and the sizzling letters spelled out *Gold Boris's Abattoir, Home of Mystery Meat!*A smaller line beneath said *Public Not Welcome.* Boxy delivery trucks pulled up to a loading dock in the back.

With a sinking feeling in my stomach, I remembered that the Mystery Meat substitute was supposedly "bug based." If Mama Fly's larvae liked to play in Dumpster Row, what if Gold Boris— whoever that was—had thugs engaged in maggot snatching, then fed the protein-rich grubs into the abattoir?

The industrial building had no windows whatsoever. One of the delivery trucks rumbled to life, spurting noxious exhaust fumes into the air, then rolled off into the Quarter to make deliveries.

I'd have to look into this further—but I needed to have more backup than a little vampire girl.

V

After putting up all the flyers and exploring the sinister Dumpster Row, Alvina and I returned to the offices. My vampire half-daughter ran into the kitchen where she was playing a game of Curses With Friends with the sentient mold growing on the wall next to the microwave.

Time was of the essence, considering the life expectancy of a fly (giant or otherwise). I needed to bring in the big guns—two guns actually: Officer Toby McGoohan's police special revolver and his police extra-special revolver loaded with silver bullets. But it wasn't all about weaponry. I wanted McGoo with me for moral support, as well as law-enforcement support. I got ready to call him.

Sheyenne flitted up and gave me an air kiss, but my attention was suddenly drawn to the office TV, which was playing her favorite afternoon talk show, *Conversations with Dick the Head*, where the decapitated host interviewed local celebrities.

I was more interested, however, in the commercial break.

Peppy circus-like music accompanied an announcer extolling the virtues of "Delicious, Nutritious Mystery Meat!" Images showed juicy, savory slabs of the undefined protein mass. The narrator promised that the substance was completely organic and that no living creatures were harmed in the production of Mystery Meat.

Inherently suspicious, I muttered, "I wonder if that means they use undead creatures."

The voiceover continued, "And no undead creatures were harmed either! It's the perfect protein, a renewable resource. Healthy, tasty Mystery Meat from Gold Boris."

I removed my fedora and hung it on the rack, then scratched around the bullet hole in the center of my forehead as I pondered. Something about the ad struck me as odd. Renewable resource—I couldn't stop thinking about how fast flies breed.

Sheyenne had watched the commercial with me. "Have you ever tasted that, Beaux?"

"Just yesterday at the Ghoul's Diner. It was their lunch special."

"I never thought of you as a possible vegetarian." She had a teasing glow.

"I never thought that myself either. I permanently gave up eating brains, but I'm not sure if I could ever do without a good cheeseburger."

But I wasn't thinking about cheeseburgers, or any food whatsoever. I had lost my appetite, more than usual. I thought back to all the questions I had surrounding Gold Boris's Abattoir.

VI

"I've studied the reports, Shamble, and quite a few maggots have gone missing over the years," said McGoo. He cocked his patrolman's cap as we met up outside the Chambeaux & Deyer offices. "If you've got suspicions about Gold Boris, then we'll check out that abattoir." He pursed his lips. "Besides, I hear Mystery Meat is pretty good."

"The Ghoul's Diner serves it," I said.

McGoo made a face. "Even if it started off pretty good, that place turns my stomach."

We made our way to the industrial park near Dumpster Row. McGoo let out a loud whistle as he scanned the giant parking lot filled with garbage containers. "You think that's where dumpsters go to die, Shamble?"

"Alvina already suggested that," I said.

"Our daughter is a smart kid," McGoo said.

"Takes after me," I replied. He just snorted.

Four more delivery trucks were parked behind the big industrial building. There were no windows in the corrugated walls, only a thick metal front door with the sign *Public Not Welcome*.

"We're not the public, Shamble." McGoo used the sleeve of his blue uniform to polish his badge. "Two-week life cycle, you say? I'd call that extenuating circumstances." He pounded on the door. "Police! Open up. We've got some questions."

For good measure, I added, "Zombie detective!" You never know what might impress or intimidate people.

We heard scuttling sounds behind the door, which remained closed in our faces. McGoo's expression darkened, hiding his freckles. He was ready to yell and threaten, but I took a different approach. I turned the doorknob. It was unlocked.

We entered a small front room with file cabinets, a water cooler, a credenza with an old coffeemaker, a folding chair, and a reception desk with a phone, a typewriter—yes, an actual typewriter—and a rat man in a lab coat stationed at the desk. He looked up at us with beady, close-set eyes, and his ears pricked up. His lips curled back, and his whiskers twitched. "No visitors! No public tours! Gold Boris's Abattoir has trade secrets."

"We're not here for a tour," I said.

McGoo leered into the rat man's face. "We need some answers about Mystery Meat."

"And missing maggots," I said. "There's a very distraught mother fly looking for her grubs."

"Maggots?" the rat sniffled. "Are you suggesting that our Mystery Meat is contaminated with maggots?" His whiskers twitched in horror. "We have never failed a public health inspection!"

"When was your last one?" McGoo demanded.

The rat man squeaked. "We're a relatively new company. Our Mystery Meat product is fresh on the market. We have patents pending, and secret recipes."

"I'm an officer of the law, and I don't cook," McGoo said. "You can't keep secrets from me. We have a lead on some missing children, and we need to know what you know."

"I know a lot of things." The rodent man sniffed. "I'm a lab rat."

"And a receptionist, I see," I added.

The rat's whiskers twitched again. "I get paid extra. Nothing here in Gold Boris's Abattoir concerns you. We have no involvement with any missing children, maggots, grubs, larvae, or otherwise." His pink nose wiggled. "I despise killing living things. So many rats have been slaughtered over the centuries it makes me shudder!" Appropriately, he shuddered. "So many rats have been eaten, murdered in traps, hunted down in the sewers. Thus, I'm a devout vegetarian."

I said, "I've been hearing a lot about meat alternatives lately."

"Yes, yes!" The rat man's beady eyes glinted, and he rubbed his little paws in front of him. "Gold Boris is changing the world for the better."

"We need to see Mr. Boris," McGoo said. "Ask him some questions."

Behind the receptionist desk, the rat man recoiled. "No, no! That won't be possible. Gold Boris sees no one. He's our trade secret!"

"We're good at keeping secrets," I said.

The rat man turned in a panic, looked toward a set of wide metal doors behind him that led into the industrial bay.

"We'll just go have a look for ourselves," McGoo said, and I shambled beside him toward the doors.

The rat rushed to block our way. "You need a search warrant."

"I also need a million dollars," McGoo said, "but I can live without it."

When the rat man couldn't stop us, we swung open the set of doors to the back bay. McGoo put a hand on one of his service revolvers. (I wasn't sure which one.) An earthy, savory smell wafted in our faces.

Stepping forward, we entered the abattoir's cavernous bay, and we finally met Gold Boris.

VII

I had expected to find caged, kidnapped maggots. Not this.

One summer vacation when I was a kid, we stayed at a lodge on a lake. I would go out fishing with a can of worms, plucking one of the wriggly critters to impale it on a fishhook. I'd drop a line on a bobber and wait for bluegills to come nibbling. More often than not, they would just eat the worm and leave the hook alone. Then I'd have to repeat the process with another squirmy worm, looping and sticking it on the sharp end of the hook.

The enormous worm that filled the abattoir bay was nothing at all like one of those.

Gold Boris was the size of several freight-train cars hooked together. A pinkish worm with tiny eyes set on the top of his blunt, rounded head. Ringed segments rolled down its long serpentine form which encircled the perimeter of the abattoir's main bay. His round mouth was like the door to a wind tunnel, wide open in an invertebrate expression of surprise. Startled, the worm reared back and pulled away from McGoo and me.

Half a dozen rat men in lab coats squeaked as they rushed to take shelter behind the worm's enormous tail. They all wore thick gloves on their paws, and their lab coats were stained with ichor. They carried sharp axes, machetes, and other ominous cutlery. In the back half of the warehouse bay, meat-processing machinery thrummed.

McGoo gawked. "What the hell is that?" He drew both types of revolvers, just to make sure, although he was a lousy shot with his left hand. I drew my .38, and we both crouched in a defensive firing stance.

The worm waved its huge head back and forth like a dancing cobra in front of a snake charmer's flute. "I am Boris," he said in a thick Russian accent. "You can call me Gold Boris, my current nickname."

That defused the tension a little.

"Uh, pleased to meet you, Boris," I said, dropping the tension down another notch, although the sharp implements clutched by the rat men still looked ominous.

The rodent receptionist ran in behind us, squeaking. "You can't see. You can't see! Mystery Meat is a trade secret."

"It's still a mystery to me," I said. I realized that the furry little butchers had been cutting off chunks of Boris's long tail, slicing it like a vermiform cucumber.

Gold Boris lowered his huge, rounded head. "You were not supposed to see this. Diners should not witness how sausage is made."

"Or Mystery Meat, apparently," McGoo said.

I was still looking around for Mama Fly's missing larvae. "But ... we thought you were kidnapping giant maggots and processing them."

"Maggots? Ewww!" Boris cried. "My Mystery Meat is pure, free range, homegrown, and harvested from my freshest, youngest, and tenderest ring segments."

At the tail end of the huge creature near the meat-processing machinery, the terrified rat men backed away and held up their goo-stained cutting implements. As we watched, the severed end of Boris's tail sprouted a pink new ring segment. It popped out of the raw tip, grew swiftly until it was the size of a life preserver, and was followed by another segment that extruded through the tip.

"As you see," Boris said, "one hundred percent renewable, sustainably produced."

"I'm still confused," McGoo said.

"You're always confused, McGoo, but I'll join you as a partner in confusion."

"Isn't it mythologically obvious?" Boris bobbed and dipped his huge head. "I thought my name would give it away! The modification seemed obvious to me, but perhaps I overestimated how conversant the average person is with classic Gnostic legends."

"Your name? Gold Boris?" I asked. "It's still not clear."

"Oro means gold," the worm said, waiting.

"And Boris? Oro Boris…" I still waited. I glanced at McGoo, but no light bulb went on over his head either.

"Ouroboros!" the giant worm said, squirming and wriggling.

"Oh, now I remember," I said. "Ouroboros, the worm that eats its own tail."

The huge creature bobbed his head. "The name was too challenging for most people to say—or spell—so I modernized it, catered to the lowest common denominator. Thus … Ouroboros became Gold Boris."

McGoo took off his cap and scratched his red hair, clearly still confused.

Defensive, the giant worm added, "Lots of famous actors do the same thing when their real names aren't catchy enough, or American enough. Martin Sheen is really Ramón Antonio Gerardo Estévez, and Ricky Martin is Enrique Martín Morales." He leaned closer to us. "Or for an even bigger mouthful, how about Anthony Quinn's original name? Manuel Antonio Rodolfo Quinn Oaxaca!"

"Okay, I get the name change," McGoo said, "but that's the only part I get."

More ring segments sprouted out of the severed tail end, and the worm kept growing longer and longer with alarming rapidity.

"So, you're the mythical worm eating its own tail …" I left the sentence dangling like a worm on a hook.

"It was like sucking on a thumb! Disgusting habit!" Boris said. "But I finally broke myself of it, pulled the tail out of my mouth, and never touched it again." A shudder rippled through the whole serpentine body. "But once I unrolled myself and stopped devouring my own tail, the tail just kept growing and growing! Something had to be done about it.

"Now, I thought that the taste of my tail meat was delicious, almost addictive. So I stopped always grabbing a piece of tail, and instead I decided to make the world a better place. I hired assistants with similar mindsets, rat men who wanted to stop the environmentally damaging and inhumane practice of raising large animals for meat, and we set up shop here. Those soy substitutes taste terrible—but not my Mystery Meat! It's real meat, solid protein, humanely harvested, and voluntarily given."

And I'd eaten one of those steaks in the Diner yesterday. My stomach churned, even though I told myself that it wasn't any more gross than eating a hot dog.

At the rear of the abattoir bay, the tail segment kept growing. The rat men by the processing machinery began to grow nervous. "We need to keep harvesting, boss, or we'll fall behind."

"Indeed!" Boris bobbed his huge head. "Get back to it. We have orders to deliver."

"I see why it's a trade secret." McGoo looked at me and shrugged.

I shrugged back. "I'll check with Robin on the legal issues, but I don't think they're doing anything against the law."

"I can give you free samples," Boris said. "Enough to fill your freezer."

"No thanks," we said in unison.

The rodent receptionist squeaked. "You can't reveal this! No one can know the source of Mystery Meat! Otherwise, we'll have competitors springing up out of the ground like nightcrawlers after a rainstorm."

The rat crew began slicing and dicing the fast-growing end of Gold Boris's tail.

"That still doesn't help us find the missing maggots," I said. "What are we going to tell Mama Fly?"

"No maggots here," said the worm. "We run a clean processing plant."

VIII

As we left the abattoir, the flickering neon sign gave McGoo's face a strange and sickly pallor, much like my own. "There's no more mystery to the Mystery Meat, Shamble," he said. "But that doesn't help solve your case."

We walked away from the abattoir, facing the vast Dumpster Row and its hundreds of dark garbage containers. The complex had no security lights, since the chances of dumpster robbery were low. Staring at the countless rows, I couldn't imagine what frisky young maggots found so enticing about the place.

Unexpectedly, Sheyenne's spectral form appeared in front of us with a faint blue glow. "Anything to report to Mama Fly? She's getting really anxious. What about Gold Boris?"

"Now, that's a long story," I said.

McGoo grinned. "Better yet, it's a long tail."

"Don't make me any more queasy than I already am, McGoo."

Across the eerily silent dumpster park, I heard the usual restless skittering, intermittently accompanied by the rhythmic thumping from before. Maybe some young scavenger demon was practicing on a drum kit. The banging increased, and it seemed to have a frantic undertone.

Sheyenne perked up. "That doesn't sound right. Isn't this where Mama Fly's grubs liked to play?"

"Maybe somebody needs help out there among all the dumpsters," I said.

McGoo regarded the endless collection of garbage containers. "How do we know which one? That'll be like finding a needle in a haystack."

"Or a maggot in a dumpster farm."

"We'll have to search row by row," Sheyenne said in a determined voice, and she flitted ahead.

I looked at McGoo. "How long could it take? There's only a thousand or so of them."

We split up, and I shambled down one row while McGoo headed along another. Unburdened by a physical form, my poltergeist girlfriend was able to cover more territory.

The urgent pounding echoed off the other containers, confusing the sound. I reached the end of one row and doubled back down the next one, but I didn't seem to be getting any closer. McGoo pounded on a dumpster, waiting for a response like some trashy game of Marco Polo.

Sheyenne circled overhead, listening closely The thumping grew louder, more desperate. I was sure we were on to something.

I went to the next row. Maybe I was getting closer. Sheyenne drifted next to me. "I think it's …"

The thumping increased.

I yelled, "It's over here, McGoo!"

Trying to locate the source of the sound, Sheyenne raced ahead and called out, "This one! Here's the dumpster we've been looking for."

McGoo and I reached it at the same time. The heavy lid had fallen shut and the latch bar clicked into place, but something inside was pounding—trapped. Hearing our voices, the banging increased.

Sheyenne hovered above the container while McGoo and I worked together to wrench open the metal bar that locked the heavy lid shut. We finally got it free and heaved up the lid.

As soon as we raised it, maggots boiled out. It was like turning over a ripe rotting corpse, except in this case the maggots were the size of thick pool noodles. They swayed, eyeless and frantic, their tiny mouths puckering and unpuckering in expressions of excitement, gratitude, and relief.

"We're saved, we're saved!" the maggots squeaked as they sprang out of the dumpster.

Sheyenne tried to be reassuring. "There, there, you're safe. We'll get you back to your Mama Fly."

"What were you doing in there?" I asked.

"Just playing like always," said one of the maggots. "We built a fort in our favorite dumpster, but then the lid fell shut, and we were locked inside. We couldn't move the latch."

"Dumpsters aren't designed with emergency exits," McGoo said. "Not even for unfortunate young maggots."

One grub wailed, "We didn't think we'd ever be rescued!"

"We've been trapped in there for days," said another larva.

A third said, "Mama Fly told us we had to get home early before it's time to pupate."

"We're gonna get a whupping!"

The grubs waved back and forth, bowing their heads. I think they were crying, but it was hard to tell, since maggots have no facial features. I couldn't identify them from the pictures on the MISSING posters, but I was pretty sure these were the ones we were looking for.

"Come on, squirm after us." I gestured as I set off with McGoo and Sheyenne. "We'll get you home."

IX

Mama Fly was buzzing with joy when she returned to our offices a few days later. She was glad to have the case solved, of course, and she was also eager to write a check for our fee. It's not often a client is so quick to pay their bills, but Mama Fly insisted that she wanted to settle up.

She entered the office, still wearing the polka-dotted head scarf. In her top sets of limbs, she cradled four capsule-shaped bundles, each wrapped in a baby blanket. "As you can see, my babies safely entered their pupae, thanks to you."

Alvina came bouncing out, smiling. "They look so cute. Can I hold them?"

At first Mama Fly flinched, but then handed over the fuzzy cocoon and blanket. The little vampire girl rocked the pupa back and forth and sang an off-key lullaby; Mama Fly rocked the other pupae in time.

Robin was satisfied, as she always was upon successfully closing a case file. "I'm sure they'll grow up to be strong, young houseflies," she said.

Mama Fly seemed to be in a hurry. "I just had my retirement party today at the manure pile." She took the other cocoon back and turned about, thanking us again.

I waved as Mama Fly took her leave. "See ya around."

She swiveled her head and regarded us with her large compound eyes. "Not likely." Her proboscis extended and retracted. "Two-week lifecycle, remember?"

She flitted off. I was glad to know that the rest of her brief lifespan would be a happy one.

STIFF AND SORE

I

At the Goblin Tavern, I was having a beer—or maybe a second one—with my best human friend, Officer Toby McGoohan, when the monster hunter walked up to me.

"Have you seen this necromancer? He's a nasty piece of work." The man dropped a photo on the wooden bar in front of me. I had noticed him going around the tavern asking questions.

I took another sip to show that I didn't appreciate having my valuable detective time interrupted. As a zombie, I couldn't really taste the beer, but I like to keep up appearances. Old habits die hard, even when you're undead.

Still wearing his patrolman's uniform, McGoo wrapped a hand around his pint glass and appeared to be deep in thought, probably concocting another dumb joke. Off duty after walking the beat in the Unnatural Quarter, he had his after-hours priorities.

I gave the monster hunter a good look before considering the photo of the necromancer in question. He was a tall, thin man with a narrow face and a pinched expression—maybe he could have used one of McGoo's jokes. He was covered with weapons and wore an impressive set of armor, like a kid with an overprotective mother trying out for the school football team. He had a full chest plate, shoulder pads, forearm pads, and gauntlets—one of which he had removed so he could handle the photograph—boots, thigh pads, and, yes, even an all-important codpiece. A long katana poked up from its sheath on his back. A Magnum pistol rested in a holster on his hip next to two long throwing daggers. The utility belt would have made Batman green with envy. He also had a grenade or two within easy reach, as well as two flasks of what I assumed was holy water. A looped cable (a strangling garrote?) completed the ensemble.

But even with all the prickly accoutrements, the vibe he gave off was more Don Knotts than Arnold Schwarzenegger.

"Hey, look at the photo, not me," he said, as if aggression might win him customer service points.

"Sorry," I said. "ADHD." I took another sip of my beer.

The photo looked more like an actor's head shot than a mug shot. The necromancer had a chiseled face, firm jaw, and a grim expression that reminded me of a drill sergeant. (Admittedly, you don't see many photos of grinning necromancers.) His black cap was embroidered with arcane symbols, and he wore a dark robe made out of 1970s-stylish velour. Around his neck hung a gaudy jewel-encrusted amulet.

"His name is Ned Kadoo," said the monster hunter, tapping his finger on the photograph, "and I've been hired to find him. Long track record of crimes, and it's time he has to pay for them."

I pushed the photo away. "Can't say that I've seen him around, but I'll keep an eye out." I hoped my tone would convey complete lack of sincerity.

McGoo wiped foam off his lips and finally paid attention. "And what's your name, Mister?"

"I see my fame doesn't precede me." The man straightened with pride, though all that body armor made his movements seem stiff and awkward. "I'm Bo Jest, monster hunter and bounty hunter, keeping the world safe from unnaturals."

That surprised me. "The Quarter seems reasonably safe, even with all the monsters."

"Oh, you have no idea," Jest growled.

"Don't like bounty hunters," McGoo said. "I'm a law-and-order man myself, and bounty hunters are a gray area. Do you have a license for all those weapons?"

"Yes I do, officer!" He had to remove his other gauntlet in order to withdraw his wallet. He spilled out a long plastic accordion-fold that contained numerous laminated cards which authorized him to carry everything from wooden stakes to rocket launchers. One plastic pocket held his bounty hunter license, backed with a personal business card.

Monsters Are My Specialty, Big and Small!

(Rates available upon request)

"I've got a zombie private investigator's license," I said, and showed him my card, hoping it would impress him or, preferably, make him go away.

When the monster hunter looked down, his eyes popped open in surprise, as if he had just seen a ghost (which is not a particularly unusual occurrence). "Hey, you're Dan Shamble, zombie P.I. I've heard of you! Even read the books about your adventures. I like true crime."

This guy wasn't earning any points with me. "It's Dan *Chambeaux*. Says so right on the card." I tapped my name, though it was always a lost cause to get people to use correct pronunciation. "And those books are works of fiction, comedic noir thrillers."

"You should read the Amazon reviews," McGoo said.

Bo Jest seemed unreasonably excited. "We should team up and find this dastardly criminal." He picked up the photo. "A zombie detective and a bounty hunter. It's a natural!"

"It's unnatural," I said.

"What a team-up," Jest continued. "With your resources and,

uh, everything I bring to the table, we'll find the necromancer in no time. I'd even cut you in on the finder's fee—say, ten percent?" He lifted his eyebrows in a hopeful expression. "So long as you do most of the dangerous work."

"You sure make a compelling argument," I said.

"If we're going to discuss this further, we need another round." McGoo raised his now-empty pint glass to get the bartender's attention. "Francine, this guy's paying."

The bounty hunter took that as his cue to leave. He tucked the Ned Kadoo photo under his chest plate and spun about, beating a hasty exit from the Goblin Tavern.

II

"You need more exercise, Beaux," said Sheyenne, my ghost girlfriend. She drifted forward in the offices of Chambeaux & Deyer Investigations to give me a playful air kiss on my gaunt cheek.

I knew she was just teasing. I hung up my brown sport jacket and patted my belly. "What do you mean? I haven't gained a pound since I came back from the dead."

Using her poltergeist powers, she held up a flyer that had come in the day's junk mail, along with coupons for harpy-claw manicures and take-out pizza. The paper was a garish neon pink, like the lipstick of a succubus, and the headline said, "Zombercize!" in a bold font with a fat exclamation point in order to get the reader excited. "Maximum workout boot camp. Limber up and laugh at rigor mortis. Every Stiff will be sore— guaranteed!"

The bad black-and-white photos were blurred on the pink paper, showing a buff instructor encouraging, or brutalizing, a group of sullen-looking, slack-faced zombies who were well on their way to advanced decomposition. They needed taxidermy more than calisthenics.

I handed the flyer back, shaking my head. "Not for me,

Spooky. I'm already a well-preserved zombie." I flexed my bicep in an unconvincing demonstration.

Sheyenne knew I took pride in my personal appearance. My skin tone has no more pallor than necessary due to embalming fluid instead of blood. I work out regularly, or at least occasionally, at the All-Day/All-Nite Fitness Club for unnaturals. Whenever I'm damaged on a case, I get myself patched up. I receive a monthly maintenance spell from Mavis and Alma Wannovich, two witch clients of ours, and I even have scheduled top-offs from Bruno & Heinrich's Embalming Parlor. In fact, my only obvious damage is the bullet hole in the middle of my forehead from when I'd been shot, but it's sort of my trademark. "I think I'll keep my gym membership instead."

"I love you just the way you are." Sheyenne put the Zombercize flyer on her desk before she began working on her computer to update records of old cases.

The door burst open, and Alvina, my cute and bubbly vampire half-daughter, bounced in, home from the Nosferatu Academy. She dropped her favorite unicorn backpack onto the floor and wiped her forehead. She was panting hard but grinned to show off her pointed baby fangs.

"Why are you all sweaty, kid?" I asked. "Is some demon chasing you? Again?"

"I just got a lot of exercise. Last period was P.E."

"I never liked gym class—not very good at team sports," I said. "I guess that's why I became a private investigator."

"You have a great team here with us!" Alvina insisted so hard her blond pigtails bobbed up and down.

"You got that right, kid," I said. I didn't know what I would do without the little vampire girl as my assistant investigator. Or Sheyenne. Or Robin Deyer, my human lawyer partner.

"Today we were playing eyeball baseball," Alvina said. "I got a home run. Knocked that eyeball right over the fence."

"That's my little slugger," I said, and she ran off into the kitchenette to grab an after-school blood box from the mini-fridge.

Robin emerged from her office, carrying a yellow legal pad. Her magic pencil floated above it, ready to take notes. "Something you should know about, Dan. Very worrisome reports, enough to make a clear pattern."

"I like patterns," I said.

"Not like this," Robin said. "Witnesses have reported zombie snatchings—likely a serial kidnapper. An unmarked hearse drives up and somehow entices them into the back of the vehicle." Her brow furrowed with deep concern. "The kidnapper targets zombies who are just standing around."

"Most zombies just stand around," I said. "But I'll be extra careful."

III

That evening, in a not-too-subtle attempt to prove my dedication to physical fitness, I went out for a walk to stretch my legs, get my steps in, circulate the fluids, and loosen up my joints. Besides, wandering around is how I get much of my detective work done.

After dark, the Unnatural Quarter is alive with the undead. The shops, restaurants, nightclubs, and abattoirs are open. Pedestrians shamble down the main boulevard, werewolves howl at the moon, and warlocks perform tricks for donations on street corners. A scaly demon with large claws attempted to make balloon animals for eager kids, but he kept popping his creations before he could finish. A listless zombie with a ratty brown beanie stood under a streetlamp with a perplexed look, as if he had simply forgotten where he was going.

I was about to cross the street and ask if he needed help—zombie solidarity and all that—when a large, unmarked hearse pulled up, its engine idling.

My senses were alert as I thought of Robin's warning about

zombies being kidnapped. And hearses are never a welcome sight.

The window rolled down, and the driver called out in a scolding voice, "Why don't you make something of yourself? Don't just stand around on the main street doing nothing!"

The zombie in the tattered beanie lurched off down a side street. "Fine, I'll stand around in a dark alley doing nothing."

Suddenly, I heard a loud yell—a cross between a Tarzan cry and an elephant being castrated—as a man in black armor charged onto the street, his long arms and legs jerking like a scarecrow turned into a ninja. "Found you, Ned Kadoo! Stop in the name of a citizen's arrest!"

Hauling ass, Bo Jest reached over his shoulder and drew the long katana without breaking stride. The samurai blade made him look even more like a ninja. I was worried for his safety because this had to be far more dangerous than simply running with scissors.

The driver of the hearse was not inclined to cooperate. The engine roared as he stepped on the gas and accelerated away. Though this wasn't my case, I knew that Ned Kadoo was a bad apple responsible for a host of crimes, and I wanted to protect the citizens of the Unnatural Quarter. What if he was also the zombie snatcher Robin had warned me about?

I had to do the right thing.

As the hearse picked up speed, I stepped into the street and blocked the way, raising both of my arms. I'm not a very threatening figure, even under poorly lit conditions, and now I was on the bright main boulevard.

I could see the figure behind the wheel, noted the black necromancer's hat, the dark robes, the chiseled and stern face. It was the same face from the photograph Bo Jest had shown in the Goblin Tavern.

"Halt!" I yelled. It seemed like the most appropriate thing to say.

The evil necromancer did not follow simple instructions unfortunately, and the hearse raced forward without slowing.

I'm not one of those slow, shuffling zombies, but I'm not a nimble gymnast either. I couldn't leap out of the way fast enough. As the oncoming hearse shot forward, I won't say that my life flashed before my eyes—it had already done that the first time I'd been killed, so this would have just been a rerun anyway. I barely had enough time to yell "Crap!" before the front of the car struck me.

I saw Ned Kadoo's face, his dark eyebrows drawn together with grim determination, and then the vehicle knocked me flat on my back.

I've suffered bodily damage before. I've been shot more than once, broken, battered, and buffeted, but I'd never been run over by a car, much less a hearse. Let's just say I'm not big on new experiences.

Fortunately, Kadoo's hearse was not a lowrider, and the big tires missed me. Tonight I was a well-aligned zombie. The vehicle was moving fast enough that I caught only a glimpse of the undercarriage before it rolled past, racing away down the boulevard.

Before I could pick myself up, the monster hunter bounded over to me. "Shamble, are you all right?" As he bent down to pick me up, he almost skewered me with his sharp samurai sword, but he shifted his grip and grabbed my shoulders, pulling me to my feet.

I was more embarrassed than injured. I brushed the front of my sport jacket, trying to regain my dignity. "He didn't even pause! What a jerk!" I picked up my fedora and tried to poke it back into shape.

"Told you he was a bastard," Jest said. "I knew we'd be a good team. We're going to catch this guy together."

"This is personal now," I said. "I didn't have skin in the game, but now I do." I looked down. "Or maybe I left some skin on the street."

IV

The well-armed and well-armored bounty hunter hadn't been able to stop the criminal necromancer, but now Ned Kadoo was up against the best zombie private investigator in the Unnatural Quarter. And even worse for him, I had a crack team.

Bo Jest had gone back to his hotel room to turn in, saying he had already put in eight hours of monster tracking that day. He was very careful to maintain a proper work-life balance.

After being flattened by a hearse, however, I was determined to make progress. I wasted no time in putting Alvina and Sheyenne to work. The little vampire girl was very proficient at tracking down outrageous conspiracy theories on both the dark web and the pink web. And Sheyenne knew her way through the backdoors, trapdoors, and dungeons of UQ bureaucracy—paperwork, forms, listings, permits, citations. She could even make sense out of the Chamber of Commerce directory of unnatural services. Those two would learn everything there was to know about Ned Kadoo.

I also told Robin about the maniacal necromancer driver and gave her a full description of the hearse. I hadn't managed to get the license plate number, even though it had been only inches from my face when the front bumper knocked me flat. (My attention had been elsewhere during that nanosecond.) I made a report to McGoo as well, so he could file an arrest warrant.

Now that my hard work was done, I took my World's Greatest Zombie Detective mug into the kitchenette. I saw on the calendar that I was due to rinse out the mug this month, after which I filled it with sludge and settled into my office to wait for results. I decided that maybe I liked team sports after all.

Meanwhile, I tried to figure out how I would handle capturing the necromancer once we learned his whereabouts. I wanted to see that smug bastard put into handcuffs—and ankle shackles for good measure—and sent away for zombie hit-and-run, plus whatever else Bo Jest was chasing him for.

McGoo had made plain his reservations about bounty hunters operating in the dead-gray area of the law. I didn't need a sidekick, but I felt honor-bound to involve Jest. He did have a lot of pointy weapons and other firepower. Most importantly, he could help me with a serious disadvantage I had when it came to Ned Kadoo.

Necromancer magic was specially attuned to corpses, and since I was a zombie, that made me susceptible to Kadoo's spells, which would not affect other people. I didn't like to be vulnerable like that. Maybe Bo Jest would serve a purpose, even in the cannon-fodder category.

Sheyenne drifted into my office wearing a concerned, frustrated expression. It was not the triumphant look I had hoped for. I tried to sound encouraging. "I'm sure you left no grave undug, Spooky. What did you find?"

"For a necromancer, he's very good at covering his tracks. No known address. Kadoo is a registered necromancer, but his business is nested inside multiple shell corporations. He may be a dark wizard, but he's also a ghost in the system. The city itself has major warrants issued against him, but I can't find any details."

I was puzzled. "If the city filed an action, there should be public records."

Sheyenne let out a spectral sigh. "You'd think so, but the original plaintiff was one of his zombie customers, and the zombie filed a claim of physical abuse, saying that he'd been tortured in sadistic rituals."

I still didn't get it. "So why did that lock up the public records?"

"Because the plaintiff complained about an *injury*, which put the filing in a medical category—and suddenly, ironclad unnatural HIPAA rules apply. Airtight medical privacy. No one can see any details about the case, not even the zombie victim's name. The whole file is redacted."

I could see how that wouldn't be helpful in solving cases.

"Robin can explain it better," she said.

Alvina skipped into my office, and her bright cuteness washed away Sheyenne's disappointment. "Just remember what Sun Tzu said. 'Know your enemy.'"

"I thought that was Machiavelli, honey," Sheyenne said.

"Not according to the comics," Alvina replied.

"I'll defer to your research, kid. Anything we find out about this guy will help us nail him."

Alvina put her laptop on my cluttered desk then proudly called up a screen. "I hacked into the private members-only site for the Necromancers' Social Society. I accessed their meeting notes—boring!—and their member directory."

"Ned Kadoo doesn't seem like a particularly social guy," I said.

"It's a very influential organization," Sheyenne said.

"That naughty man is no longer a member in good standing," Alvina said. "He was expelled from the organization for consistently failing to pay his dues."

"What a pillar of the community," I muttered.

"He left in a huff, complained that the Necromancers' Social Society does nothing but sit around and talk." The cute vampire girl blinked up at me. "He said he has a higher calling."

V

When I got to the Goblin Tavern the following night, Bo Jest was waiting for me on the bar stool next to my usual spot. He studied a glass of bourbon on the rocks with such professional dedication that I thought he might be a kindred spirit after all.

On the bar to his left, he had placed his sheathed katana, his holstered Magnum, a bandolier of silver bullets and poison darts. Wooden stakes were neatly lined up, pointed ends toward the door and ready for any threat. He had loosened his chest plate and his codpiece for comfort.

Seeing me, Jest raised his glass of bourbon. "Shamble, glad

you're here! I came early to start strategizing." He took another stiff gulp and let out a sigh of satisfaction. "And bracing myself for the ordeal to come." He raised his glass higher, waving it for attention. "Bartender, pour me another and get something for my friend here. I need him at his peak performance."

"My name's Francine," she said in her cigarette-smoke-damaged voice. "You should know that if you're going to be a regular." Her face was well-aged, but not like fine wine or cheese. She'd had a rough life, which had prepared her for the most cantankerous monster customers.

Jest flashed a broad white smile that he must have practiced in a mirror. "Francine it is, then! I might be a regular if there's steady work." He glanced around the tavern at the vampires, werewolves, gremlins, blue-collar trolls, dapper-looking mummies, and rowdy college-student ghouls who didn't know how to handle their liquor. "I think there'll be plenty of work."

"Let's take care of Ned Kadoo first." I slid a printout of information over to him. "This is what we've learned about the necromancer: his social-media presence, personal acquaintances, society memberships—or actually, revoked memberships. He has shell corporations, and that hearse isn't registered under his own name."

Jest scowled. "That hearse is responsible for a lot of very ugly violations—it's why my client hired me to bring him to justice."

I felt anger rising in my embalming fluid. "You mean I wasn't his first hit-and-run?"

Jest gave me a grim look. "A vehicle like that can have many violations." He shook his head. "You don't want to know."

"Actually, details would help," I suggested.

McGoo entered the tavern and hesitated when he saw Jest, then he walked forward. He scowled. "Not much room at the bar with all those weapons on display. You sure you want to sit so close to a grenade, Shamble?"

"I live dangerously, McGoo."

He took a seat on the opposite side of me, as far from the

armored man as he could. "Rough clientele these days, Francine."

Bo Jest sounded defensive, even as the bartender calmly poured us each our beers. "Monster hunter is a legit profession, Officer McGoohan. I keep the streets safe from genuine unnatural hazards, and I get paid for it. Nothing wrong with that."

"Didn't say there was," McGoo said and raised his pint glass in a surly toast. "As long as you don't break the law. I'll be watching."

Jest responded with a look of horror. "Break the law? Then I'd be as bad as my targets."

"Everything's relative," I said, trying to calm the situation down. "Speaking of relatives, do you have ties around here, Jest? You're not from the Unnatural Quarter." I wanted to gather information on my alleged sidekick, as well as on our target.

He took a gulp of his fresh bourbon. His eyes were already bleary. "Originally from Orlando, but I move from city to city, wherever my services are needed, and I ended up here in the Quarter. Seemed like a smart choice for a monster hunter to go where the monsters live. Better job security."

"So how did you get to become a bounty hunter in the first place?" McGoo grumbled. "That proctologist thing didn't work out?"

Bo Jest was too deep in his thoughts to rise to the bait. "After the Big Uneasy, when all the monsters infested the world, everyone was panicked. There was chaos in the streets, and my wife and my daughter were terrified. No one was safe. There were monsters everywhere."

His eyes widened, and he looked at me for support, as if he expected a zombie to sympathize with him.

"To be fair, a lot of unnaturals were upset, too," I pointed out. "Militias were hunting them down, killing even the non-carnivorous mythical creatures. It was a dark time."

Jest didn't seem to hear me. "I had to keep my family safe

and keep other people safe. I joined the Neighborhood Monster Watch, and soon they elected me chairman. I guarantee you, not a single no-good unnatural got into our gated community!" He took another drink of his bourbon, rattling the ice cubes at the bottom of the glass. "Since then, the work has found me, and I can pick and choose my assignments."

He finished his drink and took the printed notes I had given him. "I'll come to your offices tomorrow, Shamble. We can strategize our plan of attack."

He began the long, slow process of reinserting and reinstalling his weapons, taking a silent inventory, inspecting the points of the wooden stakes, checking the bullets in his Magnum. "You can't be too careful." He patted down his full armor. "Just walking the dangerous streets of the Unnatural Quarter, I take my life in my hands every single day."

"Right," McGoo said, unimpressed, since he had been walking his beat in the UQ for years. "Look both ways before you cross the street."

VI

Next morning, I was ready for a full-on pursuit of Ned Kadoo. But I would be even more ready after coffee and breakfast at the Ghoul's Diner. Albert Gould, the proprietor, ran a morning special of embryos and larvae with a side of hash browns, but I just ordered toast, since it was the healthier option.

Bo Jest wouldn't be joining me, since he had a strict personal rule of not starting work before 9 a.m., but I reviewed supplemental paperwork he'd sent about the hearse— registration and license info, the VIN number, and where and when he had gotten his last oil change. I considered just staking out the auto-mechanic shop and waiting for the odometer to roll over the next 5,000 miles, but I preferred a speedier course of apprehension.

The harpy waitress brought me my order of toast and a mug

of oily black coffee. I didn't dare stir sugar in for fear that it might dissolve the spoon. With clawed hands, Esther hurled three jam packets down onto the counter next to the toast plate. I never used jam on my toast, but she had threatened to charge me extra if I broke her routine. Esther hated working the morning shift, which was clearly reflected in her mood. But she hated working the lunch or dinner hour, too. Albert had trouble keeping other employees, primarily because they couldn't stand working with the harpy waitress. So, customers were stuck with her. Gluttons for punishment, I guess.

I sat at the counter, brooding over my coffee. Behind the kitchen window, Albert the ghoul, who was normally slovenly and lethargic, suddenly moved in a flurry, clanging and slapping his metal spatula like an over-caffeinated Benihana chef. I realized that some of the larvae had gotten away from him, but he flattened the critters soon enough, and I heard them sizzling on the griddle.

Then the door opened, and the necromancer entered the diner. He took a stool at the far end of the counter and pulled out a newspaper.

I stared, unable to believe my luck. There was no mistaking Ned Kadoo in his embroidered funny hat and his fancy dark velour robes (which must have been hellishly hot in summertime). The necromancer's amulet dangled from his neck like a piece of gangster bling.

Esther flounced over to him with a swirl of her razor-edged feathers, glowering with her pinched beak. But Kadoo seemed to intimidate her, and she showed a modicum of courtesy. He ordered the embryos and larvae special. "Make sure they're dead," he warned.

I pulled out my phone and quickly dialed Bo Jest's number. It went straight to voicemail. 8:45 a.m. After the beep, I said in a loud whisper, "Jest, I need you at the Ghoul's Diner, right now! He's here. Ned Kadoo is here! He just ordered breakfast."

I hoped the monster hunter would check his voicemail soon.

He was probably busy flossing his teeth or putting on deodorant before donning his body armor, getting ready for his workday.

To my dismay, Albert served up the embryos and larvae with hash browns—everything extra crispy—far speedier than usual. Ned Kadoo doused the whole plate with ketchup.

I knew I had to stall him.

I picked up my coffee and toast and sidled down the counter to take the empty stool beside him. The necromancer looked up from his food, and I felt a chill when I saw his dead stare (which was appropriate for a necromancer, I guess). The jewel-encrusted amulet dangled down from his neck when he leaned forward to take another bite of his food.

"Excuse me," I said. "Could I borrow the newspaper when you're done?"

"You want the sports section?" Kadoo asked.

I had never been interested in sports. "Sure," I said.

He pulled out a section of the paper but kept staring intently at me. I felt as if I was being visually dissected. "You look like a well-preserved zombie," he said.

"Yes, sir. I put in the effort." At least I could keep him talking. "I have a gym membership, a regular maintenance spell, strict regimen of embalming fluid."

"Good," Kadoo said in a stern voice. "Glad you're making something of yourself. Too many unfit zombies in the Quarter—it's an epidemic." He turned back to his breakfast. "I have no problem with you."

Doused in ketchup, one of the fat grubs still twitched and squirmed. Kadoo stabbed it with his fork, then popped it in his mouth.

I looked at my watch. 8:55. I had no idea how soon Bo Jest would show up.

"Nice weather we're having," I said, then flinched, realizing I had aroused his suspicions.

Kadoo studied my face again, noted the bullet hole in my

forehead. "Wait, I recognize you from the other night. You're working with that annoying bounty hunter."

He remembered seeing my startled face as he plowed me down with his hearse—just as I would never forget seeing his maniacal expression as he hunched over the steering wheel just before he drove right over me.

I grabbed for the .38 inside my jacket pocket, but the necromancer touched his amulet first. The jewels glowed; the symbols shimmered and seemed to spin. Dark magic rippled out, and suddenly I couldn't move. The necromancy had locked my joints like a double dose of rigor mortis.

I tried to lurch up from the stool and tackle him so I could restrain him until help arrived. Esther would call the UQPD, and we'd get this dangerous necromancer off the streets once and for all.

But I was petrified. The amulet's pulsing magic had been directed just at me, and I found myself frozen in place. I couldn't even make a sarcastic comment.

"I think I'll be going," Kadoo said. He grabbed a last bite of hash browns, dabbed his mouth with a napkin, then threw a $20 bill on the counter. Unfortunately, that would be enough of a tip to prevent Esther from chasing after him when he left the diner. I was out of options.

"It's been nice chatting with you," Kadoo said and sauntered away. I couldn't even turn my head to see him walk out the door, though I heard the jingle of the bell as it closed behind him.

"You finished with that?" Esther screeched, pointing down at my uneaten slice of toast.

With the necromancer gone, I slowly began to regain my movement.

The door banged open, and a harried Bo Jest bounded in, his katana askew on his back, his codpiece only half attached. Seeing me, he ran forward. "Where is he, Shamble?"

I was barely able to turn my head, but I managed to croak out, "You're five minutes late. He's already gone."

Jest pulled down his gauntlet to look at his watch. "Aww, man, it's only 9:02!"

"I tried to stall him, but he used necromancy on me."

The bounty hunter ran back out the door and looked up and down the street, but came back in, disappointed. "No sign of the hearse. He's long gone by now."

He slumped onto the stool beside me, glanced at my toast, then up at the menu on the wall. "I might as well have breakfast, start the day right. What's good here?"

VII

That afternoon, after lunch and a power nap, Bo Jest arrived at our offices, loaded for bear—or werewolf, vampire, and any other worrisome unnatural. But our target was Ned Kadoo, and I had already put Alvina's internet research skills to learn the most effective kryptonite against a necromancer. I'd never battled one of them before, since necromancers are, for the most part, bland and unassuming people without much of a sense of humor.

Alas, necromancers did not appear to have any unique vulnerabilities, such as wolfsbane, garlic, silver bullets, holy water, or clowns. Or cats and cucumbers. If a direct confrontation turned ugly, I figured my .38 pistol—and certainly Bo Jest's Magnum—would do the trick.

When he arrived, the bounty hunter had to turn sideways to fit through our office door, because his throwing knives stuck out from his hip in one direction, and the katana was tilted over his shoulder. "All right, Shamble," he announced, "we know what to do as soon as we find our guy."

"Well, finding him has been the difficult part," I pointed out.

The bounty hunter grinned at me. "We'll have a good partnership, Shamble. Monster hunter and zombie detective. You find him, and I bag him. And we split the bounty." He frowned slightly. "Percentages still to be determined."

Alvina hurried out of the kitchenette, where she had been feeding fresh ground beef to her pet piranha. "Oh, look at all those weapons! This doesn't suck at all!"

Jest preened at the vampire girl's admiration. "Be careful with all the sharp points, little lady."

"And the razor edges," she said. "I can respect that."

The monster hunter endured the attention as Alvina poked and prodded among his armor pieces, even tugged on the garroting rope. I could tell Jest had a soft spot for children. He said, "I have a daughter of my own, but her teeth are less pointy." A troubled expression crossed his face. "The last time I saw her."

Robin stalked out of her office, and I could tell she was also loaded for bear—but in a legal sense. "I uncovered more disturbing information that's very relevant to this case." When her dark eyes flashed, I could imagine the chill any of her opponents in court would have faced.

As Alvina continued to poke around his body armor, Jest turned. "Good, Ms. Deyer. The more information we learn about our opponent, the more ways we can fight him."

"Know your enemy," Alvina quoted. "From the Sun Tzu comics."

"My information is not about the necromancer, Mr. Jest." Robin came forward with printouts of case reports and database searches, as well as her yellow legal pad. The magic pencil drifted along with her. "I did my due diligence and a background check. Officer McGoohan was right to be concerned about your track record as a bounty hunter. I found several alarming reports filed against you."

Startled, Jest jerked back so abruptly that Alvina had to dodge a stray wooden stake. "Is it about excessive force? Things get rough out there in my world. I had no choice! I needed to protect myself. That lawn gnome threatened me."

Robin's magic pencil darted down to her legal pad and scribbled a note. "Hmmm. I hadn't located any lawn gnome complaint yet. I'll dig deeper." She held up the papers. "I found numerous complaints from former clients about non-completion of services, that you would take a bounty assignment and never deliver."

Embarrassed, Jest looked away. "Those assignments are, uh, still pending. It's hard to track down a quarry if they don't want to be found. And sometimes the danger level gets too high."

Perplexed, Alvina toyed with one of the monster hunter's grenades dangling from his belt.

"Don't touch that, kid," I warned. "And be sure you don't pull out the pin."

My vampire half-daughter doesn't always listen. Instead of leaving it alone, she unclipped the grenade from the belt and stepped away. "Hey, this is fake!"

The monster hunter spun around. "Give that back. You shouldn't play with grenades, little lady."

Alvina held it up with her lips pursed in an "I told you so" expression. "It's just a prop." She pulled out the pin, and we all gasped. Fortunately, that was the only sound we heard, instead of an explosion.

Jest grabbed it out of her small hands. "I, uh, don't exactly have a valid license for real grenades anymore, but never underestimate the intimidation factor. If my target thinks the grenade is real, they'll surrender before I lob one in their direction. Perfectly acceptable bounty hunter practice."

Unruffled, Robin continued, "I'm most concerned about these outstanding warrants filed by your ex-wife. You're late on child support."

"I'm not late," he blurted out. "Not by much. It's in process, and as soon as I get this big score for nabbing Ned Kadoo, I can pay everything I owe. It's first on my list, I promise."

Robin pointed to the damning papers. "It says that your wife has been after you for some time, sir."

"That's why I'm in the Unnatural Quarter. Peggy will never follow me here with all the monsters. It gives me breathing room. That's all I need!" He looked at me with an earnest, pleading expression, as if I was the softest, unbeaten heart there. "Please, Shamble, if you and I catch the necromancer, then I'll be right with the world."

I was torn. I didn't want to be involved with an unreliable man and deadbeat dad. But I would need his help against Ned Kadoo. I had my own grudge against the necromancer, and if I could help get a little girl's child-support money paid, that made it even better.

"I don't like this," Sheyenne said. Her ectoplasmic glow had a darker tinge that showed her anger. "But we have to do right by that family."

I turned to Jest. "Go back to your hotel room and wait. We're still doing our investigation. If something comes up, and I need you, I'll call."

The bounty hunter was already backing out of the offices, as if all the weapons and armor in the world couldn't protect him from Robin's ire.

I warned, "And you'd better be ready to respond—whether or not it's regular work hours!"

VIII

Later that evening, after Alvina went back to school for an extracurricular night class called "Fun with Mad Science," I was still searching for clues about the nefarious necromancer, when I realized it had been right in front of my face all along. Or at least on Sheyenne's desk, in plain sight.

The neon pink "Zombercize" flyer was still there next to the pizza and manicure coupons, and I wondered if Sheyenne had left it as a hint for me. I picked it up and stared down at the low-resolution pictures photocopied there. Before, my attention had been focused on the sullen zombies in their sweatsuits, but now I studied the buff and shirtless drill-sergeant instructor. How could I not have noticed it before?

"What's the matter, Beaux? Decide to take one of those fun classes after all?" Sheyenne asked.

"Nobody takes those classes. It's all just a gimmick," I said. "But that's what he was counting on. It's perfect camouflage!" I hadn't recognized him in the photo without his necromancer cap and dark robe, but there was no doubt about it. The Zombercize fitness instructor was Ned Kadoo himself!

He wasn't just a necromancer. He was also an exercist!

I was willing to let bygones be bygones, or at least give Bo Jest a chance, so long as he did some of the work. If he was a true monster hunter, he could put himself on the line to catch the evil necromancer, especially if I was vulnerable to the dark magic.

Though it was after hours, Jest answered the phone when I called, true to his word. "Get ready. I have a solid lead," I said. "I know where to find Ned Kadoo, as long as he does indeed hold nightly classes."

He was baffled. "Nightly classes? In necromancy?"

"No, physical fitness. He's made a lot of stiffs really sore. I'll explain when I see you. Bring all your weapons." I hesitated. "And any live grenades you might have."

We arranged a time and place to meet, and Jest arrived early —so quickly, in fact, that I guessed he had been sitting around in his full armor. "Tell me what you've got, Shamble. I knew you were a great zombie detective!"

I showed him the neon pink flyer and watched his expression light up with recognition. "That sadistic bastard! He's making those poor zombies do calisthenics."

"Zombercize," I said. "It's supposed to be fun." I had already found the address on the map of the Quarter. "It's in an old strip mall not far from here. We'll catch him, if he really does hold classes."

We made our way to the strip mall, where one unit had been

rented for Zombercize sessions. It was a run-down mall in a run-down part of town—in other words, a typical location. The look and feel of the place reminded me of a karate dojo or a place where people bought Pilates memberships but never actually went to sessions. Several units were vacant. Two more had gone out of business but not yet entirely abandoned. There were no cars in the parking lot, and no one seemed to be around.

The only unit with lights on had no professional sign or banner, but a poster board had been taped in the window.

ZOMBERCIZE
Are you a stiff? Limber up!
Inquire within during regular business hours

No business hours were listed, however, on the door or anywhere else. The blinds were drawn, blocking any view inside, despite the lights that glowed through from inside.

With exaggerated stealthy movements, which only made his body armor and weapons noisier, Jest crept up to the Zombercize door and rattled it. "Not just locked, Shamble—it's padlocked." He tugged on the chain that secured the handle.

"Someone must have a lot of exercise to hide," I said. "How are we going to get inside?"

The bounty hunter grinned at me, then rummaged around on his utility belt and produced a heretofore-unseen large bolt cutter. "Snip snip!"

I decided this guy might be useful after all.

Before he could make short work of the thick chain, however, Bo Jest's big tool became unnecessary. Bright headlights came down the street, and the two of us scrambled to hide from the approaching car. We ducked behind a convenient dumpster, which was full of smelly garbage, even though the strip mall seemed empty. From restless noises inside, I realized the dumpster had an inhabitant, but we were careful not to disturb it. An irate monster squatter could cause a scene.

My greatest hopes and fears were realized when the large vehicle pulled into the parking lot and stopped in front of the padlocked Zombercize door. I would recognize that hearse anywhere.

We both crouched down and watched. Jest's hands jittered and moved, as if he couldn't decide which weapon to draw first, but he was ready for anything. And clearly terrified at the same time.

The hearse's engine shut off, and the headlights died. Ned Kadoo emerged from the driver's side, wearing his black cap and dark velour robe. The garment was loose enough that he could stretch, raising his arms to make large and small circles. He went through a sequence of warm-up exercises, touching his toes, twisting his torso in a long stretch, bending backward far enough that I could hear his neck crack. He let out a sigh of satisfaction before he strode around to the rear of the hearse.

He mumbled a spell as he yanked the back open, and the amulet around his neck shimmered and glowed, just as it had done when he worked his dark magic on me. "Come out, come out! It's workout time."

Two figures shifted and grunted in the rear compartment, and finally managed to spill out onto the parking lot. They wobbled, disoriented, as they tried to regain their balance. The zombie pair moved listlessly, controlled by the necromancer's spell. One of the two zombies wore a ratty, brown beanie, and I recognized the aimless undead slacker from the night Kadoo ran me over with his big vehicle.

Both zombie captives were dressed in ash-gray sweatsuits.

"Oh my God, what is he going to do to them?" Bo Jest whispered.

"Nothing good, I'm sure. They're even wearing white gym socks."

While the two zombies remained immobile from the amulet spell, the necromancer used his keys to remove the padlock and chain to the Zombercize door. Swinging it open, he barked an order and commanded the zombies to march forward. With stiff, undead limbs they shuffled inside the gym unit. Kadoo followed them and closed the door behind him. After he entered, the blinds shifted, opening just a little.

Bo Jest and I waited several minutes, tense, waiting to see what would happen. Matching each other's testosterone, we crept forward to the Zombercize door. Together, we stood at the window and peeped in, finally able to see inside.

We gazed upon a scene of horror.

IX

Even though I had a licensed bounty hunter/monster hunter for backup, I couldn't be sure Bo Jest would have my back. So, I alerted McGoo to what we'd found at the old strip mall, and he promised he was on his way. He's a dedicated UQPD officer, and he takes zombie hit-and-runs seriously.

But Jest had no interest in waiting, even though he seemed to be quaking in his boots. "We can nab him, Shamble—just you and me! We're not going to forfeit our bounty if the police department arrests him first."

"Whatever happened to team sports?" I asked.

Impulsively and unwisely, he pulled open the door. "You and I are a team." Before I could argue, he planted a gauntleted hand on my back and shoved me inside. "Go first and create a diversion."

My expression of protest came out as little more than "Urk!"

Inside the open, well-lit gym area, Ned Kadoo preened in front of his victims. He was shirtless, clad only in red exercise shorts. For a necromancer, he was quite buff, with a well-toned chest, biceps, and a washboard abdomen. He had folded his velour robe on a workout bench nearby and placed his hat and the heavy magical amulet on top. A Zombercise-branded water bottle and a sweat towel were next to the garments.

"Five more reps!" he growled at his victims. "Don't be wimps. Make it hurt. It's a good burn!"

Half a dozen discouraged and downtrodden zombies stood there in sweatsuits, white gym socks, and tattered sneakers. They were in bad shape, I could see. Their skin was slack and discolored from decay, which is not unusual for zombies who don't take care of their bodies. Even worse in the eyes of Ned Kadoo, Zombercise instructor, they all had potbellies and flabby arms. The zombies groaned in abject misery at the prospect of more exercises.

Thanks to Bo Jest's unwelcome encouragement, I stumbled in and caught my balance on a weight rack, which rattled. Then the bounty hunter made even more noise with his clattering assortment of extreme weapons as he scrambled in and ducked out of sight behind the sign-in counter.

Distracted by the sudden disturbance, the zombies groaned, but it sounded like relief to me.

The necromancer lashed out at them, "Don't pause! I want to see you sweat!" Then he turned to me, and his dead eyes flashed with both fury and glee. "It's the zombie detective! Come join our group! Limber up!"

"Not so fast," I said, and reached for my .38 pistol.

Kadoo, however, lunged for the amulet on top of his velour robe, which immediately began to glow. The necromancy magic acted so swiftly, I barely had time to say, "But I'm still in my street clothes!" before I was seized with an uncontrollable urge to do jumping jacks.

The nightmare physical trainer cackled. "Now let's see how well-preserved you really are!"

Pulled by puppet strings, I shuffled forward. The other six calisthenic victims began to jump and wobble, sweeping their arms up and down, spreading their legs apart and drawing them back together. It was a miracle they all didn't collide and collapse. I was moving right along with them, involuntarily yelling "Hup! Hup!" I dreaded that he would order push-ups next—or worse, squats.

Kadoo yelled, "You can do it! Make it burn!"

The necromancer activated a boom box on the counter, playing a pounding disco beat we all could exercise to. Not without irony, he had chosen "Stayin' Alive" by the Bee Gees as his Zombercise theme music.

Over the falsetto singing and the dance beat, I strained to hear the sounds of police sirens, hoping that McGoo would arrive soon, since Bo Jest was still hiding behind the counter. I didn't know why he bothered with all that body armor if he had no backbone.

Against my will, I kept doing jumping jacks with so much gusto that my fedora fell off my head. I remembered the complaint of physical abuse from the zombie victim saying that he'd been tortured in sadistic rituals. Now I understood all too well.

As things looked darkest for me, and Ned Kadoo was about to order another round of exercises, Bo Jest finally grew a pair— or at least one. He lurched up from behind the counter, visibly quaking and showing his inner Barney Fife. But he had drawn his katana for moral support and kept muttering, "I can do this! I can do this!"

He let out his Tarzan/castrated-elephant yell again and charged into the fray of calisthenics. "I've got you now, Ned Kadoo! You're gonna pay for your citations."

The fitness necromancer whirled and thrust the growing amulet toward Jest, but the dark magic had no effect on the human (though cowardly) bounty hunter. As I continued my rigorous jumping jacks, I managed to gasp out through gritted teeth, "The amulet, Jest! Get the amulet!"

Jest squinched his eyes shut in fear, as if he couldn't bear to watch as he swung the long samurai sword down at his target. Given the trajectory of the blade, he should have decapitated Kadoo, or at least lopped his arm off, but the necromancer raised the amulet as a shield in the last instant. The razor-edged steel smashed into the encrusted jewels and etched arcane symbols. Sparks flew, and the necromantic glow faded.

"No!" Kadoo yelled. "They still haven't done crunches!"

Instantly, I was released from the hateful workout magic.

Jest was staring in amazement at his Japanese sword, as if he had forgotten how it worked. I knew that was likely all the action I was going to get out of him. This would be up to me.

But I also had a little help from my friends. Team sports.

"Get him!" I yelled to my reluctant workout buddies. Now that they were all warmed up, surely they could become fast zombies.

I slammed into Ned Kadoo and tackled him. His bare chest was moist with perspiration, which was gross, but I would take any steps necessary to bring him to justice. I knocked him onto the Zombercize floor, which had nice rubberized exercise mats. "There, I flattened you, just like when you ran me over with your hearse!"

Stiff and sore, the sweatsuited zombie horde closed in and piled on top of their nemesis. The physical trainer for the undead didn't have a chance.

"No! No!" Kadoo cried. "I'm just trying to get them in shape! They're dead, but they can still be fit!"

Though I might have sympathized with his point, I didn't sympathize with his methods. "You can't force them to be healthy against their will, Kadoo. They can fall apart in the pursuit of life, liberty, and happiness. It's the American way."

Now that Kadoo clearly wasn't going anywhere, Bo Jest found his courage and stepped forward, victorious. "You won't get away this time, necromancer! I'm collecting the substantial bounty on you because of what you've done."

He reached into his chest armor plate and withdrew a folded stack of papers from a hidden pocket. He slapped them down on the necromancer's face, relishing his look of dismay. "Boom! Twenty-five unpaid parking tickets for that hearse! Substantial fines and late penalties." Jest formed an expression of disgust. "I've never seen such a heinous case."

I extricated myself from the pile of zombies pinning down the evil exercist. They weren't going to let him up, mainly because they just needed to take a rest and not move for a while.

"Parking tickets?" I asked. "*That's* why you have a contract against him?"

"The bounty was large enough to pay what I owe to Peggy."

I still couldn't believe it. "But you're a bounty hunter and monster hunter. Look at your outfit and your weapons—all that for unpaid parking tickets? Aren't you embarrassed?"

He raised his chin, indignant. "It's steady work, and I ... I don't like scary monsters. I have to pick and choose the cases I think I can handle."

He pulled out his phone and snapped a quick picture of the subdued necromancer with the parking ticket notices strewn on top of him, along with the exhausted zombies. Then he turned around and clicked a selfie before motioning for me to join him in the frame.

"That's proof enough for me to collect the bounty. I'll let you and the UQPD handle the arrest and the paperwork."

He fumbled with his long katana, trying to stick it behind his back. He wiggled it around but couldn't find the sheath. I had to help him line it up. "I guess justice can be served in small ways too."

"And with a big stick," Jest added.

Finally, I heard the sirens outside. McGoo had a habit of arriving slightly after the nick of time.

Jest looked panicked and bolted for the door.

"Where are you going?" I asked. Maybe he was worried about the overdue child support, but I knew he now had a chance to make good.

Jest grinned in response. "Off to vanish into the night. It's my style." He opened the door and ducked out before he could be seen, just as the squad cars rolled up.

I watched him dash past the half-open window blinds, and I heard the lid of the smelly dumpster creak open, then slam shut. I hoped the current occupant wouldn't mind company.

Moments later, four uniformed officers charged in, guns drawn. McGoo cocked an eyebrow as he took in the situation. "Never thought I'd see you at an exercise class, Shamble."

"Just exercising my skills as a zombie detective." I glanced at my workout buddies piled on top of Kadoo. I saw that all resistance had been squashed out of the necromancer.

I retrieved my fedora, which had fallen off during the manic jumping jacks, and placed it firmly on my head, covering the bullet hole.

The officers pulled Ned Kadoo to his feet, but before they put him into cuffs, he pleaded, "Wait, at least let me use my sweat towel first."

Over the next hour, McGoo and his companions took the names and contact information from the unfit victims. The UQPD already had the hit-and-run arrest warrant, and once the overdue parking tickets were factored in, Ned Kadoo was going away for a long, long time.

Once the crime scene was processed and the necromancer hauled away in the back of a squad car, the six zombie victims were released. I knew they just wanted to run away in relief, but their bodies were so achy they barely managed to shuffle off.

"Are you all right, Shamble?" McGoo asked. I saw genuine concern on his face.

I reassured him. "I'm fine, McGoo. I didn't even break a sweat."

HOLY BALLS

Y
ou hold my balls in your hands," said the warlock. I
could tell from his expression he was uneasy. "Take good
care of them."

Actually, his balls were much too large to fit in my palms.
"They're bigger than I expected," I said. "Put them on the table
and let's have a look."

The warlock's name was Vincent, a wiry old man who looked
scrawny but not at all frail. He was bald, with a prominent
Adam's apple on his long neck, and a narrow gray beard that
hung like a dribbly waterfall of whiskers from the point of his
chin. He reminded me of a cartoon wizard, though he insisted
that warlocks were different from wizards. (As a zombie private
investigator, I accept any and all kinds of clients.)

With a grunt of effort, Vincent set the first of the two large
crystal balls on the display table in our front office. I moved
some old magazines aside to make room for the other ball. The
second transparent orb looked identical to the first.

"I need your security expertise, Mr. Shamble." The warlock
drew his bushy gray eyebrows together. "No one can see what's
in these crystal balls—especially not my nosy wife." Vincent

flicked his eyes back and forth, as if his head were filled with guilty secrets.

"I normally work as a detective," I told him, "but we also provide security services. I have a gun license and a P.I. license." Mollified, the warlock peered down into the pair of crystalline spheres. He had already met with my human lawyer partner, Robin Deyer, the week before to discuss the matter with her, and now he was back to see me specifically.

"Tell me exactly what you're looking for, sir," I said, "and we'll take care of it."

At Chambeaux & Deyer Investigations, we solve crimes and handle legal matters for naturals and unnaturals. Robin is a fierce defender of unnatural rights in court, and I often wander the Unnatural Quarter in search of clues.

"I am a powerful warlock, as you can see." Vincent spread his arms. He wore a black velvet robe with embroidered stars, crescent moons, and strange constellation diagrams. "And I can predict the future by gazing into my sacred crystal ball."

"I'm familiar with the concept," I said. "I had a magic eight-ball once."

"My wife, Dismerelda, is also a fortune-teller and future-predictor, but she prefers to use tarot cards. We both have a very similar magical skill set, but we don't perform parlor tricks. We predict the future. We're prognosticators, not prestidigitators. And we aren't ridiculous frauds like those scam telepsychics who advertise on billboards across the city."

"I've never used one of those services, nor do I intend to." I had always been skeptical about psychic hotlines and fortune-tellers—but that was before the Big Uneasy. When you see monsters shambling around every day, it's hard to be too skeptical of any possibilities.

"Good," Vincent said. "Always use real magic, I say."

I ran my palm over the nearest crystal ball, expecting sparkles, but nothing happened—not even a little flurry of white flecks, like from a snow globe. "So a witch and a warlock? You sound like a perfect couple."

He gazed down at the identical crystal balls. "We've been married for twenty years, and our anniversary is coming up." His expression suddenly hardened. "Dismerelda's a powerful witch, and I would never underestimate her abilities—or her deviousness. You must keep her from looking into my crystal ball!"

"And why are there two of them?"

"One of these is a decoy—a distraction to help keep the real one safe." Vincent waved his hand over the two spheres. "Dismerelda is always snooping and prying, digging into my private affairs, putting her nose where it doesn't belong." He raised his eyebrows. "Did I mention we've been married twenty years?"

"It's hard to imagine you still have secrets from her after all that time," I said.

"That's exactly the problem! She pries into everything. And sometimes, a man needs to have a little privacy, you know."

Sheyenne, my beautiful poltergeist girlfriend, drifted over from the reception desk to see if she could help us. I knew she had also been eavesdropping. "What sort of secrets are you keeping, Vincent?"

"They're a secret!" he said. "I caught Dismerelda eyeing my balls the other day, trying to stare into the future to find out what I'd been doing and what I was thinking. Fortunately, I caught her in time and covered them up. If she gets her hands on these, she'll ruin everything. I need you, Mr. Shamble, to keep these crystal balls under lock and key." He picked up the nearest one, hefted it in his hands, and passed it to me. It was much heavier than I thought.

"This one is a decoy. Lock it in your safe and make sure everyone knows you're guarding it there." He gestured to the second holy ball. "Then quietly hide the other in an even better place. I'll pay you handsomely to help me make sure the real one is safe and out of Dismerelda's view for one week. After that, it won't matter."

Vincent removed two large black fabric bags from a pocket in his warlock robe. "Here, keep each one hidden and protected in this special ball sack—and be very gentle with them."

II

Sometimes in the Unnatural Quarter, the days never seem to end. Still, when I can end the day with a cold beer at the Goblin Tavern, then I call it a good day.

Today was a good day.

"Hey, McGoo," I said as I climbed stiffly onto my usual bar stool. Officer Toby McGoohan had a fresh beer in front of him. He wore his blue patrolman's uniform; his cap was on the bar beside him.

"Hey, Shamble," he said. "Do you know why a mummy movie director always finishes a scene on time? Because he can't wait to shout, 'It's a wrap!'"

He knew I wouldn't laugh. I said, "My new client says he can predict the future. I'll ask him to predict when you'll tell a joke that's funny."

McGoo snorted and slurped his beer. "I like to be unpredictable."

I waved for Francine, the hard-bitten human bartender who was tough enough to put up with any sort of monster customer. Because I was a regular, she was already filling a pint of my favorite beer. When she delivered it, she looked at the two of us. "Next time, bring in that little vampire girl of yours, I'll teach her how to make a Shirley Jugular. That's her drink of choice, right?"

I nodded. "It's what Alvina orders every time we come in here."

"I have a special recipe for special customers," Francine said. "That squirt has potential. If she plays her cards right, she could be a bartender someday."

"She does like to mix weird chemicals for her mad scientist chemistry lab experiments at school," I said.

McGoo agreed as he sipped his beer. "We want to make sure Al is equipped with life skills."

I took a long drink and let out a satisfied sigh. Ever since I'd transformed into a zombie, my sense of taste sucks, but drinking beer was an old social habit and it felt good going down cold. "Any big cases today, McGoo?"

He shrugged. "It's been quiet in the Quarter all week. The worst I'm dealing with is some vandalism on those new telepsychic billboards. Big spray-painted words, like 'Fraud!' and 'Bet you didn't predict this graffiti.'"

"Probably just zombie slackers," I said.

"Not zombies," McGoo said. "They finished all the letters instead of just petering out as they lost their train of thought."

In back next to the pool table, five dusty old mummies, a college fraternity group I think, were engaged in a drinking game while a scorekeeper wrote painstakingly detailed hieroglyphics on a scratch pad.

Two other fraternity mummies were engaged in an arm-wrestling contest. The bandage-wrapped skeletal figures clutched hands, rested elbows on the tabletop, and strained, clenching their sinewy jaws as they pushed harder and harder. When I heard a loud, hollow *crack*, I cringed. The rowdy mummies scrambled to get out fresh linens to bandage up the break.

Suddenly, at the front door of the Goblin Tavern, a swirling cloud of emerald green smoke erupted, as if someone had just cracked open a gas grenade. The smoke billowed upward, smelling strongly of cabbage, and I heard a shrill cackle of laughter. Emerging from the swirl of smoke was a gaunt, greenish-skinned witch in a pointy black hat and a black dress. She had a long, bent chin and an equally long and bent nose, both of which held prominent warts. She cackled and shrieked again as she looked around with blazing green eyes.

Everyone in the tavern turned to her, waiting for something interesting to happen. The mummy fraternity group even stopped their game. The witch shouted, "Where's Dan Chambeaux? I've got business with him!"

Francine, McGoo, and many of the other bar patrons swung their gazes toward me. "At least she wants to talk business," I told McGoo. I raised my gray hand, seeing no way to duck out of this.

The witch stalked over like a battering ram. Her black dress swished and swirled. Her pointed nose and chin looked like dangerous weapons. "You've got something of mine!"

"At the moment, I don't even have your name," I said, wondering what this was about.

"I'm Dismerelda. I want that crystal ball. Give it to me!"

"Actually, it's your husband's ball," I said.

"Community property!" she snapped.

"You've got her husband's balls?" McGoo said.

I flicked him an annoyed look. "That's an obvious joke, McGoo, but I thought you'd like it."

He chuckled and drank his beer.

"Your husband engaged my services to hold the crystal ball for safekeeping, and he specifically wants me to keep it away from you."

"Where is it?"

"Locked in a completely safe place." I knew I had to be firm. "I cannot help you, ma'am. The crystal ball belongs to Vincent."

Anger flared on Dismerelda's face. "You'll be sorry for that! I'll make you pay."

"Your husband is paying. Quite substantially." I crossed my arms over my chest, standing tough against this demanding witch. Zombies can be implacable.

"I need to see what's in that crystal ball. I need to know his secret!"

"If you had a solid marriage, you could just discuss that with him," I pointed out. I knew that's what Sheyenne would have said.

"A solid marriage? We've been married twenty years!"

"He told me. Congratulations," I said, then hardened my voice again. "But I can't give you the crystal ball. Period."

In a huff, the witch swirled around and stalked back toward the door, which she flung open. Outside, against the wall of the Goblin Tavern, she had propped a long broom with a padded broomstick. "We're not finished with this, Dan Chambeaux!"

She hurled out another smokescreen of green, roiling vapors, which didn't entirely obscure her exit. She hopped on the broom and flew off into the dark, gloomy skies of the Quarter.

McGoo and I ordered another beer.

III

The following afternoon, Sheyenne and I met young Alvina right after Nosferatu Academy let out for the day. The kid was perfectly capable of walking home all by herself, but we enjoyed the company.

The vampire girl was cute as a button, with her blond hair tied into two pigtails, a pleated plaid skirt from school, her favorite fuzzy pink sweater, and her unicorn backpack. If any unnatural tried to harass her, I pitied them. She would flash her little baby fangs, and if that wasn't threatening enough, she would kick them in the gonads. For a school paper, she had researched the vulnerable testicular areas of various unnatural creatures, or the equivalent spots in asexual entities.

"So how was school today, honey?" Sheyenne asked.

"Lots of fun," Alvina said with a bright smile. "We're having a comparative apocalypse unit. It's called 'What's the worst that could happen?'"

"I like it when you're optimistic, kid." I tousled her hair, making the pigtails jiggle.

On the night of the Big Uneasy, when twisted magic had

unleashed every legendary creature, people had thought *that* was the end of the world, but we got over it just fine. It only took a few years for people to realize that the world hadn't actually turned into a horror movie, but was more like an everyday sitcom, except with an additional cast of characters.

At Chambeaux & Deyer, we had plenty of job security. Unnaturals still got divorced, still got involved in petty crimes or frivolous lawsuits. As a lawyer, Robin focused on finding justice for underserved unnaturals. I was a human private investigator and had worked cases for many unnaturals, until I got shot in the back of the head. But thanks to the new rules, I returned as a zombie and clawed my way out of the grave—back from the dead, and back on the case.

Now, we had light, comfortable conversation as we walked along the main boulevard. Vincent's sacred crystal ball decoy was securely locked in the office safe, which was the most obvious place I could think of to store it. And I'd hidden the other one, the real one, upstairs in my own small dingy apartment, wrapped in its ball sack and rolled in blankets inside the cardboard air-conditioner box that Alvina used as her coffin when she slept over.

Today the Quarter was active with local street vendors: a tentacle creature showing off with hacky sacks, a banshee with a boombox trying to sell her CDs. At a Talbot & Knowles Blood Bar we bought Alvina one of her favorite unicorn-blood frappés, because I knew the sugar rush would give her the energy to do her homework.

Surprisingly, we came upon a table with a familiar warlock and witch sitting next to each other, stiff-backed and cold-shouldered. A handwritten poster board said, "Fortunes told and contradicted. Know your future, believe it or not." A large jar sat between Vincent and Dismerelda holding loose change. It reminded me of the lemonade stand that Alvina had wanted to set up last summer.

"Can I get my fortune told?" Alvina said. "I always wanted a fortune."

"It probably costs a fortune," Sheyenne said.

Vincent and Dismerelda both saw me at the same time, but pivoted to stare at Alvina, their target. "Want to know your future, little girl?" Dismerelda cackled.

"I have a bright future," Alvina said. "Is this a scam?"

The warlock and the witch both raised their chins, making similar movements like a long-married couple. "Our prognostication is real," Vincent said.

The witch added, "Not like those fake telepsychics who don't know what they're doing."

At the mention of telepsychics, both Vincent and Dismerelda turned to opposite sides of the table and spat on the sidewalk in disgust.

"I'm surprised to see you here together," I said.

"We've got to make a living," Vincent said. "Don't we, dear?"

Turning away from him with an annoyed sniff, Dismerelda said, "My husband can't help you, because he doesn't have his crystal ball today. You'll have to trust my sacred tarot cards."

Dismerelda pulled out a pack of tarot cards and spread them on the table. As Alvina watched with intense curiosity, the witch laid out the cards in a specific pattern, flipping them over one at a time, then she looked up at Alvina with a deeply troubled expression. "You have a very dark future, little girl. I fear that you may go into … politics."

Alvina brightened. "I could be the mayor of the Unnatural Quarter."

Vincent huffed. "Dismerelda always gets it wrong, because she doesn't have my holy crystal ball. Here, let me tell your correct fortune." He reached into a brown paper bag next to him and pulled out a handful of plastic-wrapped Chinese fortune cookies. "These are never wrong." He spread the wrapped cookies on the table and gestured Alvina closer. "Pick one, child. You will know your own fortune."

Alvina slurped on her unicorn-blood frappé, then snatched one of the cookies.

"Now, open it up and reveal your true destiny," Vincent said.

She unwrapped the cookie and cracked it open. The warlock took the little tag of paper and perused it in deep concentration. "Ah, yes. I know this is accurate. Today you will meet someone interesting."

She looked at the warlock. "You're interesting."

"Fortune cookies never lie," Vincent said. "And I can go into more detail once I have my crystal ball back in a few days."

Alvina took even greater pleasure eating the sweet crunchy cookie. "Maybe I'll go into politics, or chemistry. But right now, I'm a private investigator's research assistant."

"You can be anything you want, honey," Sheyenne said.

As we continued along, Vincent called after us. "Protect my holy possessions, Mr. Shamble."

I took my job seriously. "It's locked up tight in the safe in our offices, sir. No one can get to it."

Dismerelda remained icily angry at her husband and didn't say a word.

IV

Late at night, the Unnatural Quarter is really hopping, but I felt tired. McGoo was watching Alvina (she has an identical empty air-conditioner box for a sleepover coffin at his place), so he and I didn't meet up at the Goblin Tavern as usual. After working hard on some court filings, Robin had gone home.

Sheyenne and I went out for a nice drink and conversation at her old haunt, the Basilisk Nightclub, and we returned to the dark and empty offices long after midnight—and came upon a violent burglary in progress.

I immediately knew something was wrong when I saw our office door ajar. I gestured Sheyenne to stay behind me for safety, although that was just an instinctive gesture, because nothing much could harm a poltergeist. She glided past me through the wall, while I pushed open the door.

Inside, I spotted the large rolling garbage can, the steel bucket with gray water and pungent pine-smelling solvent, and the erect mop handle. I realized that we must have interrupted the Bigfoot janitorial crew. We had hired the cleaning service to add a little extra sparkle to the office. Though Bigfeet were large and hairy and tended to leave footprints everywhere, they were quiet, unobtrusive, and rarely seen, and thus made perfect janitorial staff. I hardly ever noticed them myself.

Now, though, I spotted the tall hairy creature clutching his push broom and standing against the wall, terrified, his large eyes wide, his big, fanged mouth open with gibbering fear.

A green ectoplasmic entity, like a terrifying knot of poisonous vapor, was swirling around our steel office safe. The Bigfoot let out a grunt of terror. The green smoke churned and flailed—and I watched the safe's combination wheel spinning and whirling back and forth, back and forth, trying thousands of different combinations, one after another, like a computer algorithm made out of fumes.

"Hey, stop that!" I shouted.

The smoke redoubled its efforts, and with a *click-clunk*, somehow stumbled upon the right combination. The heavy, steel door of the safe swung open.

Sheyenne drifted forward. "Don't you dare!"

But the roiling cloud entered the open cavity of the safe and grabbed the wizard's ball sack. Sheyenne floated in front of it, trying to stop the theft, but the green smoke and the heavy bag pushed right through her spectral form.

I grabbed the push broom from the terrified Bigfoot janitor and swept at the fumes, but the floating black bag struck me in the head like a bowling ball and knocked my fedora askew. The cloud of smoke roiled and pummeled past me, then whooshed out into the hall. I staggered after the fleeing criminal vapors, but the smoke picked up speed, and the dangling ball sack swung back and forth.

Sheyenne rushed up to me as the felonious fumes hurtled down the stairs and out of the building. "Are you all right, Beaux? That looked like a hard blow."

"I've got a thick skull," I said, "and there's not much in it. I'm okay."

As we watched the greenish smoke disappear, I straightened my fedora, just because it helped restore my self-confidence. "At least that was just the decoy. Vincent gave it to me for a reason. Maybe that'll keep the witch off track."

Sheyenne was clearly angry. "Do you think that was Dismerelda? She looked different at the prognostication stand."

"She's involved at least. The green smoke is sort of her signature move." I went over to the open door of the safe. "But she left no fingerprints and no identifying features, so we can't prove anything."

Behind us, the Bigfoot was discreetly finishing up his janitorial duties. We hardly noticed him.

"Get me Vincent's number, Spooky," I said. "I'd better call him."

When I told the warlock our dire news, he actually cackled with a sound much like his wife's. "Ha! I knew she would try something like that! She just couldn't resist the temptation. I told her to leave it alone, but that just made her more angry. Oh, she'll learn her lesson soon enough."

"Sorry I let you down, Vincent. I thought our office safe was secure. It was the highest-rated model on Amazon."

"Never trust those ratings," Vincent said. "But it doesn't matter. You just need to keep the real one absolutely, positively safe. For another four days."

V

After Dismerelda had been foiled by the decoy crystal ball, she tried an even more devious and underhanded tactic to get what she wanted.

She hired a lawyer.

Fortunately, the lawyer was our own Robin Deyer, which kept the situation simple, straightforward, and incredibly complicated. If Vincent had still possessed his holy ball, he might have foreseen the complication, but his fortune cookies were inadequate to the task.

Dismerelda flung open the door and stood there so we could take in the threat. Wearing her pointed hat and black traditional dress, she carried her broomstick upright as she stalked into the office, then thrust the stick into our umbrella stand, where it rested against the wall. The witch loved to make a grand entrance. She would have done well if she tried out for the lead role in an Unnatural Quarter revival of *Wicked*.

"I'm here to see Robin Deyer, Esquire. I intend to engage her services—I hear she always wins." Dismerelda raised her crooked, warty chin and made a sniff through her crooked, warty nose.

Robin emerged from her office and regarded the witch. "I always win when the cause is just."

"Well, my cause is just *desserts*," she snapped. "I need to get what is mine—my husband's secrets. We share everything, but he won't share whatever he's hiding from me. And I must have it. I'll sue!" She held up a black clutch purse and opened it. "Let me pay your retainer, Ms. Deyer, so we can get started right away."

Robin was cool and discomfited, but I had already risen to a level of pissed off. "You couldn't get what you desired through illegal means, so now you're trying legal means?"

Dismerelda's wart jiggled on her nostril. "I have no idea what you mean."

Sheyenne sat indignant at her reception desk. "You broke in

here last night. You cracked our safe, and you stole the crystal ball."

"Prove it," Dismerelda said. "Do you have any photographs? Any fingerprints? Any witnesses that can identify me?"

I spoke up. "We saw a nasty clot of green smoke. That distinctly reminded me of you."

Robin pressed her lips together in a hard line. "It won't hold up in court, Dan, even if we know she did it."

"That fake crystal ball held no value whatsoever. It was as ridiculous as a telepsychic." Dismerelda leaned to one side and spat on our carpet.

I would have to make a note for the Bigfoot janitor to clean that spot. Carefully.

The witch continued, "I want to sue for possession of my husband's crystal ball. It is community property. His secrets are my secrets, and I need to see what he doesn't want me to see."

"There's a conflict of interest," Robin said. "We already represent your husband. I cannot represent you on the opposing side."

Dismerelda held up a gnarled finger. "Vincent hired Dan Chambeaux for security services. I intend to hire you for legal services. Completely different."

"That's not how it works, ma'am," Robin said. "I can reference any number of legal tomes."

Even I knew that the witch had a losing argument, but I could tell from her demeanor that losing wasn't going to stop her from arguing.

We were saved, or at least distracted, by the warlock's arrival. Vincent stalked in, thrusting out his chin to waggle his long, gray waterfall of beard. While Dismerelda seemed outraged and indignant, Vincent was amused. His eyes sparkled. "Now, my dear, you've never been good at admitting defeat, and you just can't leave well enough alone. If you loved me, you would trust me."

I thought the witch was going to snatch up her broom and sweep the amused expression off his face. "How can I trust you when I know you're keeping secrets? What are you hiding? You're sneaking around behind my back."

Vincent crossed his arms over his black warlock's robe. "No, my dear, I am sneaking around right in front of your face, and you just can't stand it."

He chuckled, which only enraged his wife more. "You tricked me with that fake crystal ball. Where is the real one? I want it back now. I'll sue!"

Sheyenne rose up, glowing. "Could I get anyone coffee? Or water?"

Unruffled, Robin stepped in between them with a calm, businesslike demeanor. "That's enough talk about lawsuits from both of you. I'm always an advocate of talking matters through. I would suggest an arbitration conference, so we can discuss how to satisfy both of you."

"I'll be satisfied when I have his balls firmly back in my hands," Dismerelda said.

"You need to learn a little patience, my dear," Vincent said. "You never know what surprises are in store."

"I don't like surprises," Dismerelda said.

"And that's no surprise to me," he countered, "which is why you make this so difficult." He turned to Robin, sounding very reasonable. "I'll agree to an arbitration conference. Let's schedule something for …" He paused, touched a finger to his lower lip. "Three days from now."

That was when his contract with us ended. Even though he was a paying client, I was going to be happy to roll these balls out of our lives.

Dismerelda considered. "I have a Pointy Hat Society luncheon in two days, but that time frame seems clear to me. As long as we can resolve this—in my favor."

Vincent smiled secretively as Sheyenne put the meeting on the calendar.

VI

Fully aware of the extreme measures Dismerelda was willing to take, I redoubled my efforts to guard the real crystal ball. We'd made no secret, on purpose, that Vincent's decoy had been stored in our office safe, but nobody knew the other hiding place. I worried, though, that Dismerelda could use wily magical means—whether through tarot cards or fortune cookies or something even more esoteric—to figure out where I'd hidden the second crystal ball. Talented prognosticators can be unpredictable.

Wrapping the glass sphere in Alvina's unicorn blanket then stuffing it inside her coffin air-conditioner box seemed like a brilliant trick, but I would also rely on brute force. For the final couple of days when the crystal ball was in my care, I vowed not to let it out of my sight.

For the time being, McGoo watched over Alvina when she wasn't in school. I didn't imagine that Dismerelda would genuinely threaten our vampire girl, but I wasn't going to risk putting her in danger.

That night, I sat upstairs with my .38 in hand, completely alert. I was going to be a restless zombie until this was all over. I sat hunched in my own chair next to the air-conditioner box after double-checking that the object was safe and secure.

I watched the seconds tick by on the clock on the wall, tense and determined.

Sheyenne made the stakeout more than tolerable, pleasant even. I smiled at her glowing presence in the room with me. "You can keep me company any day or any night, Spooky."

"I'm cheaper than a regular security guard," she said.

"And less at risk," I replied.

I thought of the good times we'd had together, even though our relationship as humans had been all too brief. She'd been so beautiful singing on the Basilisk stage. I was smitten with her the first time she crooned out "Spooky," and that had become our signature song.

Now as we hung out, watchful against any malevolent clouds of aggressive green smoke, Sheyenne grew contemplative. "Those two have been married for so long, Beaux. The witch and the warlock seem to have so much in common. Looking at the shine in Vincent's eyes, I can tell he cares for Dismerelda."

"He cares for his secrets even more, though," I said. "But he was right in what he said today. If she trusted him, it wouldn't be such a big deal."

"What if his secret is something terrible?" she asked. "What do you think Vincent is hiding from her?"

"We don't know that it's terrible," I said. "Could be just something he doesn't want her to know."

I wondered how I would feel if someone else could see my every action, every thought, every embarrassing moment or confidential activity.

"So would you ever keep secrets from me?" she asked.

I was about to make a joke, but I saw the expression on her face and knew I needed to take it seriously. "Spooky, we've been together long enough. I don't have any secrets from you." I tapped my head, and the bullet hole there made a hollow sound in my skull. "You can look inside anytime you want."

She leaned over to give me a glowing ectoplasmic kiss. "I know you've got nothing to hide."

VII

I didn't need a crystal ball to predict that the arbitration meeting was going to be tense. Frankly, I'd be glad to wrap up the case and get rid of the problematic magical artifact. Let Vincent the warlock handle his own balls from now on.

I always say the cases don't solve themselves, but this hadn't been a mystery—just a pain-in-the-butt security matter.

Robin had handled unnatural divorces, prenuptial agreements, transformative bonds, and custody agreements after love spells wore off. She knew all the law's fine points about community property, whether with mundane objects or powerful cursed artifacts. But Dismerelda's indignation seemed to go beyond any statutes and codes.

We sat at the conference table with Vincent on one end and his witch wife glowering at him from the other. The warlock remained stony-faced, a closed book, but I sensed a building anticipation, as if he was clutching a secret about his own secrets.

Robin produced a yellow legal pad and her ensorcelled pencil for taking notes. "Now then, shall we begin?"

"We can begin by bringing the real crystal ball here," Dismerelda said. "You, Mr. Shamble—go upstairs and get it from where you've hidden it."

I held up my gray hands. "I never said where the real crystal ball is. What makes you think it's upstairs?"

"I am a prognosticator." Dismerelda crossed her arms over her black dress. "I know things."

Vincent let out a hard chuckle. "You don't know everything, my dear."

The witch stabbed a gnarled greenish finger at me, and I saw that she'd put on a fresh coat of black nail polish. "You tricked me with a false crystal ball in your safe, but I know that the real one is somewhere else, somewhere close." She closed her eyes, concentrating. "The other ball is hidden in a … coffin, or a box. And I sense a blanket, a unicorn blanket."

For a moment I couldn't find words. Sheyenne hovered next to me, and we both exchanged an alarmed glance. "That's pretty good," I said.

Vincent was offended. "You learned all that from your tarot cards, my dear?"

"You forced me to take desperate measures." The witch sounded embarrassed. "I had to call a telepsychic and paid them to reveal where it was."

Vincent leaned to one side and spat in disgust, then faced us with a big happy grin. "Ha ha, I knew it! And they were wrong! Even the telepsychic doesn't know where my real crystal ball is."

I was confused. "Well, not exactly wrong …" I looked at Robin. "Uh, should I go upstairs and get it?"

Robin had a strange and uncomfortable expression on her face. "Yes, for the sake of this meeting. Get the crystal ball from upstairs."

I've known Robin a long time, and I usually know what she's thinking, but this time she was unreadable. Could my own lawyer partner be keeping secrets from her zombie friend?

Dismerelda said, "I'll wait."

Not sure how this would end, I left the conference room and trudged upstairs to my little apartment, where I rummaged in Alvina's cardboard coffin box to retrieve the precious object. Carrying the heavy crystal sphere, I returned downstairs and placed it in the middle of the conference table. I left the black fabric bag cinched closed, though. "It was right where the telepsychic said it would be."

Vincent spat at the side of the table again. "Please don't do that," Sheyenne said. "It's unsanitary."

"I have a right to see the crystal ball," Dismerelda said. "I want to know what my husband is keeping from me. Are you having an affair? Are you addicted to gambling? Do you have an identical twin you never told me about?"

"All in good time, my dear," Vincent said with a sniff. "You are so damned impatient, you make it difficult for me to do my husbandly duties."

The desperate witch surprised us all by snatching the ball sack, using her clawed fingernails to tear open the drawstring. As she yanked out the smooth crystal sphere, Vincent lunged, trying to stop her. "No, not yet!" he said.

But they fumbled the ball. It bounced up and off the edge of the table, then crashed onto the floor. The crystal ball cracked in half, breaking open.

Dismerelda shrieked. "What?"

Vincent chuckled. "You see, it was just a cheap fake."

I glanced at Sheyenne, then Robin. "Wait ... it was another decoy?"

Robin stood up, prim and professional. "Dan never had the real crystal ball in the first place. Both were fakes."

I gasped, which is unusual, because I don't breathe much. "Vincent, you told me the one from the safe was a decoy."

The warlock kept grinning. "But I didn't promise the other one was real."

Robin explained, "Vincent came to me the previous week and contracted my services. I've had the warlock's real crystal ball all this time."

Vincent spread his hands apologetically. "I gazed into my crystal ball, Mr. Shamble, and I knew you would fumble the job at least once. I needed to make sure."

Even Sheyenne was astonished. "Where did you keep the real crystal ball?"

Robin walked over to the conference room door. "Right in my desk drawer, where no one would think to look. I'll be back in a minute."

We were surrounded by a great deal of uncomfortable silence, until Robin returned with yet another fabric ball sack. She placed a third crystal ball onto the table, and the warlock gave her a satisfied smile. "You did an admirable job, Ms. Deyer, and your fee is most reasonable. I only needed to keep my crystal ball away from sweet Dismerelda's eyes until today."

"Vincent, you had better explain yourself," the witch warned.

He was beaming. "You have been so obsessed and preoccupied, my dear. I think you've forgotten what today is."

"Today is the day of our arbitration, when I can finally see what secrets you've held in that crystal ball."

He held up a finger and announced, "Today is also our twentieth wedding anniversary."

Sheyenne brightened. "Congratulations to the loving couple."

Vincent unfastened the drawstring on the real ball sack and pushed down the folds of cloth. "I have been planning this for some time, Dismerelda. I wanted to surprise you with a special present—but because you're always so nosy, looking into everything I do, sneaking glimpses into my crystal ball, I had a devil of a time getting you a surprise gift."

The witch fluttered her black-nailed hands in front of her mouth in astonishment. "You got me a gift? I've never been surprised before."

"That's because you always look into my crystal ball," Vincent said. "This took careful planning, believe me." He ran his palms over the smooth, curved glass surface. Glimmers of light and swirls of mist appeared inside. I saw sandy beaches, palm trees.

"What is this, Vincent?" Dismerelda said.

"A second honeymoon for us, a seven-day cruise and a relaxing vacation in the Bahamas."

"The Bahamas?" Dismerelda cried. "I've always wanted to go there."

"Are you surprised?" Now Vincent just sounded smug.

She clutched her hands in front of her chest. "I'm so sorry I doubted you. This is wonderful. I can't believe you did this!"

"You're worth it. You should see the look on your face."

"I … I don't know what to say," Dismerelda said.

"You could say you love me," Vincent said.

She leaned close and rubbed her crooked, warty nose against his cheek. Then they smooched.

Glowing, Sheyenne drifted close to me. "Oh, how romantic."

Robin closed the folders on the table in front of her. "I wish it hadn't escalated so much, but we had to maintain our confidentiality. We're happy to help you accomplish your desire, Vincent."

Still kissing, he and Dismerelda paid little attention to the legal comment.

"You could try to surprise me like that sometime, Beaux," Sheyenne suggested.

"I don't need to keep anything a secret from you," I said. "Besides, I don't think I have the balls for it."

THE EYEBALL AT THE
END OF THE RAINBOW

I

At Chambeaux & Deyer Investigations, we take every client seriously, no matter how ridiculous the circumstances might seem. As a zombie detective in the Unnatural Quarter, I never know what might show up next.

So, I greeted the distressed leprechaun with a professional demeanor and an interested smile, tilting my fedora to cover the bullet hole in my forehead. The short, spritely figure entered our offices, weaving noticeably as he led a blind, hulking cyclops through the door.

I'd heard of mixed marriages before, but I'd never seen such a striking example of mixed mythologies.

The leprechaun wore a traditional emerald jacket, jaunty cap with a prominent shamrock, and a fat black belt with a big silver buckle. His hair and beard were shockingly red, and he looked as if he were about to break into a jig, though he seemed inebriated and unbalanced.

Like an Irish seeing-eye dog, he guided an eight-foot-tall cyclops of the Harryhausen variety, with a pointed horn like a lonely antler on his bald head. The cyclops had a bare muscular chest and warty, knobby shoulders. His crooked teeth might have been prominently featured on any "before" poster for basic dental services.

His face had one prominent but empty eye socket, like a fleshy crater. Resting one hand on the leprechaun's shoulder, the cyclops strode in with misplaced confidence and bashed his shoulder on the side of our door. "Are we here yet, Bailey? Or did you stop at a pub again?"

I extended my grayish hand in greeting, though the cyclops couldn't see and the leprechaun seemed distracted. "Welcome, gentlemen," I said. "I'm Dan Chambeaux, zombie private investigator, and you've come to the right place."

I had no idea where they were trying to go, but my ghost girlfriend Sheyenne says we should always make potential clients feel welcome.

At her receptionist's desk, Sheyenne glowed with ectoplasmic greeting and wafted up from her chair. I may be the unnatural detective, but the blonde ghost always steals the show. "We're prepared to look into any matter, natural or unnatural," she said. "Dan provides zombie detective services. Robin Deyer can offer legal services on monster matters."

"Oh, it's the detective services we'll be in need of," the leprechaun said in a rich brogue that was enhanced, or slurred, from a little too much Irish whiskey.

"We need to find my eye!" said the cyclops. "Tell him, Bailey. Is he there?"

"Sure, and he's right in front of you. He can tell it's the eye that's missing!" The leprechaun turned to me with a toothy grin. "I am Bailey O'Cream, and this here is my associate, Ulysses S. Clops."

"He's my sponsor," the cyclops growled. "And he lost my eye."

The leprechaun looked embarrassed. "Ulysses and I serve as each other's sponsors, help each other out, have each other's back, as it were."

Robin Deyer emerged from her office, eager to help.

"Sponsors for what?" She's a beautiful, professional African American woman in her mid-thirties, with a passion to prevent injustices against unnaturals. She was accompanied by Alvina, a cute-as-a-button little vampire girl, my half-daughter. The kid wore a fuzzy pink unicorn sweater, and her blond hair was in a pair of bouncy pigtails.

Seeing the leprechaun, Alvina squealed with delight. "I've seen him on my boxes of Unlucky Charms!"

"Oh dear," said Bailey O'Cream, blushing until his cheeks matched the color of his beard. "'Twas one of my early celebrity endorsements, and it's embarrassed me ever since." He sniffed. "Myself, I'll say no more about it."

"It drove him to drink," said Ulysses.

After making introductions, we got to the basics of the case. "Sponsors for what?" I pressed again.

"Err, well, I'll tell you it's a kind of support group. UTI would be what we call it—Unnatural Total Inebriants."

The cyclops grunted. "For monsters who want to go on benders responsibly."

Although I frequented the Goblin Tavern, my zombie metabolism and the formaldehyde in my bloodstream prevented alcohol from having much effect on me.

I could see Robin's disapproval. She rarely drank anything but green tea or club soda with lime. "These benders—are they a regular occurrence?"

Both the cyclops and the leprechaun shook their heads. "Oh dear, oh dear!" Bailey said. "Not at all, you see. They're only for special occasions."

"Only on Catholic or Jewish holidays," said Ulysses.

"So, a regular occurrence then," I said.

The cyclops's shoulders slumped. "I drink with Bailey, but I prefer to use giggle weed myself—the very best marijuana strains. Less of a hangover."

"Himself, he likes to pass the days stoned as could be," the leprechaun said.

The cyclops blinked his empty eye socket, which I found very disturbing. "Yeah, stoned. It reminds me of when I would stand on a cliff and hurl big stones down at those pesky Greek ships."

"Greek ships?" Robin asked. "But your name is Ulysses, the Roman variation of the Greek Odysseus. Don't you mean Roman ships?"

"Doesn't matter. I never hit a one of them anyway. Poor depth perception." The cyclops scratched the warty skin on his left shoulder. "I still like to get stoned, though."

"He's happy to imbibe in my Irish whiskey when I share, so," Bailey said. "And that's all to the good, since I have a magic whiskey bottle that refills itself. The drinks are always on me."

"Can I pour some of the whiskey on my Unlucky Charms?" Alvina asked. "I want to see if it turns red like milk does."

Robin, Sheyenne, and I all answered the little vampire girl simultaneously. "No."

I still didn't understand what mystery these two wanted me to solve. "Let me get this straight. As sponsors for Unnatural Total Inebriants, you two watch over each other and make sure neither one gets in trouble."

"It's designated nondrivers that we are," said the leprechaun. "Best that way."

"But something went wrong," the cyclops said.

"As it usually does on repeated benders," I said, trying not to sound judgmental. "Did Mr. Clops trip and poke his eye out with a stick?"

Both the leprechaun and the cyclops reacted with horror. "No!" Bailey said. "Sure, and I'd be failing as a sponsor, then." His brogue thickened as he grew more upset.

Robin had taken out her yellow legal pad and her spell-bonded pencil, which was ready to take notes all by itself. "Then how did Mr. Clops lose his eye?"

Ulysses muttered in his deep voice. "*I* didn't lose my eye. *Bailey* did."

The leprechaun scuttled forward, wringing his hands.

Ulysses followed, still gripping the little guy's green-clad shoulder. "Now, it's not that I *lost* the eye, you understand, so much as *misplaced* it. We didn't want anything to happen to my friend's one and only eye, so we took precautions, don't you see? Removed his eye is what we did, and then hid it safely away in a secure place."

I tried to follow along, but I felt I was missing an important piece. "So … this cyclops has a detachable eye?"

The leprechaun tugged the front of his frock coat in indignation. "Now, sir, have you ever met one who didn't?"

I could honestly answer that I had not.

"And now the eye's gone missing!" said Bailey. "And it's you that we would like to hire to find it again, Mr. O'Shamble."

"It's pronounced Chambeaux," I corrected, knowing it was a lost cause.

"Where exactly did you lose it, Mr. O'Cream?" Sheyenne asked.

"Misplaced it, truly," the leprechaun insisted. "Even though I took precautions. Sometimes after a mighty bender, I have a bit of inexplicable memory loss, so."

"Inexplicable?" Robin muttered.

"So I wrote down careful instructions on where to locate the eyeball again. I'm not entirely unprepared, you know."

From the pocket of his green jacket he withdrew a folded sheet of paper, a Chinese takeout menu, on which a few words had been scrawled. The writing looked like the tracings of a heartbeat monitor from a werewolf undergoing a bad monthly transformation.

I looked at the menu, but the scrawl made no more sense to me than the Chinese letters did.

"I wrote down precisely where I stashed the eyeball," Bailey said. "Now we just have to go there and find it, you see."

"I can't see," Ulysses said, "but I know Bailey has terrible handwriting even when he's sober."

The leprechaun scoffed. "Ha! When have you ever seen me

sober, Ulysses?" The cyclops had no answer for that. Bailey lowered his voice. "These are clear instructions."

"Clear instructions written in illegible handwriting," I replied.

Alvina tried her best, but even the vampire girl couldn't decipher what the words said.

"So, will you take the case?" the cyclops asked. "Translate Bailey's handwriting and track down my eyeball?"

"Of course we'll take the case." Sheyenne took the scrap of paper and studied the scrawled writing.

Robin interrupted in a no-nonsense voice. "Mr. O'Cream, are you willing to take care of Mr. Clops in the meantime? He's required to have assistance, thanks to the Unnaturals with Disabilities Act." She had helped pass that particular law, and she was very proud of the results.

"You got to take me to the dispensary, Bailey," the cyclops said. "I'm running low, and I don't want to get stressed."

"In good time, Ulysses, in good time. Sure, you still have plenty in your stash. Soon enough, these good people will read my handwriting and find your eyeball. Then all will be right with the world."

II

The cases don't solve themselves—that's my motto. And the leprechaun's handwriting didn't read itself either.

After Bailey O'Cream had led the blind cyclops away, suggesting they stop for a quick nip at the pub, I held the Chinese menu under a bright light so I could look for fine details.

Alvina, who was always helpful as my detective's assistant (for extra credit with her schoolwork at Nosferatu Academy), wondered if I had the paper upside down. I turned the menu around, but to no avail.

The kid rummaged in her science kit and took out a large

magnifying glass that would have made Sherlock Holmes the envy of Victorian society. Even enlarged, illegible handwriting was still illegible handwriting.

Meanwhile, Sheyenne dug into unnatural histories and guidebooks, brushing up on facts and figures related to leprechauns and cyclopses. (She discovered that detachable eyes were not, in fact, all that uncommon.) She studied leprechaun magic and lore to determine if the little guys had some secret language that we would have to decipher, old Irish runes or special calligraphy. Although their thick brogue could be incomprehensible, there was no specific leprechaunese.

No, this was just a case of criminally bad handwriting, and it was up to me and my team to decipher it. Ulysses S. Clops's monocular vision depended on us.

As a zombie detective, I know I can't do everything myself. I have a network of experts and confidantes, both humans and unnaturals, who have knowledge where I have deficiencies. Since I have a lot of deficiencies, I know a lot of experts.

The Unnatural Quarter's foremost expert—and practitioner —of terrible handwriting was Dr. Zonda Nefarious, whose scribbled prescriptions were both renowned and feared.

Several years ago, a trio of shady gremlins who were seeing the witch doctor for persistent toenail fungus discovered that no pharmacist, apothecary, or alchemist in the Quarter could interpret Dr. Nefarious's writing, so they convinced an unwitting pharmacist that they needed the most expensive and dangerous controlled substances—with unlimited refills—which they then sold on the black market.

In her defense, Dr. Nefarious claimed that medicine was not an exact science, nor was handwriting. If anyone could unravel Bailey O'Cream's penmanship, it would be the witch doctor.

Alvina and Sheyenne insisted on going along to the Brothers and Sisters of Mercy Hospital. It's not often that a little kid, vampire or otherwise, is eager to go to the doctor, but she loved the hemoglobin lollipops Zonda Nefarious gave her as a treat.

Sheyenne called ahead for an appointment on a "medical matter." We whisked past the hospital's front desk, but had to meet with Dr. Nefarious's Igor physician's assistant (who was no help at all because of his acute nearsightedness).

Finally, the witch doctor came in to see us, clucking her tongue. She had a stethoscope and a severed hangman's noose around her neck, and a medical chart tucked under her elbow. Like all witch doctors, Dr. Nefarious had bristly black hair under a pointed hat with stars and crescent moons. The significant wart on her chin indicated her status among witches.

Looking at me, the doctor noted the hole in my forehead, then she glanced at Sheyenne, but her gaze passed right through her ectoplasmic form. When she saw Alvina, though, she bent down and extended a gnarled finger to touch the kid's delicate baby-teeth fangs. Satisfied, she whipped a hemoglobin lollipop from the pocket of her surgical coat. "Here you go, dear. You need more sugar to take care of those little fangs." She clucked her tongue again. "Now then, what seems to be the matter?"

Sheyenne spoke up. "We need your help reading."

"Oh, reading problems?" The doctor looked at Alvina with immediate concern. "Does the dear child have undiagnosed dyslexia?"

"No, it's about a leprechaun client who suffers from incomprehensible autographia." I figured by speaking in a medical-sounding language I could better get through to her.

"Ahh, sounds serious. Let me see."

I pulled out the folded menu and pointed to the scrawl. Dr. Nefarious studied it carefully, pulled out her ear probe and squinted through the lens, pointing the light down on the written clue. "It appears he crossed out an order of General Tso's chicken."

"I wish it were that simple, or that spicy," I said. "This message contains the whereabouts of a highly valuable object, and we urgently need a translation."

"Please help us," Alvina said. "If we can figure out the words, then we'll know how to solve the case!"

The witch doctor studied the whorls and loops, the scribbles and lines of Bailey's handwriting. "Ah, I think I see now. I'm familiar with this type of notation, though it's rarely used." She blinked her eyes. "And not often this badly."

"Can you make out any of it? Any words at all?"

"This one here …" She tapped the paper with a long, pointed fingernail. "I think it says … *Gold*. Yes, that is quite clear to me."

I saw nothing clear at all on the smudge of ink.

"And this appears to be *Pot* … I think. Who did you say wrote this message?"

"A leprechaun," I said, and the wheels were already turning in my mind.

Pot and *Gold*.

We needed to find the leprechaun's pot of gold, and then we'd have the eye of the cyclops!

III

Although leprechauns are notoriously tightlipped about their hidden pots of gold—I knew that much from folklore as well as from the cute summaries on Alvina's Unlucky Charms cereal boxes—I decided the best approach was to ask Bailey O'Cream directly.

Chambeaux & Deyer needed to be paid for our services, but I wasn't in this for a pot of gold. I was looking for an eyeball. Maybe the leprechaun would make an exception, especially if his brutish friend and sponsor twisted his little green arm.

In our new client paperwork, Sheyenne had (legibly) written the address of Ulysses S. Clops. I decided to go see him and the leprechaun by myself, since Alvina had schoolwork to do.

The cyclops lived in a modest but homey cave that was part of a new cave development on the south end of the Quarter. All of the cave openings in the subdivision looked the same, though many were adorned with culturally specific decorations, windsocks, lawn ornaments, even a few pink flamingos.

With the luck of the Irish, I found a subdivision map at the entrance. Since I had the specific cave number, I eventually located the dank and dripping grotto where the two lived. The doorbell let out an incongruous series of Westminster chimes, and soon the spritely leprechaun wobbled to the door, half dancing a jig and half tripping over the uneven cave floor. He held the refillable bottle of Irish whiskey in one small hand.

"Well, if it isn't O'Shamble!" he said with a wide grin. "We hope you solved the case. Ulysses is getting intolerable." Then he frowned so deeply that his shamrock drooped. "Alas, I can see from the expression on your mug that you're not bringing us an eyeball."

"These things take time, Mr. O'Cream, but I do have a strong lead. I've managed to decipher your clue." Triumphant, I pulled out the folded Chinese menu.

Bailey doffed his stylish hat and gestured me inside with a bow. "Delighted to hear it! And next time, I promise I'll send my clues by text. That'll be more readable than handwriting, don't you know."

I wanted to give my news to the leprechaun and the cyclops at the same time. It wasn't exactly clear which one of the two was our actual client, and Robin was a stickler for legal details. I followed him into the central living grotto.

Holding his whiskey bottle, Bailey plopped down on a threadbare, plaid sofa that looked like free furniture left on the sidewalk for large trash day. Sitting on the opposite end of the sofa, the cyclops stared at me—actually, he turned his face toward me, but even without his eyeball, he didn't seem ready to see or hear anything.

"Better tell me the details, O'Shamble," said the leprechaun. "I've only had a few snorts, so I'm sharp as a tack. But Ulysses smothered his sorrows in a raft of reefer smoke, and now he's Blarney stoned, you might say."

"I have something to cheer you up, Mr. Clops." I raised my voice, although increased volume didn't have any obvious effect on the well-lit cyclops.

Ulysses blinked his empty eye socket and flared his nostrils. "Where did Bailey put my eye? You better find it. He never should have lost it."

The leprechaun sniffed. "Once again, boyo, I didn't lose it. I kept it safe."

"You kept it *lost!*" the cyclops grunted.

I cut them off before they could get into an argument. "I consulted an expert on professionally bad handwriting, and she was able to interpret the clue. Now I know where the eyeball is. Mr. O'Cream, you hid it in your pot o' gold."

"My pot o' gold!" Bailey cackled. "That's only nonsense for the gullible. It's a myth that leprechauns have a pot o' gold!"

"You're just greedy," said Ulysses. "You've got my eyeball! Give it back—and some of the gold that you've been holding out on me."

I raised my hands. "Everyone says a leprechaun's pot o' gold is at the end of a rainbow, though I did plug that into my GPS without success. We'll need your leprechaun magic, Mr. O'Cream."

"A rainbow? And where do you think I'm going to find a rainbow in the Unnatural Quarter?" The leprechaun took a long swig of Irish whiskey, draining half the bottle, though by the time he set it back upright, the amber liquid had refilled to the top again. "It's always cloudy and gloomy here, the way the unnaturals like it."

Ulysses was growing more agitated. He picked up a fat, claw-rolled joint and inhaled deeply, holding the acrid smoke in his lungs. Even so, he showed no sign of relaxing. "You suck as a UTI sponsor."

Now the leprechaun flushed scarlet. "It's *you* I'm protecting you from, ya daft gimp. Sure, even when you do have your eye in its socket, you can't see how much I do for you."

"Ugh! What you can do for me is *turn around and leave*! You're evicted, and I don't want you as my sponsor anymore. I'll file a report with the local UTI chapter."

The leprechaun furiously stomped his heel on the floor as if he were channeling Rumpelstiltskin. "Aye, I'll leave—and good riddance to you, too. I'll share no more of my rare Irish whiskey. Go and get stoned all by yourself. You and I have bent our last bender!"

In defiance, the cyclops inhaled a huge breath of pungent smoke, then exhaled with lungs like a blacksmith's bellows, choking both of us, even though I rarely needed to breathe.

Growing more enraged, Ulysses expressed his anger in a demonstrably physical fashion. He pounded on the cave wall and flung an ash-laden ashtray like a frisbee. I barely ducked out of the way, but the object still knocked my fedora askew. Then he grabbed the plaid sofa cushions and hurled them about. Now I understood why they looked so frayed.

Bailey and I made a hasty exit. "You'd better find your pot o' gold, and quick," I said.

"I'm giving out about that dolt and his eyeball! Or his sponsorship … or even his friendship." He sounded defiant, but also hurt. "I knew I should have brought my shillelagh and cracked it right on his noggin!"

"I thought all that marijuana would make him mellow," I said.

Bailey grunted. "That *is* mellow."

As we walked away, he offered me a snort of Irish whiskey, and I accepted just to keep the client happy.

IV

My regular watering hole was the Goblin Tavern, a place where everybody knew my name, but no one held it against me. Sitting with a beer, I could propose improbable solutions to the world's problems with the sarcastic and curmudgeonly

Officer Toby McGoohan. By now, our usual barstools had been worn into the specific configurations of our buttocks. (Those are as distinctive as personal fingerprints—few people know that.)

McGoo was already there, dressed in his blue patrolman's uniform after a day of walking the beat. He had slurped a couple of inches of beer from the pint in front of him, nursing it on the fast track. "Hey, Shamble," he said.

"Hey, McGoo." It was the start of what would surely be another pithy conversation.

Francine, the hard-bitten human bartender whose rough-and-tumble life had prepared her for rowdy customers—monsters or otherwise—started pouring my beer as soon as I walked in the door.

"It's nice to be known and liked," McGoo said, nodding to Francine.

She slid the beer over to me, and I smiled with gratitude as I replied to McGoo. "Or in your case, just *known*."

"Somebody's having a pissy day," McGoo said. "I was going to tell you a new joke, but now I'll hold off."

I smiled. "That does brighten my day."

He sounded sincere now. "Rough case?"

I told him about the cyclops and the leprechaun and the search for the missing eyeball and the fabled pot o' gold. He responded with a grave nod. "Mixed mythology. Those cases can be tough."

"The two are mutual sponsors for Unnatural Total Inebriants. Their bond was strong before, but now I think it might be shattered."

"It's all fun and games until somebody loses an eye," McGoo said.

As if by magic, the tavern door swung open, and a small, green-clad figure bounded in, belting out a chorus of "Oh, Danny Boy." Bailey O'Cream was taking the drinking establishment by storm, at least a little one. He spotted me and strolled toward our barstools. "By my four-leaf clover, it's Dan O'Shamble!"

"It's just Shamble," McGoo said.

"It's Chambeaux," I corrected.

With some effort, and a little bit of levitation after touching the side of his nose, the little guy nestled himself on the barstool next to us. "It seems I am in need of new drinking companions, so. Have you two lads had your first bender yet?"

McGoo raised his eyebrows. "Had my first one of those back in police academy days."

"Then you're due for a whiskey!" the leprechaun observed.

I introduced the two of them, and Bailey was mollified when he heard the name McGoohan. They shared their Irish heritage, though the leprechaun seemed more intent on consuming Irish whiskey, but he had not brought his bottle with him. He loudly ordered the best Francine had to offer, and she came by to pour him a shot. Then another. Though she didn't have a magically refilling bottle, Francine did her best to keep up with his thirst.

Over time, Bailey grew more maudlin, and it was not an improvement. "You guys are the best drinking buddies ever!"

McGoo and I stuck to beer, and we wisely did not attempt to keep up with a proud member of Unnatural Total Inebriants.

"I miss my cyclops," Bailey moaned. "What am I going to do without the big guy? I didn't mean to misplace his eye."

"We'll find the eye," I reassured him, but if the leprechaun had no idea where to find his own pot o' gold—even when he was semi-sober—I couldn't even begin to look.

"He needs me," Baily sniffed. "Ulysses can't take care of himself, with or without his eye, don't you know? It's myself who takes him to the dispensary, and myself, to be sure, who gets him home. I've never held it against him, but he partakes too much."

He slugged back another shot of Irish whiskey. "Did you know how many times I've had to stop him from running with scissors? And now I don't have a sponsor at UTI—and neither does he. Would you two fellows watch over me?" he asked in a plaintive voice, then dropped his forehead to the bar and fell into a stupor.

"Francine will," I promised. I paid my own tab and even bought McGoo's beers. But the leprechaun was going to have to dip into his own pot o' gold to pay for all that expensive Irish whiskey.

V

Bailey O'Cream was not going to be in any shape the next morning to help out in the investigation. In fact, I expected him to be in the tavern restroom bent over a pot o' porcelain and vomiting something emerald green.

I went back to the office for some heavy thinking. Usually, I prefer to do private investigating by wandering around the Unnatural Quarter. The cases don't solve themselves, but I might bump into just the right thing at the right time. Now, though, I refilled my World's Greatest Zombie Detective coffee mug with offensive black sludge and sat behind my desk to ponder the mystery of the illegible clue.

How could I find a leprechaun's stash? It must be somewhere close and accessible, because Bailey had intended to give the eyeball back without any hassle. And neither the cyclops nor the leprechaun was the type to take long and complicated precautions when they were about to start one of their legendary Catholic or Jewish holiday benders.

Alvina bounced in and plopped herself on the chair on the opposite side of my desk. She nestled a bowl of breakfast cereal on her lap and slurped one spoonful after another. The Unlucky Charms had turned the milk—and her lips—a bright arterial red, as advertised. Her smile showed little white fangs. "This is helping me to think like a leprechaun," she said. "Do you want some?"

"I'll use my own methods, kid." I tapped my forehead,

hoping that the answer would fall right out of the bullet hole there.

I took out the now-rumpled Chinese menu and stared at the scrawl, unable to see how Zonda Nefarious had deciphered either "pot" or "gold" out of that mess. "I need to find the pot o' gold at the end of a rainbow, but rainbows are rare around here."

"Maybe it's a metaphorical kind of rainbow," Alvina said.

I tried to think of a fabric store, or someplace that sold ribbons or flags, or even a Tibetan monastery with prayer reels and colorful banners. The Unnatural Quarter had a few fabric stores, but no Tibetan monastery that I knew of.

Sheyenne poked her head in, asking if I needed help, just as I had a sudden idea. "Spooky, does the Quarter have a Gay Pride parade? Maybe Bailey put the eyeball there somehow."

"Three so far this year, Beaux—Zombie Pride, Vampire Pride, and Werewolf Pride, but they were all last month."

Well, it had seemed like a good idea.

I continued to ponder, and that usually led to walking around. "I'm going to stretch my legs, keep the rigor mortis at bay. Maybe I'll think of something."

Taking my fedora and sport jacket, I left the office and strolled down the main boulevard. The day was gray and gloomy as usual, but the murk seemed to be thinning. The weather wizards had issued a vampire advisory that today's forecast might include patches of unexpected sun.

I considered starting at the cave subdivision and wandering in a widening circle, trying to follow the leprechaun's train of thought. Bailey had wanted to protect the precious eye from any hazards they might encounter during their bender, and he would have stored it in a place he could conveniently retrieve—but a place uncommon enough that he'd needed to write a note to himself.

Bailey O'Cream was not an imp of deep thought or unnecessary complexity. The eyeball had to be close.

I looked up in the sky and suddenly, in what should have

been accompanied by an angelic chorus, a rainbow glimmered through the misty, drifting clouds—the full spectrum from red to violet. Roy G. Biv!

I stopped in my tracks, trying to remember the last time I had seen a rainbow in the Quarter. That must be a sign! Or a clue! Or a weather incident!

The arc of the rainbow seemed to terminate in the south end of the Quarter, near the new subdivision of cave dwellings where Ulysses S. Clops lived. Exactly as I had thought!

I ran, glancing at the sky, but also watching my feet and careful to look both ways when I crossed a busy street. I can be a fast zombie when necessary. I felt like a fool from folklore trying to find the end of the rainbow in order to grab a pot o' gold. But this was work related.

Before I got halfway to the cyclops cave, the perspective shifted and the rainbow seemed to end in a completely different part of the Quarter. So I changed course, still trying to find the rainbow's end.

Alas, by the time the rainbow faded, I had reached only the garbage dump, where the stench was decidedly unmagical. I still had no pot o' gold and no eyeball.

VI

Since I was in the neighborhood after chasing rainbows, I decided to check on Ulysses S. Clops. Maybe he would have some idea where I could find his former UTI sponsor's pot o' gold. The big brute had been wasted when I'd previously brought up the subject, and by now I hoped he had calmed down and sobered up.

When no one answered the Westminster chimes, I grew concerned—where would a blind cyclops go? I decided to venture inside (which was not difficult because the cave had no door). "Hello? Ulysses, are you here?"

I heard sniffling and sobbing ahead in the main living grotto.

The air reeked with so much marijuana smoke that I wondered if zombies could get a contact high. "Hello?"

None of the mess had been cleaned up, and it was fortunate Ulysses couldn't see the household disarray he had caused. The cyclops hunched on the creaking sofa with his head bowed so that the sharp horn pointed at me. With both big-knuckled fists, he rubbed his eye socket, where the tears continued to flow.

"I got nobody," he blubbered, then turned his blank face to me. "Except you—but who are you? I can't see."

"It's Dan Chambeaux, Mr. Clops, and I'm still working on your case. We'll have your eyeball back if I could just learn the location of Bailey's pot o' gold."

"I need him to take me to the dispensary! That's my first priority. I used up my stash."

"Shouldn't your eyeball be your first priority?"

"I have immediate goals and long-term goals." His eye socket suddenly filled with hope. "Can you take me to the head shop?"

"Do you know the name of it, or the address?"

The cyclops shrugged his warty shoulders. "I'll know it when I see it."

"So … we won't be finding it anytime soon."

He lifted his head. "Did you happen to bring any Irish whiskey?"

The leprechaun had imbibed enough for a small army the previous night. "I thought you didn't care for the stuff."

"It reminds me of Bailey," the cyclops said. "And I smoked my entire stash just to make me forget. I depended on him for so much. Please?" He turned his head as if trying to echo-locate me. "I'll put my hand on your shoulder and we can wander around the Quarter. Maybe we'll bump into the dispensary. It's my favorite one. I use it all the time."

I tried to withdraw. "I was hired to find your eyeball, sir, not be your caretaker. If I can just find the connection between that leprechaun and the end of a rainbow, then I'll know what his handwritten note means."

"But I don't have any friends," the cyclops sobbed.

My dead heart was heavy on his behalf. I thought of how often McGoo and I teased each other, but what would I do without my best human friend?

He clutched the tattered, plaid sofa cushion in a bear hug and buried his face in it. He reminded me of the leprechaun drowning his sorrows in the Goblin Tavern. Those two were made for each other, more than just UTI mutual sponsors.

I was more determined than ever, even though I had hit a wall on the case. I wasn't sure I could solve the mystery of the illegible clue.

But I could solve this friendship. I knew exactly what I had to do.

VII

Somehow, I intended to salvage this oddball eyeball case. I had hope again, or at least more focus and less confusion. Getting those two back together as sponsors and friends would be a good thing—at least I could accomplish that.

Sheyenne had taught me much about the nuances of unnatural relationships, but I decided to handle it myself. Though my clients were a leprechaun and a cyclops, this was still a "bro thing."

Then I thought about bringing in McGoo for moral support, especially if we had to knock some heads together. We could play good cop/bad cop … but McGoo didn't like to be called a bad cop, because it was too judgy, so I would go it alone.

Ulysses S. Clops was sure to be huddling miserably in his cave, bemoaning his lost leprechaun, his empty stash of medicinals, and his lost eyeball. And I knew exactly where to find Bailey O'Cream.

Though it was still early in the day, the little leprechaun was in the Goblin Tavern sitting on the same barstool. His jaunty black hat and its shamrock rested on the bar top. He must have left and returned, because now he had his magically refillable bottle of Irish whiskey. He poured himself another shot and slammed it back with a sigh. "Magically delicious."

"I'm still charging you for those, you know," Francine said in her raspy, cigarette-smoke voice. She had stacked chairs on the tables to sweep the floor. "This isn't a bring-your-own-bottle party."

"But, lass, I did bring my own bottle."

"There's also a surcharge for my pleasant company," she said.

"And grand company it is!" As he poured himself another shot from the full bottle, he noticed me. His wide grin made his red beard stick out. "Ah, it's himself, here again, my boon drinking companion Dan O'Shamble!"

"I'm your zombie detective, not a drinking companion. You need your own UTI sponsor if you're going to go on a bender."

The leprechaun made a raspberry noise. "That cyclops is blind to everything I do for him! Though I have to say I miss the big guy."

"And I'm here to fix that," I said. He offered me a drink. I offered him the door. When he didn't get my hint, I grabbed him by the shamrock and pulled him off the stool.

When that wasn't good enough, I tweaked his ear and he let out a high-pitched yelp like a banshee. But I had met actual banshees before, and I was not intimidated. "I'm going to drag you to the cave, and I'm going to sit there while you two work it out."

"But it's no use!" he wailed.

"Believe me, Mr. O'Cream, I have spent more than my share of time on pointless endeavors."

The leprechaun kept struggling until I realized he was just trying to reach for his whiskey bottle. Once I let him have it, it served as a kind of pacifier. As I hauled him out of the Goblin Tavern, Francine called out as she wiped down the far side of the bar. "Shamble, you know I love you, but who's going to pay his bar bill?"

"Sorry, Francine," I said, embarrassed. "Put it on McGoo's tab."

Though the leprechaun's legs were short, he hopped and skipped along, scuffing his black boots on the sidewalk. "Meself, I'd never underestimate a cyclops with an eyeball grudge, O'Shamble. The only way he'll forgive me is if you solve the case and decipher my note."

"I brought the note with me so we can all solve it together. And if that doesn't work, at least I'll make you bury the hatchet."

"Oh, don't ever give Ulysses a hatchet! He's blind—imagine what he might hit."

"We'll make do with a metaphor. Real hatchets are too dangerous."

At the cave subdivision, I knew I'd find the one-eyed brute (minus one eye) still moaning in the main living grotto. Nervous, Bailey hid behind me as if I could protect him from the wrath of Ulysses.

His former sponsor was sprawled on the cushionless sofa with his eye socket staring at the ceiling in a typical "depressed cyclops" pose. Right away, I noticed the distinctively clean air and the unexpected lack of marijuana smoke.

I tried to wake him gently. "Mr. Clops? I brought someone who wants to make amends. He says he's sorry."

Ulysses lurched into a sitting position, and the springs creaked. "Bailey's back?" He sounded delighted.

"And he's sorry," I said.

The leprechaun grimaced. "By my four-leaf clover, I never said I was sorry!"

"You're both sorry, or I'm going to make you both sorry." It was the best threat I could imagine. McGoo would have been proud of my tough-guy imitation.

"I'll have him back," the cyclops said, facing the wrong

direction. "I'm sorry, too. I need my leprechaun sponsor so much."

Bailey simmered with indignation, but I could tell he was softening. "Well, no need to get my shillelagh in a knot … as long as Ulysses apologizes, too." He lowered his voice to a mutter. "I didn't mean to misplace your eyeball."

"I sure wish we could find it," Ulysses said.

I took out the note for handy reference, but the squiggles still made no sense.

The cyclops straightened. "Right now, though, can you two take me to the head shop? Please? You know the way. I'm starting to get really bad cravings. I need my special blend of pot—the Acapulco Gold you always get for me. Remember, you put in a special order with Consuela? It's got to be there by now."

"Yes, laddie, it should have arrived a few days ago, but I wasn't inclined to pick it up for you." He straightened his hat, still holding on to a bit of his pride.

"Wait a minute," I said. "Acapulco Gold? Pot?" I held out the Chinese menu with the leprechaun handwriting. "Does this say *gold* and *pot*?"

Bailey hopped into the air and clicked his heels together. "You've done it, O'Shamble! Why didn't I see it before? I wrote a reminder to retrieve the eyeball when I picked up his special order." He jabbed his small finger at the scribble. "That scrawl right there—it plainly says Acapulco next to gold. And pot. It's clear as day."

"It's not very clear to me," I said.

The leprechaun scratched his red beard. "I meant clear as a soft day in Dublin, where it's almost never clear."

The cyclops lurched up from the sofa. "Does that mean you remember where you stored my eye?"

Bailey chuckled. "Sure and I do, every bit of it. I put that eyeball of yours in a neat little box and took it to the head shop. Since we're such frequent customers, Consuela was happy to put it in safekeeping for us." He sniffled. "Mind you, I just forgot what the note meant, that's all."

VIII

Consuela's dispensary was conveniently, and accurately, called Head Shop, and the proprietor was, also accurately, just a head.

Consuela had large brown eyes, full red lips, and long raven hair draped around the base of her neck—which was where she stopped. The head rested on an ornate silver platter with two burning novena candles behind her. Her expression lit up when we entered the shop, the leprechaun leading the blind cyclops. I closed the door behind us.

"Ai, my friend Ulysses! I thought you'd never come back."

"Grand to see you, Consuela," Bailey said. "Ulysses and meself, we've had some wee relationship difficulties."

"And also handwriting difficulties," I added. "Not to mention memory difficulties."

The head shop was a dim and crowded place. Racks of shelves held glass jars of dried buds labeled with clever or arcane names. Display shelves at the front counter held packaged and delicious-looking edibles, which were heavily regulated because unnatural species reacted differently to medicinals. I saw packages of dried leaves, dried flowers, and dried mushrooms, as well as mandrake root and exotic herbs. The labels suggested they were beneficial for any sort of health disorder suffered by any sort of creature, as well as the perfect ingredients for all witches' brews.

The cyclops blundered forward, knowing his way by instinct. He stopped in front of Consuela's head. "Do you have my order ready?"

I added, "More important, do you have his eyeball?"

Consuela turned her dark eyes toward Ulysses, which was the best she could do because she had no muscles to turn her entire head. "Both important questions, and the answer is yes to both. You are one of my very best cyclops customers, and I am honored you trusted me with such an important responsibility."

Ulysses swelled his bare chest with pride. The leprechaun danced another jig.

"Your order is packaged up in the back as always," Consuela continued. "And your eyeball is perfectly safe, just as I promised." Her expression flinched and her jaw clenched. Her eyes moved back and forth, and she seemed to be straining, then she sighed. "I'm afraid one of you will have to fetch it for me. I keep forgetting that I don't have any limbs."

"And it's still in the little box?" Bailey asked. "It's a family heirloom for holding curios. And eyeballs."

"It is right under the counter—beneath my vertebrae."

Since I'd been hired to solve the case, I wanted to be the one to end it. I stepped around the counter, searched behind Consuela's flowing dark tresses, and found a lower shelf. It held a dirty coffee mug, a cashbox, a small bottle of hand sanitizer— all of them dusty from lack of use—and a small wooden curio box with a carved four-leaf clover.

"Found it!" Holding the box in my palm, I lifted the lid. A bloodshot eye the size of a navel orange stared back at me. Normally, that would have been alarming, but right now it meant complete success.

Ulysses held out his hands, fumbling in the air. The leprechaun bounced up and down. "Here, let me help, laddie!" He reached into the curio box and snatched out the eyeball.

"Oww! Be careful," the cyclops said. "You poked me in the eye."

"Don't worry. I brought saline in my bag o' holding."

"Good thinking," I said.

Bailey handed the eyeball to Ulysses, who popped it firmly into the center of his forehead. "Ahhh!" He blinked furiously, then rolled his eye around and stared at me. This was the first time he'd actually gotten to look at his zombie private investigator. "I can see clearly now!"

The leprechaun returned from the back room, skipping along as he carried a package marked *Ulysses S. Clops*. The cyclops's eye widened with anticipation.

"Here you go, boyo, your Acapulco Gold. And I am glad to be your UTI sponsor again."

"I hope you'll be more careful next time," I said. "Or at least more legible."

"We will," Ulysses said.

"It'll be a real shindig!" the leprechaun said, and the two left arm-in-arm.

"They'll be back," Consuela said to me from her platter, still smiling. "I love repeat customers."

"That's a good business practice," I agreed, but I hoped I would not be seeing those two again.

HEART OF CLAY

I

It makes me feel all hollow inside, Shamble," said Officer Toby McGoohan, my best human friend, as we looked down at the mangled corpse of the golem on the grass of the overflow parking area.

Someone had opened the clay guy's chest from the base of his throat down to his waist, splitting him like an orange. He was completely empty inside.

"Not a good time to joke, McGoo." I tilted my fedora and scratched my forehead around the hard edge of the bullet-hole scar from the night I'd been killed.

McGoo pulled out his notebook. "I always make jokes. You know that." He wore his usual blue patrol officer's uniform and cap from the Unnatural Quarter Police Department. At his side, he carried a .38 Special police revolver and a .38 Extra Special loaded with silver bullets for troublesome monsters. His belt also had pepper spray and a squirt bottle of holy water. "These days, if I don't think all the ghosts and goblins are funny, I might get nightmares."

I knelt down on stiff knees next to the dead golem. Despite lingering rigor mortis, my joints worked rather well once I got warmed up, but I was due for a top-off at the embalming parlor again.

I touched the clay of the golem's body. It was still soft and pliable, but drying out. From the hardness of the stone, the coroner could determine the time of death. According to the three letters imprinted on his forehead, his name was Joe.

Golems were hard-working but downtrodden, second-class citizens even among the unnaturals, fashioned by wizards and animated to do the dirty jobs that even slime demons liked to avoid. Since all golems looked alike, and because they often had trouble distinguishing themselves from one another, each golem had his name imprinted right on the forehead, or sometimes on the back of the head (for privacy issues).

"I wonder what he was like as a person," I pondered.

"He was probably like a golem, Shamble." McGoo used his radio to call in the report. Backup would arrive soon, but there was no emergency. Joe had been murdered out in the vacant parking ground for Dred's Real Renaissance Faire, but the Faire's gates had been closed for the day when Joe met his untimely end.

Looking at the dead gray mud of the corpse, I muttered, "Ashes to ashes, dust to dust." I ran my fingers along the skin, smearing a soft line. "And Play-Doh to Play-Doh."

"They can just scrunch up the clay again," McGoo said. "Moisten it with a little water and squish it into shape. Reanimate another golem."

"But it wouldn't be *Joe* anymore. And you know Robin would give you one of her famous stern looks if she heard you talking like that."

"Not the stern look!" McGoo cried. "Point taken. It's a murder, plain and simple, and we better solve it."

I lurched back to my feet, drawing in a deep but unnecessary breath. My lungs no longer needed air, although it did make talking a lot easier. "Sounds like a job for a zombie detective."

McGoo looked up at the lights of the Renaissance Faire camp

that had taken over the empty land outside of town, saw the smoke of cookfires, watched the nocturnal monsters dwindle down to lethargy as the day grew brighter. He glanced at the dead golem again. "Whew, and this is the second one in a week."

II

The dragon was the star attraction, no doubt about it, but Dred's Real Renaissance Faire had jousting matches, swordfights, minstrels, jesters, elaborate costumes, and souvenirs to fit any budget, so long as it was high. Food vendors served fantastical concoctions for all digestive systems, whether carnivorous, demonic, or health conscious. One pushy vendor offered me a brain gelato and didn't want to take no for an answer.

I'd been meaning to take Sheyenne, my ghost girlfriend, here on a date, and now I had a reason to go to the Renaissance Faire because of work. Sheyenne glowed with ectoplasmic delight when I bought tickets for all of us, including my partner Robin and cute little Alvina, the little vampire girl who was either my daughter or McGoo's. (We weren't sure who was the real father, since we had both been embarrassingly involved with the mother back in the day. But based on her cuteness and intelligence, I was betting on my genetics, not his.)

Sheyenne had altered her spectral form to look like a regal lady with her blond hair done up in extravagant braids. Her gown came out of a Disney princess movie.

"You look gorgeous," I said.

Not surprisingly, she shimmered. "Thank you, Beaux. I wanted to look the part." I wore my usual fedora and sport jacket with the stitched-up bullet holes.

Inside the main entry gates, Talbot & Knowles had set up a medieval-looking tavern with a wooden sign that said YE OLDE BLOOD BAR, where they filled tankards of blood for rowdy vampires, and also served coffee, iced tea, and soft drinks for their less sanguine customers. I treated Alvina to a unicorn-blood frappé, which was more sugar and caffeine than hemoglobin, but it made the girl even cuter than usual with her pigtails and a grin that showed off pointy fangs.

The Faire was gaudy and colorful, filled with noise, delightful diversions, and expensive things at every turn. After all the mythical creatures had returned, thanks to a cosmic alignment and accidental virginal blood sacrifice, the vampires, ghosts, mummies, werewolves, zombies, ghouls, trolls, gremlins, etcetera, congregated in the Unnatural Quarter, a place where they could feel at home.

But other mythical creatures—especially the dragon, the wizard king, enchantresses, and Jabberwocks—took their lives on the road. Dred's Real Renaissance Faire performed around the country, and they were doing quite well on their month-long stop here in the Unnatural Quarter.

"Can we watch the jousting?" Alvina asked.

"People just go there to see knights crash into each other," I said.

The kid beamed. "Sounds great!"

I looked at the program. "Next match is in half an hour."

As Robin walked with us, I could tell the wheels were turning behind her dark eyes. I had told her about the murdered golems, and now we saw numerous other golems hauling barrels, tightening ropes, lugging heavy sacks, emptying dumpsters, scrubbing Tow-a-Toilets. I was sure some of them had known the two eviscerated victims.

Around us, the crowd paused and pointed into the empty sky. Robin glanced at her watch, and her face flashed a real smile. "Stop right here. This is a good place for us to watch."

"What is it?" I asked. "And how much does it cost?" It was an instinctive question here at the Renaissance Faire.

"The show is every hour on the hour, Dan," Robin said. "The dragon!"

At the far side of the site, beyond the crew tents, storage

areas, and dumpsters, a scaly monster lurched into the sky, flapping broad wings that were as large as billboards. The dragon—named Alice—had a long, barbed tail and a sinuous neck, as seen on all the posters. Her eyes flared scarlet fire as she swooped over the Renaissance Faire and then dive-bombed, letting out a roar as she streaked over the heads of the cheering spectators.

Alvina laughed. Sheyenne drifted close to me, and I could feel her thrumming spectral presence.

"Don't worry, we're safe," Robin reassured us. "The dragon may be powerful, but city ordinance limits her destructive activities."

Alice did a barrel roll in the air to more cheers, then cocked back her neck and opened her jaws wide. I thought she was going to breathe fire, but instead she released only a series of humorous smoke rings. After a five-minute performance, the dragon glided overhead, tipping her outstretched wings as if in a bow, and circled back to her large tent the size of an aircraft hangar, where she reportedly kept her treasure hoard.

"Can we have a dragon?" Alvina asked.

"We don't have the room in our apartment," I said, though I hated to disappoint the kid.

"Please? I'll take care of it, I *promise*!"

"It would be too big, honey," Sheyenne explained.

"Let's just get a little one. Hatched from an egg. If we go to the UQ Animal Shelter …"

"Little dragons grow into big dragons," Robin said.

"Let's start out with a salamander," I suggested. "Maybe we can work our way up."

That satisfied the girl, and we went off to find the jousting field.

As we went around back of Ye Olde Blood Bar, a golem waiter with a tray—Jim, according to the name on his forehead—was delivering dirty tankards to another golem, Don, who was wearing an apron and yellow dishwashing gloves. Standing at a large barrel of sudsy water, Don sloshed the tankards in the soapy water to remove the bloodstains, then dunked them in a separate rinse barrel.

Since we were away from the crowds, I paused to do some detective work. "Excuse me, gentlemen. Are you aware that last night another golem was found murdered in the parking area? His chest had been pulled open, and he was empty inside. His name was Joe."

"Oh ... Joe," the golem said, sounding sad. "Joe was a good guy."

"What about your working conditions here at the Faire?" Robin asked. "Why would someone murder golems?"

"We just do our work," said Don, raising his yellow dishwashing gloves. He dunked a tankard in the soapy water and swished it in the rinse barrel before setting it on a wooden drying shelf. "Whenever a master hires us, we're just putty in his hands."

I remembered the hollowed-out clay corpse. "What's inside a golem? Why would anyone want to take it?"

Both Jim and Don answered in unison. "We have a heart of clay." They each brought a hand up to their chests. "And Art has the heart of a lion. Art will save us all."

"Who's Art?" I asked.

Alvina tugged on my hand. "We have to get to the jousting."

"Just a minute, honey."

"Art is Art," said the golems. "He will free us."

"Is Art another golem?" Robin asked. "How do we find him?"

"You will find him," intoned Don and Jim.

When Alvina kept tugging, I realized that we really did need to go or we would miss the beginning of the joust.

Thankfully, it was a cloudy, gloomy day, so all types of unnaturals could enjoy the spectacle outside. Golem ushers herded the crowd to bleachers on the edge of the jousting field. On opposite ends, two armored knights sat on black nightmares that pawed at the ground with sharp hooves. The knights wore full regalia, visored helmets, and doublets that should have borne the insignia of noble houses but instead sported corporate logos, the sponsors of the jousting teams. Each jouster held a long wooden lance.

On a raised reviewing stand beside the bleachers stood a man with curly, golden locks, wearing a jewel-studded crown and impressive black velvet robes. The black velvet was adorned with painted images of sad-eyed puppies and Elvis Presley. When the crowd was seated on the bleachers, the regal-looking man raised his hands, as if expecting roars of approval. He got a smattering of applause.

"I am Mortimer Dred, king of the Real Renaissance Faire." When he raised his hands higher, his ballooning black velvet sleeves dropped down to his elbows, revealing scrawny arms. "All fantasy-based unnaturals are here to perform for your entertainment, and tips are gladly accepted." The next round of applause was markedly subdued.

"Today's first match is between two of our greatest jousters. Sir Anatomy of Bone!" One of the knights raised the squeaking visor of his steel helmet to reveal a grinning skull. The skeleton knight opened his metal chestplate to reveal an empty rib cage.

"And on the other end of the field," King Dred roared, "Sir Fangsalot of Jugular!" The second knight doffed his helmet to reveal the pallid skin of a dapper vampire, a widow's peak, and slicked-back hair. He flashed his fangs.

"Those aren't real names," Alvina said. "They're silly stage names, like in WWE."

The kid was smart. Very smart. Took after me.

The skeleton knight lowered his lance, pointing it at his opponent. The vampire knight showed no concern about the long wooden stake pointed toward his chest.

When the Renaissance king waved a pennant, the two knights kicked their nightmares and charged directly toward each other like street racers playing chicken. The hooves pounded, the audience held their breath. We all stared, tense. The riders came closer and closer.

Out of the corner of my eye, I watched King Dred hurry down the steps of the reviewing stand, as if he had an important appointment. I turned back to the charging nightmares. The lances were leveled, the demonic horses were reckless. The two knights seemed not to care for their own lives or safety.

At the last moment, Sir Fangsalot raised his shield, knocked the threatening wooden staff to one side, but held his own pole firm and plunged it through the armored chest of Sir Anatomy. The lance skewered the skeletal knight and knocked him off his horse. He landed with a clamor of armor on the jousting field.

The crowd's gasp was like thunder. The vampire knight rode past and wheeled around, holding up a gauntleted hand in triumph. "Victory is mine!"

The skeleton fumbled on the ground, grabbing at his metal chestplate, barely able to move due to the long lance thrust directly through him. He pulled his armor plate open to reveal that the wooden shaft had passed harmlessly between two widely-spaced ribs.

"You hit no vital organs!" shouted Sir Anatomy. "I demand a rematch."

"It's all fake," said Alvina, "like WWE."

"All in good fun, honey," said Sheyenne. "No real knights were hurt during the performance."

Golems lumbered onto the field to extricate the long lance from Sir Anatomy. They rounded up the snorting demon horses and started to prepare the field for the two o'clock jousting round.

Having finished her unicorn-blood` frappé, Alvina wanted another treat. Leaving the jousting field, we strolled among the vending stalls, sniffing the odors, some delicious, some nauseating.

I heard subdued shouting up ahead, clearly an argument that was not part of any performance. My eyes were drawn to pointy objects at a sword vendor's stall. A scrawny old gremlin with patchy fur and immensely thick glasses squirmed on a stool behind a counter. He was surrounded by broadswords, throwing daggers, battleaxes, and morning stars. A sign in front of the stall promised *Gifts for the whole family!*

King Mortimer Dred loomed in front of the stall, waving his arms. "I want that sword! You were supposed to hold it for me."

"Sorry, sir," said the gremlin in a raspy voice. "We can't do layaway plans."

"I am the Renaissance king," Mort insisted.

The gremlin leaned forward like an astronomer peering through a telescope, but he couldn't see much through his glasses. "I told you last week, and the week before, that someone already bought the sword." He gestured toward his cornucopia of weapons on display. "But I have plenty of others. Why not choose a different one?"

"Because a different one is not Excalibur."

Attracted by the shouting, Robin, Sheyenne, and I approached the stall, ready to help if the situation grew ugly.

"Can I have a sword?" Alvina asked. "A long, pointy one?"

"Not today, honey," Robin said.

The gremlin brightened, sensing new customers. "I am Noxius, purveyor of sharp objects! I have blades of every shape and design, ranging from mortal combat weapons to kitchen cutlery. Talk to me if you see something you like." He leaned forward on his stool, peering down at Alvina. "How about a double-bladed battle axe for the cute little girl?"

"Oh, so now you can see just fine?" Mort huffed.

"She's cute," explained the gremlin.

Alvina grinned bashfully, showing her fangs.

I butted in. "What seems to be the problem?"

Robin said, "I know several members of the Unnatural Quarter's Better Business Bureau."

"I should file a complaint!" Mort glared at Noxius. I saw that the painted puppies and Elvis figures on his black velvet robes were quite well done. "Excalibur is missing, and I need to find it. The sword belongs to me! I am the proper king!"

The gremlin shrugged. "First come, first served. The dragon lost the weapon from her hoard, fair and square. She just can't resist a bet."

Mort clenched his hands and worked his jaw. His eyes became very hard. "That damned Alice and her gambling problem." He leaned over the rickety wooden counter, and the gremlin flinched behind his thick glasses. "I'll buy it back. I'll pay you double. Just tell me who has it."

"I told you before, they all look the same to me," said Noxius. "Couldn't read his name."

"Why would a golem want a legendary sword in the first place?" Mort demanded. "What are they going to do with it?"

That immediately piqued my interest. "Excuse me, sir? I'm Dan Chambeaux, zombie private investigator, and this is Robin Deyer, my partner at Chambeaux and Deyer Investigations. Could you tell us more?"

Mortimer Dred gave us a dissecting look. "I'll do more than explain to you—I'll hire you! If you're a detective, I need you to find Excalibur, the sword of kings. He who holds the blade rules the land, as well as the Real Renaissance Faire. I will pay you greatly if you find it for me."

As our business manager, Sheyenne immediately took charge. Somehow she produced a sheet of paper from her medieval costume. "This is our client engagement form. If you'll fill this out, Mr. Dred, we can begin our investigations right away."

III

As a zombie detective, it's my passion to solve crimes. I had a golem murderer to catch, but we also had to pay the bills.

"We'll find the missing sword," I promised.

"Always take care of the client," Robin said, satisfied, "but our real work is in the name of justice."

"And keeping our business afloat," Sheyenne added. The two didn't always see eye to eye.

"Don't forget about my college fund," Alvina said.

Since Excalibur had been part of the dragon's treasure hoard until it fell into the hands of the gremlin sword vendor, we decided to go ask Alice. The vampire girl was eager to meet her very first dragon, even though fantastical beasts were commonplace in the Unnatural Quarter.

Outside the main exhibition area, the dragon's tent was impossible to miss, being big enough to hold a giant flying reptile with elbow room to spare. We made our way through the hubbub, passing a fire eater who was being heckled by an actual fire demon, and a juggler who was a multi-armed squid creature wearing colorful medieval clothes.

Before our band of merry friends could get there, however, we encountered an unexpected attraction. Standing on a wooden crate, a golem raised clay fists to the sky and shouted in a hollow voice that belonged at a political rally. "Golems have been downtrodden for too long! We will no longer let our mud be trampled underfoot and tracked all over the house. We were made to serve, but we were not made to suffer. Golems have rights."

"Serve, not suffer," the crowd chanted.

I saw a handful of curious onlookers like ourselves, but most of the crowd consisted of golems dressed like peasants, laborers, beasts of burden. One wore a low-bodice dress with rounded clay breasts scrunched up in a bad imitation of a lusty barmaid.

"Serve, not suffer!" they chanted. Someone bellowed, "Three cheers for Art."

They all yelled, "Art! Art!"

The golem speaker stood straight-backed, strong and confident, his clay smooth and moist. The name "Art" was imprinted on his forehead. "I am on a crusade for my fellow golems. We want better conditions at the Real Renaissance Faire."

"And in the whole Unnatural Quarter," called another golem.

There was something about Art. Though most golems were subservient walking lumps of mud, this one was a *leader*, filled with charisma.

McGoo sidled up to me, dressed in his beat cop uniform, which meant he was on duty. I shuddered to imagine him in a Renaissance costume. "Hey Shamble. Seen anything suspicious?"

"If you don't see something suspicious in the Quarter, then that in itself is suspicious."

He tipped his cap toward the golem firebrand still shouting from his soapbox. "Who's that?"

"A rabble-rouser," I said.

"A crusader for justice," Robin interjected.

"That's what I meant to say," I corrected myself. "His name is Art."

McGoo nodded with mock seriousness. "You could frame him and hang him on the wall." When I responded with a blank look, he added, "Then he'd really be *art*." He waited for me, or anyone, to laugh. He was about to explain the cleverness of his joke when, fortunately, we were interrupted by several huge ogre guards bent on violence.

"Break it up! Break it up!" The ogre voices sounded like rocks rattling out of a gravel truck. They carried thick spiked clubs.

The golem workers scattered, knowing they weren't supposed to be on a coffee or crusading break. The burly ogres elbowed people aside as they pushed their way toward the defiant Art, swinging their clubs.

One of the smaller golems, obviously a convert to Art's cause, threw himself in front of the ogres, and they squashed him, bending his body and smooshing his shoulder and arm as they knocked him with a club. The damaged lump of clay twitched and crawled away.

McGoo charged in. "Hey, I'm law enforcement here. I'm a peace officer."

"We're chaos officers," said the nearest ogre. "Private contractors."

Art sprang from his soapbox and ducked down as he melted into the milling crowd. He ran a palm over his forehead to smear out the letters of his name, leaving only a blank gray patch as he disappeared.

The ogres—generally about as bright as golems—were easily confused.

After the impromptu crowd dispersed and the ogres strutted in circles holding up their heavy clubs in search of something to do, I nudged Alvina along. "I better get you away from this."

Robin's nostrils flared, and she flashed a venomous glance at the ogre guards. "We were all witnesses to that!"

While McGoo went to have stern words with the overly enthusiastic ogres, I hurried my companions toward the big tent on the outskirts. "We're off to see the dragon."

IV

Two more security ogres stood outside the dragon's tent, though I couldn't understand why an enormous creature like Alice would need bodyguards.

"To keep the paparazzi away," said one of the ogres.

"And autograph hounds," said the other. "Now, piss off."

Robin was incensed, but I tended to be calmer, more relaxed. After coming back from the dead, I found it easier not to be bothered by little things. I stepped forward. "We've been hired by King Mortimer Dred to investigate a missing sword that recently belonged to Alice. We're here to interview her."

Alvina piped up, "It's an important part of the case."

Sheyenne produced a copy of the client engagement contract,

which enlisted our services for the locating the sword called Excalibur, and thrust it in front of the ogres. "See, here's proof." They squinted, tugged on their drooping fat lips, and pondered. Ogres were too embarrassed to admit they couldn't read, so they let us pass.

Reptiles had a certain smell about them, and even though my senses were dulled thanks to the embalming process, I could instantly tell that some giant lizard lived within the tent. Of course, I could *see* the huge dragon, which was my second clue. Alvina pinched her fingers around her nose.

"Oh, visitors!" boomed the dragon in a lilting female voice. "I'm on a break between performances." Alice leaned forward with a gigantic scaly head, slitted eyes the size of basketballs, and fangs that would have made a great white shark pee in the water. Her green and gold scales were like garbage-can lids. "Did you come to interview me? King Dred likes the publicity, but he never sends the press anymore." She snorted. "Once, I ate a reporter who asked an embarrassing question. Is this a softball interview?"

Alice settled herself on top of a pile of treasure—gold coins, chains, chests of jewels, battered suits of armor, swords with gem-inlaid hilts. The wealth I saw was enough for a comfortable retirement account, even for a long-lived dragon, but the amount did look a little disappointing. When Alice shifted her position, coins, chains, and gilded blades rattled beneath her. "Is this my good side?" She turned a head the size of a rowboat.

"We're here to talk to you about a sword, ma'am," I said, using my best professional P.I. voice. "The Renaissance king hired us to find Excalibur."

Alice grumbled. "Excalibur, Excalibur! I have plenty of treasure, and all anybody wants to talk about is Excalibur."

"Isn't the sword famous?" I asked. "From a movie, or something?"

Alice blinked her huge eyes. "You don't know the story of Excalibur?" Sheyenne and Robin both looked at me in surprise.

Alvina sighed. "Excalibur was the sword of King Arthur. Only the rightful king can draw it from the stone." The little vampire girl was constantly getting her information from the internet, so she was better informed than I.

"That must be why King Dred wants it," Robin said. "It legitimizes his rule over the Real Renaissance Faire."

"Isn't it all just fun and games?" Sheyenne asked. "Costumes and jousting acts? It's not a real legendary sword."

"After the Big Uneasy, who knows what's real anymore?" I asked. "If dragons can be real, then Excalibur can be real." I turned back to Alice. "So, can you tell us what happened to the sword?" I stepped closer, trying to be congenial. I could smell the dragon's breath.

"Excalibur was part of my hoard. So many riches! Once, I needed seven warehouses just to keep my treasure, but, alas, much of it is gone now, dwindled away." She raised her head and snorted one small smoke ring. "This losing streak is bound to end soon, though! I'll win it all back. I know I will." She flapped her giant wings, rattling the tent fabric overhead, then settled back onto the mound of gold and jewels.

Robin thought she understood. "You gambled away your treasure?"

"And Excalibur?" I added.

"I still have some riches." The dragon sounded defensive. "A big win is right around the corner. I know it. Dragons can sense these things."

Sheyenne drifted close and whispered in my ear. "The dragon has a gambling problem."

Dragons also had extremely acute hearing, as I should have remembered from *The Hobbit*. "Yes, I have a gambling problem—I admit it! It's the thrill, the risk … and the winning." She clacked shut her fanged jaws. "Texas Hold 'em is my preference, though it's hard to hold the cards with big claws like these."

Alice raised a huge, scaled hand. "I lost a chest of gold and Excalibur two weeks ago in a big game. That gremlin is a good player! Noxius would win a few hands, then I'd win, then he'd win a few more. He'd egg me on until I bet the whole pot." The dragon snorted smoke, flapped her wings, and tried to settle down. "I don't know how he can even see the cards with glasses that thick, but I kept raising the bet, because I *knew* I was about to start a winning streak!" Her slitted eyes had a disturbing obsession. "I'll win it back—I'll win it all back."

"You need help, Alice," Sheyenne said in a sincere voice. "It's an addiction. Gambling makes you lose everything."

The dragon hung her head and her groan of sorrow was a rumble deep in her throat. "I know ..." Then she perked up. "Would you like to play a round now? Who's got a deck of cards? I could use the practice!"

"Sorry, ma'am, I'm on the job," I said. "We need to find Excalibur."

"Talk with Noxius. He put it up for sale in his sword vending stand."

"He did. Sold it to a golem, but we don't know which one."

"Sure you don't want to play a game? Not even one?" Alice whined. "Low stakes, I promise! A buck a round. I'll bet on anything." She sounded desperate.

Sheyenne looked concerned. "I think the Unnatural Quarter chapter of Gamblers Anonymous accepts legendary creatures."

The dragon's need was so great she actually trembled. "It's a terrible disease." She closed her basketball-sized eyes. "Go away. I need to rest before my next performance."

Out of courtesy, we hurried out of the tent.

V

Rettop the cavewight had hands like lawn rakes covered with thick mud. A big grin crossed his pale, sallow face. Sitting on a stone bench next to a wheelbarrow of fresh clay, he whistled as he worked. He pumped his potter's wheel with his feet and slapped on more mud, building up a mound that he shaped into a circular vase. His hands and fingers were so large he could manipulate a lot of mud at a time.

Werewolves, ghouls, and vampires watched him with interest as he shaped the sides, pulled up a fluted oblong container, then poked his fingers down inside to make it hollow, expanding the waist. Next to his potter's wheel sat a table filled with his wares, pots, vases, and ashtrays.

"Can you make Canopic jars?" asked a curious mummy.

"One of my specialties," said Rettop. "I take commissions."

Alvina had paused to look at a crudely fashioned flowerpot. She looked up at me with those big eyes. "I'm thinking of getting a present for you and McGoo. Father's Day is coming up. How about an ashtray?" She picked up a lumpy object that looked like a project I had made in third grade.

If my heart were still beating, it would have been filled with joy. "That's beautiful."

"I'll take you shopping separately, honey," Sheyenne said, lowering her voice. "We'll make it a surprise for both half-daddies."

With a loud muttering, the crowd parted and a damaged golem lurched forward, twisted and misshapen. "Rettop! Need repairs! Now!" The deformed golem could barely move, trying to get its clay legs to work. I realized it was the golem smashed by the security ogres at Art's rally. His name was Tony, according to his forehead.

The cavewight clucked his pale tongue against crooked, brown teeth. "What a shame! That's why King Dred keeps me around. Step right up." He helped the golem to his potter's wheel and let out a long sigh. "I just want to make vases and pots, but I spend half my time repairing damaged golems." He clucked his tongue against his teeth again. "Let me see what I can do."

With spatulate hands, the cavewight seized the golem's chest and shoulders, then worked like a chiropractor, twisting him, straightening him. The clay was pliable enough that Tony eventually straightened. Rettop took palmfuls of fresh clay, using it on the golem instead of his pots. "Lucky you got here in time. If the damage had been more severe, your animation spell might have been broken." He slathered Tony's skin, bulked up his back, added to his biceps, even finished with a flourish of a cleft in the golem's chin. "There, good as new!"

"About those canopic jars?" said the mummy, his rattling dry voice tinged with impatience.

Then, not far away, someone screamed a high terrified shriek, which was always a good way to get attention.

As a ghost, Sheyenne could move faster than any of us, and she streaked away, waving for us to follow. Robin and Alvina bolted, and I shambled as quickly as I could, getting my body warmed up. Being a detective, I was great at solving mysteries, but chase scenes and action-packed brawls weren't my specialty.

A crowd had gathered by the dumpster bins behind Ye Olde Blood Bar. McGoo was already there, trying to hold off the onlookers. A banshee barmaid with big hips and a layered skirt screamed and screamed, breaking nearby windows and nearly deafening us all. Sheyenne hovered in the air, her translucent form sparkling with intense anger. McGoo was red-faced.

Sprawled on the ground in front of the dumpsters were two more dead golems, side-by-side, their arms at odd angles and their chests split open, the clay pried apart and leaving them hollow: Don and Jim, the golems we had met earlier. Don still wore his yellow dishwashing gloves.

McGoo bent down beside the eviscerated clay figures. "It's too late."

"Why would anyone want to kill golems?" Robin asked. "And why open them up like that?"

More clay figures pressed closer, still riled up from Art's crusade. "Serve, not suffer," one grumbled. I heard the same words muttered among the others.

"Something bad is happening here, McGoo," I said. "Somebody's cracking open golems, like shucking oysters and hoping to find a pearl."

My best human friend had had enough. He bellowed, loud and clear, "Four golem murders in two weeks! This is a crime scene. This entire Renaissance Faire is a crime scene!" He pulled out his radio and called to request backup. "By order of the Unnatural Quarter Police Department, I declare this Faire closed. The public must leave immediately in a calm and orderly fashion."

Security ogres lumbered in to see what the fuss was all about. "Knock some heads!"

"No, no, just a peaceful evacuation," Robin insisted. The ogres looked disappointed.

McGoo said, "Call King Dred. I want all Faire employees together on the jousting ground. I need to interrogate everyone." Sighing, he looked at me. "This is going to be a long day."

VI

Squad cars arrived before the Faire workers had managed to organize themselves on the jousting field. The security ogres got into several brawls (with each other, since they'd been given orders not to harm the paying customers), and eventually all of the patrons made their way to the overflow parking lot, creating a huge traffic jam as they headed back to the Unnatural Quarter.

King Mortimer Dred stood on the reviewing stand as if this entire meeting had been his idea. McGoo and I sorted the Faire workers by species so we could interrogate them better. Robin made sure that every accused monster was properly read its rights. Sheyenne had gotten a treat for Alvina, roasted frogs on a stick, because the little girl was hungry.

Trolls, mummies, and werewolves in blacksmith aprons gathered around, as well as Noxius the gremlin and Rettop the cavewight. The vampire and skeleton jousters stood shoulder to shoulder, and I realized that they were actually close friends, not mortal enemies as the audience had thought. Even Alice the dragon thundered in, landing not far from King Dred's reviewing stand. Twenty or so golems crowded together, identical except for their various Renaissance costumes.

McGoo strutted in front of the reviewing stand. "Now that you're all here, I've got—"

"I'll take it from here," Mort boomed from the platform above. When he lifted his hands, his black velvet sleeves fell down to his elbows again. Thunder sounded across the sky, and dark clouds began to form. "I am King Mortimer Dred, your boss." He strode down from the reviewing stand and marched onto the field, heading straight for the gathered golems.

McGoo and I hurried after him, trying to regain control of the situation. "What are you doing, sir?" I asked.

"We have this handled," McGoo said.

King Dred ignored us. As he walked past the nearsighted gremlin, he grabbed the furry creature by his scrawny neck and dragged him to stand in front of the golems. "Now that you're all here in one place, I can get this done in a far more efficient manner. I need Excalibur. I know one of you golems bought it. I know one of you is hiding it." The king glowered, and his eyes crackled with sparks.

I looked at the smooth clay golems and wondered where in the world they could manage to hide something as large as a sword.

"I demand to know which one of you has Excalibur!"

After a long petrified silence, one golem pushed forward from the back. He seemed taller than the others, exuding power. It was Art, the leader of the golems' crusade. "And I demand justice for all golems! We will serve, but not suffer."

The wizard king seemed shocked and intimidated. "You demand nothing! Where is my sword?"

"The sword belongs to the rightful king," Art said.

"Or it belongs in my treasure hoard," the dragon piped up, "until I lost it in a poker game."

"Lost it fair and square," chirped Noxius.

"I am the king of the Real Renaissance Faire. I, Mortimer Dred, must draw the sword from the stone as was foretold in the legend."

Without flinching, Art placed a gray fist against his soft clay chest. "What if the sword is inside the stone already?"

I suddenly figured out the only place a golem could hide something as large as a sword, and I knew that Mort Dred understood it as well. "He was looking for the sword!" I said to McGoo, who clearly hadn't yet received the same revelation. Now the murders all made sense. "Excalibur! Art has it—inside of him."

Like a flasher about to tear open his trench coat, Art plunged his clay fingers down the soft clay of his chest as if pulling a zipper, then he stretched his clay torso apart, opening himself up to expose a golden hilt and the polished steel of a sword blade that ran all the way down inside his back. Excalibur! The legendary blade hidden inside the soft stone body.

"I have Excalibur," Art declared. "I *am* Excalibur! The sword is in the stone."

The cavewight cackled. "It fit perfectly. I thought it was clever." He held up his splayed hands and waggled his long fingers. "Sealed it right in there for safe keeping."

"It's mine!" Mort lunged forward to grab the golden hilt that protruded from Art's open chest. "Mine!" He pulled at the sword, struggling to draw Excalibur out of the golem's body.

The other golems shifted angrily, getting even more outraged and unruly. The Renaissance Faire employees watched, and even the dragon peered down as Mort yanked, tugged, dug his feet in the ground and pulled, but Art held the sword inside him. Mort strained to wrench the legendary blade free, but it wouldn't budge.

Finally, red-faced, weak-kneed, and exhausted, he staggered back. His golden crown hung askew on his head.

With perfect timing, Sheyenne appeared in front of him, holding a piece of paper. "You engaged our services to locate the sword Excalibur, Mr. Dred. There it is. Our work is now complete, and here's our invoice. Payment is due upon receipt."

Mort flew into a rage. His curly, golden hair crackled, and his crown popped off his head like a champagne cork as his body filled with sorcerous energy. "I am King Mort Dred, and I am also a great wizard. I call upon the powers of dark magic to give me the sword that is my due. I need Excalibur!" He raised his hands and lightning crackled from his fingertips. Angry black thunderheads gathered. The ground began to shake.

Art stood fearless with Excalibur still protruding from his open chest. He wrapped a clay hand around its hilt. "I do not have a heart of clay. I have the heart of a lion! I should be king."

"I will destroy all of you," Mort screamed, and thunder cracked around him for emphasis. "I will shatter every single golem and take the sword from the rubble of your bodies." He lurched back to summon a huge blast of terrible energy.

Knowing what I had to do, I didn't hesitate. I shambled forward, raised my voice. "You look really powerful, King Dred. I bet a hundred dollars that no one can stop you."

Mort let out a maniacal laugh. "Of course not—"

Then a huge reptilian foot stomped down on his head, a dragon's claw that smashed with all the weight of an enormous monster. The blow crushed the Renaissance king into a puddle of bones and flesh.

Alice let out a roar, and her slitted eyes were wide and bright with delight. "I'll take that bet!" she said. "Did I win?"

VII

Afterward, McGoo and I wrapped up the case while Robin wrote notes on her yellow legal pad for the final summary.

Sheyenne took Alvina to get another sugary treat, while we arranged a petty-cash invoice to pay back the hundred-dollar bet.

McGoo scrutinized the red stain and the crumpled black velvet robes. The painted puppies looked extra sad now. "We know Mort Dred was the murderer, tearing open golems in search of the sword hidden inside." He wiped his shoe on the grassy ground to get rid of goop he had inadvertently stepped in. "Nothing left to arrest, though."

"Case solved," I said. "My two favorite words in the world."

"I like Payment Complete," Sheyenne said, leading Alvina back from a vendor with a frozen blood-pop. "Maybe we can get the Renaissance Faire treasurer to pay our bill?"

Robin shook her head. "Mr. Dred engaged us as a personal matter, not as a corporate contract with the Faire itself."

Moving proudly among his fellow golems, Art met each one, read their names aloud from their foreheads. The hilt of Excalibur still protruded from his chest like a badge of honor. He had also retrieved the golden crown worn by King Dred, and now he placed it on his own head, the king of the golems and possibly king of the Real Renaissance Faire.

Art said, "Serve, but not suffer. We must have rights for all golems."

Robin walked among them, listening to their grievances. "We can file a formal motion, and I'll approach the proper governing bodies. I will help ensure that you have good working conditions and proper maintenance."

"I'll help with the personal maintenance," said Rettop. The cavewight was busy making commemorative clay medallions to sell to everyone present at the event.

"And regular mud baths!" said the golem Tony. Robin dutifully wrote it down.

Alice flew overhead, thrilled now. Without her knowledge, King Dred had claimed the dragon's entire treasure hoard as collateral, which he leveraged to finance the Real Renaissance

Faire. Now that Dred had been properly squashed, Alice found that she now owned the entire operation. She was so ecstatic she did barrel rolls and loop-the-loops in the air.

"She still needs counseling for that gambling problem," Sheyenne said, "or she'll lose it all again."

Art strode up. "I will be her business advisor. Instead of the Real Renaissance Faire, we will call this the *Fair* Renaissance Faire, so that all can feel good about themselves when they attend."

The armored vampire knight and the skeleton knight joined each other on the jousting field, practicing with their swords. The dragon crashed down in front of them, and the two costumed knights ran forward to challenge her in a mock battle. With a beat of her wings, Alice knocked them both flat, but the unnatural knights sprang to their feet and ran into the melee, all in good fun.

"I still want a dragon," Alvina said.

"Maybe when you're older, honey," Sheyenne said.

"You could keep one at McGoo's apartment for the nights you stay with him," I suggested.

He glared at me. "Let's start you out with a salamander first."

PREVIOUS PUBLICATION INFORMATION

ACK-NOWLEDGMENTS

Maintaining a well-preserved zombie detective, and his entire series, is a lot of work, and I depend on a lot of people. Undead and undying gratitude goes to Marie Whittaker and Tracy Griffiths who keep track of a million moving parts and details for the Kickstarter fulfillment and the book publication and distribution. Hannah Sheldon is a sharp-eyed beta-reader and continuity expert to make sure that Dan Shamble's brains have the right consistency. The Ukrainian art and design team of Miblart gives Dan Shamble just the right look and feel. And Rebecca Moesta gives her support throughout the writing and tells me I'm always in a good mood when I'm writing Dan Shamble.

Special acknowledgments to dedicated Kickstarter backers who keep the undead guy alive and kicking: Erwin Bush, Sean Smith, Stephen Ballentine, Scott M. Sidney, Andrew Bulthaupt, and Gary Randolph Iber.

Shamble on!

ABOUT THE AUTHOR

Kevin J. Anderson has published more than 180 books, 58 of which have been national or international bestsellers. He has 24 million copies in print in 34 languages.

He has written numerous novels in the Star Wars, X-Files, and Dune universes, as well as the unique Clockwork Angels steampunk trilogy with legendary Rush drummer Neil Peart. His original works include the Saga of Seven Suns series, the Wake the Dragon and Terra Incognita fantasy trilogies, the humorous Dan Shamble, Zombie P.I. series and The Dragon Business series.

He has edited numerous anthologies, written comics and games, and the lyrics to two rock CDs as companions to his Terra Incognita trilogy.

Anderson is the director of the graduate program in Publishing at Western Colorado University, and he and his wife Rebecca Moesta are the publishers of WordFire Press.

READ THE COMPLETE
DAN SHAMBLE
ZOMBIE P.I. SERIES

If you liked *Stiffs and Stones*, you might also enjoy:

Death Warmed Over

Unnatural Acts

Working Stiff

Our list of other WordFire Press authors and titles is always growing. To find out more and shop our selection of titles, visit us at:

wordfirepress.com

9 781680 577402